DEMON DOJO

An Aikido Adventure

by Liese Klein

Cover Image by Matt Stevens
www.mattstevensart.com

CHAPTER ONE

Friday

A s my arm tightens across his neck, my attacker starts to pass out.

"Don't fight me! The more you struggle, the worse it gets!"

The guy just wriggles a bit, refusing to submit.

"Tap out, tap out now!"

I hate that my voice is so high and squeaky even as I'm supposed to be taking down an opponent. I struggle to scrunch up my face in a fierce scowl to compensate.

"OK, I warned you!"

I pull my right arm tight across my chest, as if I'm pulling open a jacket. The back of my hand digs into my opponent's neck as he squirms and bucks. He aims a kick back at my knee-cap. It connects and I feel a jolt of pain – but the blow is too weak to take me down. My arms pull apart even as my muscles ache with the effort. The attacker squirms.

The guy's pulse, which I can feel at the back of my wrist, speeds up then slows abruptly. His body goes limp in my arms – I've done it! Some kind of dark joy wells up in me as my arms pull tighter.

"Cherry, that's enough!"

Thierry, the senior student leading the class, calls out. His voice is deafening, even from across the room. Thierry has been watching the whole encounter from the edge of the mat.

I explain myself: "He wouldn't tap!"

I'm not letting this guy go, after what he tried to pull. If the attacker doesn't tap out, he hasn't submitted. That means that technically, he's still attacking. The guy's like a ton of wet laundry collapsed in my arms right now, but he's still the attacker. How did he get so heavy all of a sudden?

How far can I take this? The guy's pulse slows a bit further and his body twitches. The tang of his sweat fills my nostrils. I tell myself that it's not sweat I smell – it's fear. Fear of me, the mighty ass-kicking girl warrior. I pull harder as my muscles protest.

"Stop that! You're going to kill him!" Thierry strides across the mat and he reaches for me. His fingers claw against my grip, expertly loosening the hold. On autopilot now, I let my other hand drop to the guy's shoulder and I grab a handful of his uniform, easing his limp slide to the mat. I keep my wrist against his neck.

The man's pulse jump-starts as he hits the tatami. He shakes himself awake and lets out a groan. Thierry's expression slides from concern to relief, then anger as he turns to glare at me. Back to concern again as the attacker comes to. The guy coughs a few times then starts croaking.

"Wow, I saw stars. You really got me."

"Come on, tap out already, Diego! Admit when you've been beat. It's stupid to let yourself be choked out."

That was my attacker's name, Diego. I don't bother to learn most people's names until they've been practicing Aikido here for at least month, and this guy looked like a knucklehead who wouldn't last a week. Thought he could take down the little female, did he?

Thierry, the senior student in the dojo and Sensei's assistant, tugs at my victim's uniform, annoyance on his sharp features.

"Don't mess around when someone's pushing on the carotid artery in the neck, Diego. One wrong move and that artery can rip. Then you're dead, macho man. Bleed out in like five minutes. Not worth testing this, trust me. Just tap out and call it a loss."

"I wanted to see if Aikido works," Diego says, rubbing at the reddening stripe across his neck. "My friend says Aikido is all fake and set up. I wanted to see what happens when you really crank on these techniques. That little girl is strong!"

"Now you know." Thierry's smile fades as he turns to me. "I'll talk to you in a few minutes." His voice reaches across the mat to me like a slap.

I can't help but snort and turn away, wiping secretly at the tears in the corners of my eyes. Yes, I'm happy that I'm good enough to nearly kill Diego. But I also have the pathetic weakness of starting to cry whenever I'm yelled at. And Thierry knows how to yell. There's also the sadness that comes up every time I succeed at something major. Someone's not around for me to brag to. My mom died six years ago and she would have really enjoyed this.

Nice, I've just nearly killed a guy just because his buddy said something stupid about Aikido. But I can't help but also smirk a little behind my tears: Even exhausted and with my legs cramped up, I can still take down a full-grown man.

Not bad for a 17-year-old girl who's just a little taller than 5 feet. I'm "solidly built," as they say, but hardly pure muscle. I'm not the strongest person in the world, but I've been practicing that choke technique for nearly half of my life, along with the rest of Aikido's range of nerve pinches, joint-locks and throws. I may be small, but I can use my size to sneak into someone's weak spot and take them down.

The rest of the students scatter to the edge of the mat now that the "Young Girl Schools a Knucklehead" show is over. The senior students gather on the mat with me to finish the last stage of an Aikido class, folding your hakama.

A hakama is a wide-legged pants-like garment worn by senior students and serious Aikido trainees like myself. Each of the hakama's seven pleats is supposed to represent one of the seven virtues of Budo, the Japanese way of martial arts: benevolence, honor, courtesy, wisdom, sincerity, loyalty and piety. The folding of the hakama at the end of each class should be done with full mindfulness and appreciation of each virtue. But I rush through the job, half-crying and shivering as my sweat dries and the winter chill settles into the cinderblock box that is our dojo, or training space. Better hurry up to clean the dojo, get changed, showered and dressed for the long, cold night ahead. After all, this is my first night as an official live-in student.

Thierry's slim form is still hovering around Diego, the jerk I almost killed. Thierry is in charge of the Aikido dojo for today, and concern and annoyance play across his dark features.

"So I guess Cherry answered your buddy's question about Aikido, right? Next time, I'll be happy to show you a thing or two about how Aikido works." Diego sits on the side of the mat, still catching his breath. He smiles but looks at bit uneasy. Thierry smiles, and his booming laugh dispels the tension. "Just kidding! Aikido is about challenging yourself, not dominating someone else. We're here to have fun, right?" Diego looks relieved.

"Sure, Thierry Sensei. Sounds like fun."

"Yeah, and on the serious side, don't make Cherry do that again. One bad angle and you'll bleed out inside your brain. Have I mentioned that Goffe Sensei told me there's a $10,000 payout limit on our insurance? Hope your wife is ready to pay the bills for the brain injury rehab. A million bucks a year, at least."

"Don't worry, I get it. I'll tap next time."

"OK, enough with the challenges. Let's get this mat clean and get you all home. Our young trainee student here is getting hungry, and her ramen noodles need nuking!"

Thierry's tone is as commanding as Goffe Sensei's, and there's a rush for the cleaning supplies. He turns to me again and lets his anger twist up his face.

"We need to talk after class."

I'm in trouble again, and it's only my first day on my own.

* * *

My name is Sakura Mendoza. Sakura means "cherry blossom" in Japanese: pretty, pink, flowery – everything I'm not. My friends just call me Cherry, and now everybody in the dojo is calling me that. To be honest, Thierry is the only person I can call a friend in my present location and situation, but I'm working on that.

For the past three months I've been training full time at this martial-arts school as a *soto-deshi*, or "outside" student, living at my teacher's home. Now I'm finishing up my first day as an *uchideshi*, or "inside" student who lives in the actual dojo space. It's a big step up in intensity and seriousness, especially considering the circumstances.

Our dojo is not some kind of quaint temple in the countryside, surrounded by rice fields and friendly townspeople. It's a former ammunition testing lab on the fifth floor of a mostly empty factory building that has been rotting from the inside out for fifty years. The rent is cheap – but not cheap enough, considering that the neighborhood is the poorest in the city.

To be an uchideshi here would be challenging enough at any time of year, but my live-in period is happening in the middle of winter, thanks to the last-minute trip to Japan that Goffe Sensei is taking. And this is not just any winter: We're in the dark depths of the coldest winter in living memory, with a huge blizzard coming in from the west at the end of the week. The storms are being amped up by yet another polar vortex caused by climate change.

As I get ready to clean the dojo for the last time today, more doubts fill my head. Camping out alone in a broken-down building for ten days sounded like a good idea when Goffe Sensei suggested it. The experience would toughen me up and give me time to meditate, time to "intensify my practice," as she likes to say. Now panic whirls through my skull as my hands go numb in the bucket of icy water used to clean the practice mat and my legs shudder with cramps.

Next to me are three people who actually pay money to spend their free time pushing rags across a mat and getting their arms and necks twisted. These students have been drawn to the building by Belinda Goffe Sensei, the chief instructor of this dojo and one of the best teachers of the martial art of Aikido on the East Coast. She's why I'm here as well, but she left for Japan this morning and I'm feeling my enthusiasm for this whole "dojo camping" idea drain away.

Once these people leave for the night, I'll be here in the dojo alone for the first time, part of a promise I made to Sensei to "cultivate my martial spirit." No phones, no electronics. Sensei will be mostly out of contact during her ten-day trip to Japan – she's staying with her sword teacher in the countryside. I convinced her I could handle the entire ten days living in the dojo day and night, keeping myself busy with classes, cleaning, study and meditation.

Maybe *medication* would have been a better bet: My heart feels like it's going to beat out of my chest right now with anxiety at the thought of spending a night here by myself.

First things first: cleaning the training space. We do this after every class, and the routine will empty my mind for a few minutes. We all line up at one end of the mat, each person laying both hands across a dampened rag and pausing in a crouch. Someone says *"hai,"* something like "let's go!" in Japanese, and we push our rags in front of us in line as we scamper forward, wiping clean a lane of vinyl practice mat. Hair and dust collect at the other end and are mopped up with a rag by the person closest to the wall. Another pass across the mat, a bit slower this time. Two more and we're done.

I think to myself, How can I slow this down even more? – even as I make a show of pushing my rag the fastest and doing the most thorough job of chasing down hairs and lint balls. I'm exhausted, and it's late enough that I should be able to go right to sleep. But I'm not quite ready for everyone to leave.

"Dojo" means "place of the way" in Japanese, but right now, the dojo is more like a "place of the frostbite." The propane heaters high on the wall warm it up a bit during class time, but Sensei can't afford to run them much, and Thierry switched them off before practice even ended tonight. And I certainly can't run them all night to keep me warm in my futon or I'd bankrupt Sensei. So these are my four walls, inside a giant refrigerator with no easy way out – at least until my teacher gets back.

* * *

Here's a tour of my world for the next ten days.

From the outside, you'll drive past police cars and burned-out buildings to get to a hulking former factory. The landlord painted the street side of our building a puke-green color, but ran out of money before he could finish the job. You'll park on the side, right about where the puke-green runs out and the dirty white patched with gray takes over. The side door is a bit more to the back of the building: glass woven through with wire and flanked by security cameras. Those cameras haven't worked for a decade, Sensei tells me, but they're supposed to scare off criminals. I think that no criminal in his right mind would want to break into this place.

Swipe your key card to push through the door and into the huge first-floor entryway, which is lined with stacks of flattened packing materials and piles of old machinery. Climb up five flights of stairs that are lit with flickering old-school fluorescent lights every other floor or so.

Out of breath – unless you've being doing Aikido every day for three months – you'll come to a central elevator lobby lined with peeling paint and ending in a blast door. That's right, a blast door: Fifty years ago this was where a gun company used to test bullets for their explosive power. Our floor was where the magic happened, or something pretty dangerous, at least. We usually keep the foot-thick blast door outside the lobby on our floor open for convenience, but it still slides into place on well-oiled hinges just in case someone's energy on the mat gets out of control. Or that's what Sensei says.

That door, along with the foot-thick walls and mysterious power transmitter on the roof, means no phones or wearable devices work in the building, even if we were allowed to use them in the dojo, which we're not. You have to go tech-free or use a fiber-optic line to get any information in or out of here. That's fine with me – my dad and I took the tech-free pledge last year, so I don't even miss devices. He expects me to write a letter by hand twice a month to keep in touch except in case of emergency. Others in the building have to go to the few tenants who have hard-wiring to send and receive messages from outside. The conditions tend to attract a bunch of broke, crazy and secretive tenants. Only a few of those people are crazy enough to actually pay rent and stay more than a month or two: most of the units in the building are empty, from what I can tell the times I've wandered around.

Push past the door at the fifth-floor landing and head right, down the hallway. The building's hallways run from the side that faces the street to the side on an access road that dead-ends against the rotting remains of another gun factory. Puffing from the walk up, you'll shuffle past the worn-out elevator and bathroom through a thick carpet of dust, wondering if you've gotten the address right after all.

The first door on your right, unmarked except for a piece of wood carved with Japanese characters for "Aikido," is the entrance to the dojo. The threshold and door-frame are what Sensei calls the *genkan*, or entry area. In Japan it would be a little stoop or recess; here it's just a dirt magnet I'm expected to clean twice a day. No tracked-in salt or sand is supposed to be left to crust up, and no spider webs above the door, ever. Sensei tries to keep the hallway floor clean, but dust seems to cluster on every surface in the winter, shellacked down by frost, so we've given up on cleaning it for the winter.

As you open the door to the Aikido dojo, there's a rack on the right where everyone stores their shoes before entering our footwear-free space. The rack is a repurposed bookshelf that needs cleaning at least four times as day as people track in stuff from the outside, lately a slushy mix that hardens to a dirty crust during class. Again: my job. Cleaning up crust four times a day.

Turn left to see the heart of the space: A broad expanse of vinyl mat, crowned at the back wall with the *kamiza*. *Kamiza* means "front seat" in Japanese, and it consists of a shelf with a picture of the founder of Aikido and various objects that make it the spiritual center of the dojo. There's a wooden knife, a tea-cup of water, a mirror in a bronze frame and a dish of salt. I'll explain what they all symbolize later – just know that each object attracts an unbelievable amount of dust and needs to be wiped down multiple times a day. My job.

For the next week or so, I'll be spending most of my time in the area right in front of you as you walk in the Aikido dojo: The lounge. Not a carpeted, relaxing space, as implied by the name, just a jumble of worn-out chairs and a futon couch clustered around a storage cabinet up agains the wall. Underneath them is a concrete floor cushioned with some foam tiles, and a few framed pieces of Japanese calligraphy hang on the walls. Not much lounging happens here, except when Sensei declares an official "social night." Sounds like a great place to sleep over, doesn't it?

The people who come to the dojo to practice Aikido every night get to go home to their warm houses after class – I get to pull out the futon frame, plump up the mattress, unroll my sleeping bag and settle in for the night. I gave dojo-camping a trial run a few weeks ago and survived, but that was before the polar vortex moved in.

The idea for me to move into the dojo was hatched a month or so ago, before news of the approaching weather. I insisted to Sensei that temperature didn't matter after the forecast came in, and I was determined to show her I've got what it takes to become her long-term trainee. Then she got word she had to go to Japan, but I insisted it didn't matter. Ten days alone didn't seem like a big deal this morning. Now, with shadows gathering in the corners of the space and my breath already steaming in the cold, I'm not so sure.

The polar vortex forced Sensei to leave when she did: The huge band of arctic weather, intensified by volcanic ash from the recent Green Mountains eruptions, is moving in this week. It will disrupt the entire region, along with magnetic storms said to block satellite communication. If Sensei hadn't left for Japan today, she wouldn't have made it in time to attend the ceremony marking her sword teacher's promotion to the highest rank. In addition to Aikido, my teacher is also an expert in Iaido, the art of the Japanese sword. That's also what I'll be practicing this week, trying to get good enough to qualify for the advanced class. Iaido forms are a solo practice, so if the polar vortex keeps people away, I'll still have plenty to do on the mat.

Even as we drove Sensei to the airport this morning we could feel the temperature drop ahead of the front. Since the Green Mountains blew, the ash cloud has created mini-ice ages wherever it goes. Tonight is expected to be the coldest night of the year – perhaps even the decade – but snowstorms are expected to warm it up a bit the rest of the week.

"The weather will be a good thing for you. After all, smaller classes mean less cleaning," Sensei announced on the drive to the airport earlier today, perhaps sensing my doubts about the whole insane project.

"Don't people usually show up anyway?"

"Yes, but this time of year you get vacations, people get sick...That plus snow means small classes and no-shows...One more time, Cherry. Are you sure you want do to this? You can just go with Thierry after class tonight to his place and stay in the guest room."

"No, I'm ready to do it. Fewer students mean more time to study and meditate, right?"

"Just remember that I won't think less of you if you do decide to stay with Thierry and Tom. Understood?"

"*Hai!*" The Japanese word for "yes" just sounds better sometimes. Especially when you want to emphasize how fearless you are, even though you're ready to pee your pants.

* * *

Anxiety is starting to really cloud my mind as we finish up with the cleaning.

The rags are wrung out and hanging on the rack – they're likely to be frozen into stiff sheets before they have a chance to dry tonight. My legs are quivering, protesting the hard practice after hours in the car earlier today for the airport trip. The students have changed and are clustered at the front of the dojo, putting on their shoes.

My challenger, Diego, his face still blotchy, waves and smiles. He's a youngish guy and chatty, especially now that we've settled the "Does Aikido Work" question. Tonight I'm ready to talk, although my bare feet are starting to get numb with cold. Conversation means he'll stay longer.

"Thank you again for practice, Cherry. So when exactly do you start college? Shouldn't you be on the beach somewhere before you have to hit the books? Sensei says you might study medicine."

It's a question I get a lot, even though I've explained it a million times. People meet me and assume a quiet, half-Asian girl like me should be memorizing organic chemistry texts or drafting papers on post-colonialist literature. I have a canned answer ready that usually stops the questions.

"I'm looking into programs that start in the fall. Science definitely interests me...I'm looking at a few schools. Nothing solid yet, though. Who needs the beach when I've got this place!" That always gets a laugh.

What the curious students – and my dad and stepmom –

11

don't know is that this girl has no intention of ever sitting in a classroom again. This "gap year" will become a permanent way of life if I've got anything to say about it. Unfortunately, others have a say in my life for now, at least until I turn 18 in nine months.

That's another thing I have to finesse, the whole age thing. Sensei assumed I was 19 because I finished high school last summer, but with homeschooling and all I actually finished early. I turned 17 about three months before I flew to the East Coast to start the *uchideshi* program. Sensei introduced me as a 19-year-old to the senior students at a dojo meeting when I first arrived. Let's just say I never bothered to correct her. Good thing, because my age would probably have been an issue when Sensei got the call about her trip to Japan. Who in their right mind would leave a 17-year-old alone in a falling-down building for ten days?

"So tell me again why you're choking people out in an Aikido dojo when you should be having fun and shopping? I hear you're supposed to clean all day when you're not practicing. You should be relaxing before starting school, not working that hard."

Is Diego reading my mind? I'm tired of explaining myself, all of a sudden. Now all I can think about is changing out of my damp uniform and bundling up in as many layers as possible. Keeping warm can't be as difficult as making conversation. But I can't be rude when this guy helps pay the dojo bills.

"Well, this is all part of my Aikido training, and I want to become a teacher. I started martial arts as a kid in homeschooling, and gradually my schooling became less important. Then Aikido became my school. Not to mention the great workout I get climbing up the stairs at this dojo!"

"Yeah, that walk up five flights was enough to break a sweat before I even got my gi on!" Diego says.

"You'll get used to it. The regulars here all have strong knees from stair-climbing. Just don't be tempted by the freight elevator in the lobby. The cold freezes up its works. There's just enough power to open the elevator door to let you in but not enough juice to let you out. We won't find you until spring. It's getting cold so you better leave soon."

Smile here, I tell myself. Make him think you're eager to get cleaning and not scared out of your mind.

"Yeah, well thanks again, Cherry. See you next time."

"Sure, thank you for class, Diego." Hope you learned your lesson, knucklehead, I think to myself. Thoughts of my choke earlier fill me with a burst of pride. I'm strong, I'm tough. I'm ready for this challenge.

Okay, I'm ready for everyone to leave now. The rest of the students cluster by the shoe rack, bundling up and talking about the coming storm.

Standing in her socks at the door is Ellie, a large woman who seems to draw power out of the ground to smash me every time I try to show off. Next to her is Walt, who works in IT at the university and has arms as limp as udon noodles that seem to absorb any attack and redirect it back at you. Quan is still in high school, comes to every class that he can and seems perpetually distracted by something just out of sight. When he does focus, however, his technique is unmatched in power. Even Sensei says he impresses her, and she never gives compliments. Then Diego, who – if he sticks with it – has a lot of potential, with some quick reflexes and a strong neck. Thick skull, too.

A strange mix of people, with nothing in common that I can pin down. Ellie has lots of advice, and Quan seems to be the best match for me age-wise. Could we become friends by the end of next week? Seems unlikely, as we've never had an actual conversation. Another goal for the ten days ahead.

❋ ❋ ❋

As I finish wiping down the corners of the main dojo space, the students say their goodbyes and file out. Now only Thierry is left, writing a record of the class in the dojo logbook, a list of the Aikido techniques he taught and who attended. He's got his parka on, but he's rubbing his hands and chattering his teeth as he writes. Is he doing it just for show to get me to give up on staying over? He's also taking his time, knowing I'm sitting here – starving and chilly in a damp uniform. I'm not supposed to change until the last student leaves.

Thierry is in his early 30s, lean and lightning-fast with his joint-locks and *atemi*, or strikes to the face. He's the best student in the dojo and talks about opening his own Aikido school someday. He's got Sensei's trust and respect, so I've got to watch my step. He summons me over to sit next to him, and I automatically tense up in preparation for something painful. His French accent gets stronger when he's mad.

"So what was that about? I thought I told you to be careful with the beginners."

"Careful? Why are they doing a martial art if they want to be careful?"

"You know what I mean, Cherry. There's hard training and then there's angry training. You let your emotions rule your practice. I know Sensei has talked to you about that. Have you been doing sitting meditation? We can do a few minutes now."

Sitting meditation, great. Exactly what I need now when I'm freezing to death in a sweaty uniform. Thierry is talking about Zazen, sitting silently on a cushion for hours at a time. There's not supposed to be a goal with Zazen, but Sensei has told me that it will help me step back from my emotions and live more fully in the moment. How is that supposed to happen when every time I sit for meditation, my legs hurt and my nose itches like crazy? I do meditation because she tells to me to, but I'm pretty sure it doesn't work on me.

"Well, I'd like to do some Zazen, but haven't eaten since this morning and the temperature is supposed to drop way down tonight. Anyway, this damp uniform is going to really strain my immune system if we meditate right now."

Thierry sits back from the table and gives me a steady, appraising glance. His family is originally from Africa, then

France, and some kind of Old World iciness creeps into his tone. I can really see him chopping off my head at the guillotine right now.

"Damp clothing has nothing to do with the immune system, Cherry. Don't give me superstition masquerading as science. You're right, though, it makes no sense to meditate now. But you have to shape up this week, Cherry. Sensei's only gone ten days, but you've got a lot to learn about being in charge of this place. And you've really got to control your temper. The last person who should be practicing or teaching a martial art is someone with anger-management issues."

Now I'm really starting to feel cold. Tears spring back into my eyes. I slump back and try to pull my damp uniform top around me like a blanket.

"Understood. Really, I know it's a problem, the anger-management thing. I just feel like anger gives me special energy. I'm so tired and sick of everything sometimes. No one notices when I get mad, anyway. I'm not good enough at Aikido yet."

"I notice, and Sensei notices. She can see you cranking someone's wrist from across the room, trust me. She's busted me before for 'teaching people a lesson.' See this scar above my nose? That happened years ago after Sensei saw me kicking the knees out from under an annoying beginner. She hit me with a bokken, right on my skull."

A bokken, or wooden sword, feels like a hammer when it hits you. They're not supposed to make contact with the body, but I've felt that hammer blow on my fingers and wrists numerous times in the past few months. Only one trip to the hospital, though, and I'm proud of that. But Thierry as an angry young guy getting smacked on the head with a bokken? That I can't see.

"You beat someone down? I always think of you as the ultimate peaceful warrior."

"You should have seen me fifteen years ago. I'll tell you about my life before that time someday. Either way, there's no excuse for using your skills to hurt people. No excuse at all."

Shame and anger and loneliness swirl in my as I sit there,

my knees knocking together as I shiver.

"You can tell me about your childhood now, if you want. When did you first start Aikido?"

"We can talk at my place. So you up for some hot noodles tonight? Tom would love to see you."

It's a trap.

Thierry knows I'm scared about staying here alone tonight, and he's giving me a way out. His partner, Tom, is a great guy and he probably has a gourmet meal waiting. Sensei would understand if I packed up a bag and gave up on the uchideshi plan, but I need to stay strong.

"Thanks, Thierry, but I've got some reading to do tonight, and with morning class, I better stay put."

"Right, I forgot about your new life as an uchideshi."

He lets the statement sit for a minute or so, waiting for me to ask to put off my dojo camping for a few nights. He waits some more, and I fight the urge to speak up. Finally, Thierry shakes his head and zips up his bag.

"Got it, uchideshi girl. Don't stay up too late working on your presentation – social night is a long way off. What is it about this time? Must be pretty major to take three weeks."

One of my tasks this week is to prepare a talk on an Aikido-related subject for when Sensei gets back. It's another responsibility, but this one is going to be fun. And take up a lot of empty hours.

"It's on the Tengu, a mythological Japanese creature who taught swordwork to a famous warrior named Yoshitsune, who taught swordwork to everyone else in Japan. There's all this mythology around the Crow Tengu and demons and foxes and swords…so much to read."

"Wow, sounds like more fun that the last one – not that I didn't enjoying hearing about exactly how our swords are made."

"Yeah, this one is less technical but more work. Lots of crazy stories in Japanese history. It seems like the whole country was infested by demons up until pretty recently."

I try to think of some good demon stories to tell Thierry, but all I can see in mind is a bowl of hot noodles. With reading and getting my dinner ready and all tonight, I won't have time to get lonely and scared, right?

"Nice, looking forward to the talk. When Sensei gets back, right?"

"Yep, the dojo social night the week after she comes home."

"Well, I'll let you get back to your demons. Good night, Cherry. Take care. Please."

"Good night – *oyasumi nasai*, Thierry."

"You show-off, with your Japanese. *Oyasumi nasai*, if you insist. You're sure about staying tonight?"

"*Hai!*"

* * *

I close the door behind Thierry and slide the latch closed – I'm all alone in the dojo now. All alone in the world. I hear his footsteps echoing in the hall, then in the stairwell for a few seconds, then nothing.

Silence except for the rushing of wind outside and various creaks and groans from the walls and ceiling as the building adjusts to the plunging temperature.

No time to waste. I shuffle into the changing area – a curtained corner by the mat – trying to keep my damp uniform pants from touching skin to keep from chilling my legs further.

First I quickly strip off my uniform, then my soggy sports bra. Thermal underwear goes on, topped with two thermal shirts, then a layer of thick wool. Last, my winter kimono, a quilted garment Sensei gave me that works something like a puffy jacket without the bulkiness. Two layers of thermal leggings, then sweatpants. Two layers of socks, then slippers. All that's missing is a hat – no head coverings are allowed in a traditional Japanese dojo because it's disrespectful or something. I've decided that I'm suspending that rule tonight when I'm inside my sleeping bag. After all, the dojo lounge is now my bedroom, technically a different space, right?

In dry clothes at last, I pull the rice cooker off a shelf along the back wall to start heating water for my dinner. I've got some leftover rice in a container in the fridge, but I can use the cooker for boiling water to make noodles, heating up boxes of soup and everything else. Sensei said she had no other cooking pot during her years in Japan, so I can certainly live out of a rice cooker for ten days in the dojo.

The lid of the cooker opens to an unpleasant surprise: last week's instant-ramen experiment petrifying in the inner pot. The gluey strands have hardened and lie encrusted along the bottom. I must have forgotten to clean it out last week in my eagerness to start my first dojo camping adventure. That night, Sensei stayed here too, setting up an air mattress on the mat. We ate our noodles and chatted until late then before you know it, it was time for morning class. I must have skipped the cleanup.

Great. With the utility sink in the hallway broken, I'll have to try to get the pot clean in the bathroom sink before I make dinner. Quick switch from dojo slippers to the special bathroom slippers, then I ease open the latch of the dojo door and head into the frigid hallway.

My stomach drops as I glance down to the end of the passage to my right: pitch dark. At the other end, only a glimmer of light makes its way from the central elevator lobby, lit by some half-dead fluorescents. Most of the dozen or so units on this floor have doors with small windows, but not a single window shows any light tonight. Since many panes are papered over, that's not too surprising.

I listen for free jazz squawking from the bald artist's space on the right side, or oceanic bass from the band that likes to practice late downstairs. Nothing. A brief surge of panic makes my mouth go dry, but then my meditation training kicks in: fear is an illusion. I'm better off all alone in the building on a night like tonight than have to deal with weirdo neighbors, right? To be on the safe side, I practice my ninja walk across the hallway, side-stepping with such delicacy that my slippers barely whisper across the concrete. The coast is clear. No one can hear me and no one knows I'm here.

Inside the bathroom, my nose fills with the faint aroma of decades of pee trapped in rotten plumbing. The familiar 1950s-era tile of the bathroom walls, in poison pink, scatters the last of my jitters and I get to work. My hands go numb with cold after a few minutes of pot-scrubbing – no such luxury as hot water in this building. This week's rare showers will be possible only with the use of a wrench on a pipe behind the stall – Sensei's greatest secret, she said. Sweat from class has dried on my skin already and I don't actively smell bad right now. No way am I dirty enough to warrant stripping in this cold, I decide. No shower tonight.

One by one, the strands of noodle loosen and crumble into the drain. Once the rice cooker is finally clean, I fill it up to the line with fresh water and scurry back to the dojo to get it boiling and my ramen cooked.

After dinner, my belly full and topped off with hot tea, I reconsider one last trip into the hallway for the night: Seems like I really need a shower. Sensei said that the only way she survived winter in Japan was by heading to the *sento*, the neighborhood bathhouse, right before bed. Once she got home still warm from the bath, sleep came easily. I'm okay now, but the cold has already numbed my nose and fingers. Dried sweat warmed up by my meal sends a sour smell up from my shivering body. A shower is going to have to happen for me to get any sleep, I decide reluctantly. I pick up a wrench from the bottom of the shoe rack and slip on my slippers again for another trip to the bathroom.

* * *

Not quite a quaint, bamboo-trimmed bathhouse, the

shower stall is draped with yellow "caution" tape and a hand-made sign: "Out of order." You'd have to pull back the curtain and really look to see that the stall is spotlessly clean, with bottles of shampoo and body wash stacked on the floor. A quick fiddle with the wrench on the pipe behind the shower, then a blissful couple of minutes in the near-boiling spray. Three minutes, no more, Sensei said, or the landlord might notice from his bill that we've figured out how to get hot water flowing.

The water's off and I'm completely dressed again, replacing the caution tape on the shower stall, when I hear a distant clanging and muffled shouts. My heart jumps in my chest before the sounds resolve themselves into something familiar.

Someone is stuck in the elevator.

This late? Which idiot got into that relic on a cold night like this?

We've all done it at least once in this building – gambling that the gears on the freight elevator will work in the cold. There are two elevators to this floor, but only one that's on after hours and accessible from the building's side door, out of sight of the security cameras. The "passenger" elevator near the office gets switched off at night.

A clanking relic of the building's days as an ammunition factory, the freight elevator is only a little tricky in the summer, when its juices are flowing. As fall's chill descends, it might take a few tries to get to your floor: The pull-up door gets stubborn on certain levels. Then, as winter's cold settles into the building's foot-thick concrete walls, the elevator plays a cruel trick on newbies, opening easily on the first floor, heaving itself up to the higher floors, and then refusing to open up again on any floor. You end up trapped and panicked, unless there's someone nearby who can break you out. A half-hour or so of trips up and down will warm up the works and the door will open eventually, but you have to learn that lesson the hard way.

It happened to me in my first week of training with Sensei, and she used the incident in a pointed talk to the class on the foolishness of taking shortcuts in Aikido training. Once you learn the elevator lesson, you take the stairs until late spring. Good for your cardio fitness as well.

But who would be stupid enough to try the elevator on a night like tonight? Don't they deserve to suffer a bit? Could be a burglar or serial killer, but I decide to take my chances and shut down my fear to serve my fellow man. This will be my first test as a full-time martial artist. Full of myself and basking in my own bravery, I shuffle over to the elevator in my slippers and set my shower caddy by the dojo door. Wrapping my hands in the towel, I grab a crowbar stashed for this purpose in the corner where the hall meets the elevator. The car is a few floors below, the trapped occupant silent for now. I pry open the outer doors a crack and yell down into the elevator shaft.

"I hear you! Just stay put and press the five button again." My voice is high and squeaky in the cold. Can the trapped person hear me?

Muffled shouts. This person sounds mad.

"Five! Press the five!

The response sounds like something affirmative in a male voice, and I squat down, Japanese style, in the hallway to wait. My breath rises in visible puffs in the air. The crowbar wedged in the outer door allows me a half-inch or so to see the idiot's progress.

First the grime-covered top of the elevator inches into view, followed by a few feet of scarred metal. Then a face floats up out of the creaking, clanking darkness as the outer doors hiss open. I stand up to keep the face in view. The elevator finally stops with an exhausted sigh as dark hair and eyes come into focus in the porthole, along with an expression somewhere between exasperation and panic. I lean in to get a better look. I haven't seen this guy in the building before, and I know I'd remember it if I had.

I'm a minute away from my first meeting with someone who will nearly destroy the world.

I hold a palm up to the glass and shout.

"Wait here – I can open it!"

The crowbar is so cold it burns my bare hands through the towel; wish I had thought to grab some gloves from the shoe rack. I start clawing at the elevator doors with the straight end, wedging open the side-to-side crack with my free hand. As the gap widens between the battered metal edges, I jam a foot on the bottom edge and lunge forward. My weight is enough to get the gears going so the doors open. A quick grab at the strap that raises the inner mesh elevator cage, a tug downward, and the dark-eyed guy is free, quickly climbing over the doors and muttering under his breath. I keep the bottom door propped open with my foot until he's clear.

I step back and everything clangs shut behind him with a clap like a gunshot. We both jump, then sheepishly smile at each other.

"What the hell just happened?" His voice is faintly accented and surprisingly deep. "That thing is a real hazard!"

"It's some kind of old-school hydraulic system and when it gets below zero, it doesn't have enough juice to open sometimes. It lets you in then traps you. No one told you about that? It happened to me once."

The visitor's face is slack with relief. His eyes look smudged in the dimness but sparkle behind long lashes. He's not that much older than me.

"Aren't we inside a closed structure here? How can it get below zero inside the elevator shaft?

"This building is some kind of temperature vortex. Colder than outside in the winter, hotter than outside in the summer. Guaranteed discomfort all year."

"So that's why rent is so cheap."

"That and trick elevators and the toxic dust coating every surface from the days it was an ammunition factory. If you don't die of the cold, you'll get cancer soon enough."

"Nice."

"So how long were you stuck in there?"

"Not sure. I don't have a watch. Not too long, really."

"No phone? There's a sign downstairs that warns people

not to go into the elevator without a phone."

"No phone. I'm tech-free, you know."

Great, I think to myself. All we need is another tech-free fool in the building who needs to be rescued from the elevator. I'm annoyed, but curious about this guy.

"Hey, you want some green tea? I've got an electric pot. It will take only a few minutes. You're probably freezing."

He looks doubtful, but also chilled to the bone.

"Thanks, but some other time. I, um, forgot something in my space. That's why I'm here, to go get it. Some important files."

"What floor are you on? The lights on the stairs are on a timer, so you may need a flashlight to go down."

"Actually, I'm on this floor, the fifth floor. Down there."

He gestures toward the dark end of our hallway, past the dojo and the bald artist's unit.

"All the way down there? On the right or left? Are you in that old photography studio?"

At the end of the hall before the stairs is a high-ceilinged room with no doors and scaffolding for lighting. Sensei tells me a photographer uses it when it's warm enough.

"Next door to that studio, closer to here. Though my space could have been a studio of some kind. Or a salon. Nothing on the walls but lots of old hairspray and makeup in one corner when we moved in."

"Nice. That's probably the room the models were using to get ready for photo shoots. It's warmer in there because it's right below the power transmitter on the roof." We look at each other and I can't think of anything else to say. Isn't he curious about what I'm doing here late at night?

The guy takes a few steps down the hall and I take a few quick steps to catch up with him. The dojo sign is barely visible in the dimness – it's in Japanese only to deter casual visitors. I point toward the sign and try not to look too geeky.

"I'm right here. I'm working in a martial arts school. Not actually working, working without getting paid. Kind of volunteering. As a student."

"Really? What martial art?"

"Aikido, it's a modern Japanese movement practice."

"Aikido, of course. I know all about it. 'The Art of Peace,' right?"

"Yeah, that's it."

I can't think of anything else to add, in that moment. I can't really explain that I'm staying over in the Aikido dojo, since it's not allowed under building rules and it's probably not smart for me to mention to a complete stranger. Not that he seems threatening.

The elevator victim is probably a little older than me, but not much. Also only a little bit taller than me, and scrawny enough that I should have no problem taking him down. Unless he's got that skinny-guy superpower strength that Thierry has that's impossible to deal with using anything but a vicious joint lock. Tough to tell without grabbing his wrist.

The guy's rubbing his hands and visibly shivering, so my feelings don't get too hurt when he starts backing away down the hall.

"Thanks again. I really appreciate you rescuing me. You'll be okay getting downstairs to your car?"

"Uh, sure, I'll be fine. Just have to finish a few things in here and I'll see myself out. Stay a little late sometimes to get things done."

I'm such a bad liar.

"Great, see you around. Thanks again!"

He's walking briskly down the hall and has almost been swallowed by the darkness when I call after him.

"Cherry! My name is Cherry, by the way. Stop by for tea during the day. I'm here…a lot of the time."

He turns around and gives me a smile that warms me to the core. Perhaps these ten days will pass pretty quickly.

"Sure, nice to meet you, Cherry. My name is Dar. D-A-R. Rhymes with 'car.' See you around."

"*Oyasumi nasai!*"

You stupid show-off, what are you trying to do? Of course he doesn't know Japanese. He'll probably think I'm insulting him.

"*Oyasumi*, Cherry-san!"

Hmm, he knows some Japanese, too.

Next time, I'll grab his wrist.

CHAPTER TWO

Saturday

Can tears freeze on your cheeks? If they puddle around your eyelashes, will they ice up and weld your eyes shut and do some kind of damage? Will frozen tears cause frostbite and leave scars on my face?

Ugh, I shouldn't have made that last pot of green tea after my noodles. Now it's 2 a.m. and I'm wide awake, and some kind of grief has settled like a lead weight on my chest. My eyes are closed, but I can see my father's face, and I feel the fuzzy gray form of my cat sleeping next to me on my bed back home in California. It all seems like another lifetime and I'm missing it all so terribly. Then I start thinking about my mom's death and the tears start to burn like acid as rage mixes with sadness. All alone in a broken-down building and I'm falling apart.

I can get out of this. I don't have to stay here.

In my head, I write and rewrite my "I quit" email: "Thank you for the opportunity, Goffe Sensei, but I feel that I'm needed at home and I need to prepare for applying to colleges. I'm sure the students will carry on fine without me." In my fantasy, Sensei's face crumples with disappointment that her most promising student has abandoned the path of Aikido, but then her face glows with respect and appreciation for all I've done and the sacrifices I've made.

Two paragraphs into my "I quit" message to Sensei, my eyes close and I'm drifting away in a warm wallow of self-pity. As I'm about to doze off, I feel my futon frame jerk suddenly. Another strong jolt: It's almost enough to throw me off the side of the bed and onto the concrete. What's going on? Was that me? An earthquake? Did I have some kind of nightmare muscle twitch?

The futon jerks again, letting out a hoarse screech of wood against concrete as it's pulled sharply away from the wall.

I'm sure I'm fully awake now as I peel back my damp ski mask to see better. I see the glow from the window above my head, but nothing else. Sitting up seems impossible, so I carefully shift over to my left side to get a view of the space around me.

What the...?

My eyes adjust to the dimness, cut by light from the street and a fading moon that casts a cold gleam across the concrete and cinderblock inside the dojo. Wide open, my eyes focus with a snap to movement near the door. There's something moving by the shoe rack – a shadow or flicker of some kind. The shadow seems to glide across the floor toward me, and I let out an involuntary yelp.

"Hey, stop!"

The shadow keeps coming.

Something dark and shapeless rises up from the floor right next to my bed, and I feel myself starting to pee my pants. Damn that green tea! Forget my Aikido training – I'm trapped in a sleeping bag and this thing is hovering over me. I close my eyes and prepare for death. The futon frame jerks again, harder this time. Then a booming voice seems to force its way into my very skull.

"NAMAKEMONO!"

It's Japanese, but I word I don't recognize right away.

Another jerk of the bed. Now my nose is prickling with a blast of smells: smoky fireplace and a piney scent that's somehow familiar. I lie still for a few seconds, awaiting some kind of

27

blow or murdering action. What kind of maniac wants to kill people when it's this cold? Something damp and warm seems to slip into the bottom of my sleeping bag – have I really peed myself?

A bigger lurch of the futon – this time the frame tilts and dumps me right onto the floor, where I land with a painful crunch. Luckily Sensei set up some foam mats on the floor in my sleeping area or I'd have a shoulder fracture.

"*Namakemono!*"

The Japanese word sounds like something I should know, but the meaning doesn't come in my panic. All I can think of is how sad my father will be when he hears I've been murdered, and I start crying again. Tears start running all over my cheeks, then a few data points align in my brain and identify that piney scent: it's Jintan, the super-strong Japanese breath mints that Sensei keeps in her desk. She said her teacher in Japan used them in morning class to mask his whiskey-drinking the night before. Sensei pops one of the Jintan now and then to boost her energy, and it's a sure sign that we're going to be tossed righteously in Aikido class.

Do late-night hallucinations have whiskey benders or down days? Do they need fresh breath? My fear seems to seep away as I ponder the craziness of the situation. The thing still hasn't touched me, and the dojo falls silent again. I open my eyes a bit and turn my body, still encased in the sleeping bag, toward the door. Perhaps I can stay in the warmth and crawl my way to safety. The shadow-shape is by the door again, and seems to be twirling or flapping around in front of the shoe rack.

"*Namakemono!*"

What does that Japanese word mean again? Sensei's used it when talking about her time in Japan, something about her teacher finding a moldy stash of laundry at the back of a closet in the uchideshi quarters. Everyone had to do extra sword practice for a month and one guy got kicked out over the scandal. How did that word come into it?

As my eyes adjust, I see that the creature seems to be

wearing a dark kimono-type garment, and he comes up only to the top of the shoe rack. He's practically child-sized. I could take this thing if it came to a fight, I think to myself.

I pull down the sleeping bag a bit from within and plan my leap up when I feel something rough and stinking flung at me, landing on my head and blocking my view. Is this when the murdering starts? But the scent is familiar. The stinking thing slides down my face and I can see again: the kimono-clad shadow is still moving by the shoe rack. I sit up a bit and see that it's sweeping its arms across the shelves of the rack, back and forth. Bits of grit tinkle on the concrete.

"*Kitanai yo! Namakemono!*"

Of course. *Kitanai* means dirty. The thing is telling me that the shoe rack is dirty. Huh?

Now I remember. *Namakemono* means "sloth," like the animal, but it also means lazy slob in Japanese. *Kitanai* is dirty. So I'm being terrorized by some kind of ghostly, pint-sized neat freak with an anger problem. And he's pelting me with damp cleaning rags from earlier today. That familiar smell is the funk of the rags we use to clean the mat, especially strong when the cloth is damp.

My fear ebbs a bit. Being yelled at about cleaning the dojo is something familiar.

What would Sensei do in this situation?

Asking that question makes my next move obvious. I push down the sleeping bag the rest of the way, then lift myself up to standing. I slide my feet into slippers, then scrabble a bit on the floor to pick up the rags. Now that I'm at my full height, I summon the guts to take few unsteady steps toward the shoe rack. The shape glides away from me and toward the mat, hovering and silent.

I grab a bottle of cleaning spray from the shelf next to the shoe rack and start at the top, wiping carefully along each level. More spray and more wiping as grit from outside showers to the floor. I *have* been lazy about this – I usually wipe down the shoe rack on my way out of the dojo after classes, and I didn't leave last night so I forgot. It's become "my job" to clean the shoe rack so no one else has taken the time to do it in the past month or so. I skipped the chore this morning before the airport ride and after class tonight. None of the other lazy slobs at class noticed the dirt, a blend of dust with sand and salt from snowy sidewalks. The shoe rack is filthy.

"*Baka!*"

Something solid lands on my forearm with a thunk. It stings, but no permanent damage done. My still-sleepy brain processes the familiar blow – it was a strike with a bokken, or wooden sword. Next into my brain comes the translation of the newest shouted Japanese word: "Stupid." I'm not sure how to react – I just keep wiping the shelves with more energy.

Once I finish the shelves, I do what Sensei would do and start over with a fresh rag. Another two rounds of spraying and wiping, spraying and wiping, long after the patter of grit stops. You could probably eat off the shoe rack now.

I take the rag that looks dirtiest in the dim light and sweep the grit on the floor into a pile, then drop it into the trash. I'm in cleaning mode now, and my fright has faded into background noise. The next-dirtiest rag follows to sweep up the last crumbs of grit, then the last few rags become makeshift mops as I swab the entire floor surface around the shoe rack until the concrete gleams, using water left over in a bucket from the mat cleaning last night.

I look up from my labors, and the angry little guy in the kimono is gone.

What the hell just happened?

* * *

A body sails through the air then crumples into a broken-looking heap.

My heart stops for a minute: Have I killed a small child? Sensei depends on the children's Aikido class for cash flow to keep the dojo open. A dead kid can't be good for business. But the crumpled heap soon emits a gurgle, then a full-fledged giggle. The boy flops onto his back and wiggles his arms and legs as if in the midst of a seizure.

"Splatter roll!"

He then pops up and bolts across the dojo to wrestle with his brother.

Whew, no deaths so far today. It's amazing the spectacular Aikido falls the little kids can take with no harm done. But one wrong move and they're crying in the corner – only to recover completely in the next minute. Except when they don't recover and don't come back. I had better tone it down a little. Quan, my assistant for today, herds the kids into the corner for some rolling practice.

A shudder passes through me; I haven't been able shake the chill all day. The morning started with some meditation, me and Quan sitting silently for an hour. My mind swirled with images from my dream the night before. It was a dream, wasn't it? I must have had a sleepwalking episode of some kind, because when woke up, the shoe rack was gleaming and the futon frame was out of place, as if someone had been yanking it. My sleeping bag was damp, but not stinking of urine, much to my relief. Instead it appeared that one edge of the bag had fallen into a bucket of dirty water from mat-washing, which was sitting in front of the futon on the floor.

Another *namakemono* lazy move – that bucket should have been emptied last night after class. Unlike most containers of water sitting for any length of time in the dojo space, however, it didn't have a crust of ice on the top.

Strange.

Guilt over my laziness must have brought on a very vivid dreaming episode. At least that's what I'm telling myself. That's the logical explanation, and I'm sticking to it. Weird that the shoe rack would be so squeaky-clean, with all the sand and salt in the parking lot. I know I didn't clean it last night after class. Perhaps someone else did as they were leaving and I just didn't notice. It was just a dream, more like a nightmare. I try not to dwell on the vision of the angry clean freak, even as his shouts echo in my ear. And that bruise across my arm must have been from class yesterday. Funny that I don't remember getting hit by anyone – anyone human, that is.

"What game are we playing today, Cherry Sensei?" The kid who took the big fall earlier, Thayer, looks up at me, tired of rolling practice. Great, I promised a game early in the class to keep the kids obedient, but my mind goes blank. Then, as my eyes hit the shoe rack for the hundredth time today, an idea comes to me.

"Let's play Demon Swordmaster!" Quan gives me a quizzical look – we haven't played this game before with the kids.

"What's that!?" chorus a half-dozen eager voices. I've learned over the past months that the kids love anything scary that involves monsters and swords.

"OK, everybody line up at the back of the mat. You all are going to try to knee-walk by me and not get hit by a sword. One hit, and you have to act like you're dying a horrible death. Really show me that you're dying! The more dramatic the death, the quicker Quan Sensei will bring you back to life!"

Some parents might not approve of having their precious babies play dead, but the kids seem to love the idea. The rest of the class flies by. Only ten minutes left before the kids go home I can have another cup of green tea and try to shake off the strange feeling I've had all morning.

Kids' class is finally over and I'm standing at the window, dodging the occasional strike from a foam sword as the kids wind down with some free play. Outside the sky is dim and bruised looking, smudged at the horizon by an approaching cloudbank. Even in here I feel the heaviness in atmosphere as the first blizzard moves in. The parents chatter of a coming storm, stockpiled food, the impossible energy of snowbound children.

The kids have collected their coats and shoes and are leaving in a flurry of "*sayonara*" and "see you next week." No casualties, except for one little boy who can't seem to stop crying. Quan is getting changed in the dressing room area, so I guess I'm the one who needs to be the nice Sensei today.

"Krishna, what's wrong? Does something hurt? Did you take a bad fall in rolling practice?"

The kid shakes his head and whispers.

"I don't like that man. That sword man is mean."

"It was just a game, Krishna. Cherry Sensei and Quan Sensei are very nice in real life."

Talking to little kids is not my strong point, so I go for the easy fix, rummaging in Sensei's desk to find a seaweed snack.

"See, I'm the sword man and I'm nice. I know you like seaweed snacks."

Krishna takes the papery square and munches intently, but tears are still pooling in his eyes.

"Feeling better? See, the sword man is nice and won't hurt you. It's me, Cherry Sensei."

"You're nice. Quan Sensei is nice. But I don't like *that* sword man." Krishna points to the windows beyond the mat and starts sniffling again. "He says I'm lazy and wants to hit me!"

My stomach drops.

The boy jabs his finger again toward the back corner of the dojo. Nothing there but a wan patch of sunshine shimmering with a few motes of dust. The kid's mom leans over with his shoes and gives me an amused look.

"He's such an imaginative boy. Come, Krishna, take another piece of seaweed and let's get you home."

Krishna brightens up the at thought of leaving and the pair move toward the shoe rack. I can't stop staring at the back corner, looking for shadows or movement.

A mean "sword man" who wants to hit people – sounds very familiar. What could the boy be talking about? And I never said the word "lazy" in the class. Is there something in the air today that's making people see things?

＊ ＊ ＊

"Um, can I help you? Interested in trying a class?"

A short African-American man in a puffy jacket that looks like a space suit steps into the dojo after a tentative knock. I've got a break before the afternoon classes, and I've been enjoying some tea and cold noodles. Unannouced visitors to the dojo are rare, but Sensei insists that I act "customer-friendly" with anyone stopping by. As far as I'm concerned, the dojo has enough clueless beginners already, but Sensei needs to make a living, I guess.

"Do you want a brochure?"

The man's face opens up into a smile and he pushes his hood back a bit.

"No thanks! No falling down and wrist-twisting for me. Actually, I'm supposed to be checking on you. You're Cherry, right? I'm Jean-Baptiste from downstairs."

"Oh, you're Jean-Baptiste. Sensei told me about you. Come on in and have some tea."

My visitor shakes off his hood completely to uncover angular features and short hair. His eyes are wary, but something in his manner puts me at ease.

"Thanks, I could use something hot right now. You guys keep it so cold up on this floor." He shivers and pulls the hood back on.

Sensei told me about Jean-Baptiste: He runs a startup tech company on the second floor, in one of the few parts of the building that have been fixed up. The rest of the place is falling apart, but the tenants on that floor actually live in this century.

According to Sensei, landlords in New York own the building, but they stopped putting money into it as soon as they found out that the inches-thick metal plates in the walls blocked all cell, power and drone-surveillance transmission. The few tenants who rent space here either don't need wireless signal or don't want wireless signal – or they improvise. She hinted that Jean-Baptiste is working on something big and secret, and that he might like this building because it's practically invisible to spy drones. He's got the squinty look and the scrawny body of a tech guy, I've got to agree. But he seems nice and there's another hour or so before the last class of the day, afternoon free practice. Having someone to talk to will help keep me awake after the exhausting morning and bizarre dreams last night.

"Thanks for stopping by our Aikido dojo. Try this – it's called kukicha and it's made from twigs and stems." I push a tea-cup full of brown liquid toward him.

"Hmm, tastes kind of like dirt. Is that what it's supposed taste like?"

"Yep, exactly. Dirt and dry leaves. It's super healthy."

He grimaces at his cup, but goes back for another sip. We sit in silence for a minute or so, and I study the little I can see of his face. He's practically mummified in the insulated hood, which is lined with some kind of shiny scarf. What I can see is eyes, a bit of facial hair and lips with a definite bluish tint.

"Well, at least this is warm dirt water. Kind of suits this space. You know, you seem a little young to be staying here by yourself. Belinda said you were 19. Really?"

"I'm almost 19, and I've stayed overnight in dojos before. Lots of people live in dojos in Japan. And in China. Like tens of thousands of people. It's just another lifestyle choice and it saves resources."

Jean-Baptiste doesn't look like he's buying it, and the silence gets a little uncomfortable.

I can't help myself: I blurt out something that's supposed to be a secret.

"Sensei says you stay here in the building sometimes, too."

Jean-Baptiste pulls back his hood a bit and looks me straight in the eye. I see some suspicion, but his golden-brown eyes quickly light up with amusement.

"Right, she told you that, did she? Well, I guess we both have some secrets. My work keeps me up late, and I don't like running into the spy drones in this neighborhood after dark. I have heat in my office, though."

"Makes sense to stay over sometimes, right? In the Aikido world, we think of it as the best way to learn from a teacher." I'm feeling guilty about spilling the beans, but Jean-Baptiste's smile and gentle eyes tell me that both of our secrets are safe.

"So, tell me how you ended up here, living in a martial arts school on the top floor of a mostly abandoned building in the middle of winter? When you're not even 18?"

Busted.

"Long story." I sit cross-legged on the futon couch as Jean-Baptiste settles into a chair. Sitting in the lotus posture is difficult the older you get, Sensei says, but my legs seem to fold up naturally and I've gotten to prefer it over slumping back on the cushion.

"I'm here for the experience of being an uchideshi, or live-in student. You may not realize this, but Goffe Sensei is one of the best Aikido teachers in the country. She also roomed with my mother at the university here in the city years ago."

"Interesting. Does your mom fight like a samurai as well? Is she an Aikido sensei?"

I snort and nearly spill the dregs of my tea.

"My mom pursued the martial art of tax law. She died six years ago."

My statement hangs in the air – I could explain how my mom died at this point and how it ties into my Aikido and why I'm so screwed up and why I'm living in this freezing hellhole instead of having fun at college. But I'm already jittery from last night, and I push right into more small talk.

"Weird that my mom was 100 percent Japanese and had no interest in martial arts, while Sensei is as Anglo as they get. I'm half Mexican and I'm the one in the family who's interested in exploring my roots. Third-generation Asian identity crisis and all."

"That makes sense. I've got the second-generation Caribbean-identity thing going on. I majored in Caribbean studies at the university – I was there the same time as Belinda, your sensei. She majored in Japanese, of course."

We sit again in silence, more relaxed this time. Outside a few hailstones begin to fling themselves again the windows with a chattering sound. Jean-Baptiste pours himself another cup of kukicha and we both turn to watch the clouds shift beyond the panes.

Because my mom was Japanese, I can use the "exploring my roots" line when people ask me what I'm doing here in the dojo. But I can't really explain what it is about Aikido that hooked me. Most of my life I had no interest in Japan or martial arts. Then I tried an Aikido intro class in my hometown and something clicked.

Even now, for a moment or two every Aikido class I feel like my body, my mind and the universe are all working together. When I'm in a classroom or online, I feel like a broken piece of some giant evil machine. The choice between school activities and the dojo: no contest. Aikido is my path, my career, my future. Yes, I'll be making barely enough to survive, but at least I won't be enslaved by student loans.

"But what about retirement? Don't you ever want to have a house or your own car?" I can see my stepmother smirking and rolling her eyes at the suggestion that a smart but aimless girl skip college. Not that I've revealed my whole life plan to her and my dad yet, just my intention to delay college a bit. Only a few more months to 18, then a few years of study with Sensei and a few more in Japan. Then my own Aikido dojo where I'll be free of everyone's expectations forever.

My "retirement plan" is a quick death in a duel before I'm 50 and my joints are shot – or a broken neck from a bad fall when I'm 25 and at the peak of my beauty. Lying there on the mat, my skin at its most luminous, my hair fanned out around my head as my last breaths echo in the silence... A boyfriend would be good before that, for a few years – only so he can wash my dirty uniforms and have dinner ready for when class is over.

I can dream, can't I?

Jean-Baptiste hugs himself a bit, then reaches for the teapot. I forgot he was here for a minute.

"So how did you end up alone here? Belinda said she had to leave town, but she didn't go into detail. I would think she'd want you to stay at her place."

"Someone needs to be here to cover the Aikido classes every day in case someone cancels. I don't have a driver's license yet, and it's too icy to ride a bike. Sensei got the call last week about going to Japan and she had to rush to get it all arranged. Someone needed to take care of the dojo and I promised her my dad wouldn't mind. Anyway, you're one of, like, twenty people who are supposed to be checking on me the whole time, so I'm not so alone, I guess."

"Belinda said you're serious about the martial arts life. Impressive. But don't forget to visit me if you get scared or hungry. Second floor, second room to the left of the elevator on the right. I'm actually going to be here full-time this week due to some… domestic challenges."

"Right, I understand. If you want to share a meal, come on up – no microwave here, but ramen noodles come out great in the rice cooker if you watch them carefully."

"Sounds good. Well, I'll let you get back to your duties. Nice to meet you in person, Cherry."

"Nice to meet you too, Jean-Baptiste."

"You can call me JB, everyone dones."

"Great, JB!"

Finally, a real friend. With a microwave! Things are looking up around here. I'll be OK this week, as long as it stays light out.

✳ ✳ ✳

Afternoon free practice is over.

The students are gone, eager to scuttle out after Thierry's lecture on their many faults and lapses of martial awareness. The hell with it, we're not exactly customer-friendly around here. Aikido is supposed to be about improving yourself, and most of the students just want to have fun. Pathetic, really. Don't they see how much suffering I endure to stay on this path? Anger keeps me warm as my damp uniform chills. Evening classes are canceled due to the storm so this is the last session of the day.

I stand by the door and take deep breaths of relatively fresh air from the hallway. Thierry offered me a meal and a bed at his house again, but I'm more confident turning him down this time, knowing that I've got a friend downstairs in JB. Theirry gives me a frustrated look, puts on his shoes and leaves. No chat, no lectures. What a relief. With the slam of the dojo door, I'm alone again.

Now it's time for the essence of uchideshi life: a thorough cleaning of the dojo. The heat's been off since the middle of the free practice, but at least something in this room is warm: I've heated up a kettleful of water and dumped it in the bucket, where it sends up clouds of steam in the frigid air. I've got my rags ready.

Now for the plunge: a first batch of floor rags, stiff from use the day before, into the water; my hands exploding with sensation from the warm bath after hours of chilled dojo air. Wring the rags out carefully – too much water means I'll be slipping and sliding on the floor hours from now. Luckily it's a bit warmer inside today; yesterday a few minutes of swabbing yielded a glaze of ice on top of the concrete.

Start in the corners and make sure the cobwebs and particles of grit that came in on students' boots don't start accumulating. Stretch the rag between your splayed hands so it forms a kind of mop then bend down so that your hands are about three feet from your feet. Once you've got the optimal angle, push off with your feet and sort of sprint forward so the rag becomes a power mop that covers lots of ground in a short period of time, pushing up a respectable little pile of dirt, hair and lint.

That was uchideshi lesson Number One: proper floor-cleaning technique using rags. No floor robots, commercial mops or disposable wipes in a traditional dojo. We clean the mat and the floor like they do in the Zen monasteries in Japan, by hand and with damp rags. A splash of bleach for the mat, a splash of vinegar for everywhere else. At the end of every class I draft the students for mat-cleaning. But the rest of the thousand-plus square feet of the space is my responsibility, and Sensei expects it to be cleaned before the first class and at the end of the day. That's a dozen times a week, and by now every rusty bolt on the wall and divot in the floor is burned into my brain.

After the floors comes the dusting and wiping and emptying of trashcans. Then I record all the day's Aikido classes in my dojo diary – who taught, who was there and what techniques we did. In all, about three-quarters of my waking hours are taken up in cleaning and other tasks with Sensei away. Not much time to get lonely or bored, really. But I've always been really good at squeezing the maximum amount of daydreaming and drama into my day.

At last it's all done, the dojo's usual sweaty funk replaced by the sharp edge of bleach and vinegar. All the surfaces shine. No *namakemono* lazybones here.

Cleaning done, I head to the bathroom to rinse out the buckets and rags. As I wring out the last rag in the sink, I pause to study myself in the bathroom mirror. In my Aikido uniform I look more Asian, the white of the kimono-style *gi* setting off my dark eyebrows and irises. My features loom a bit too large to fit the Japanese ideal, however, and something about the cast of my eyes and angle of my jaw marks me as *hafu* – half Japanese and half something else. People always babble on that mixed kids are especially beautiful, but some of us end up just looking like a little bit of this, a little bit of that.

In middle school I wasn't Asian enough to hang with the immigrants and first-generation kids, and not quite pretty or exotic enough to attract the boys with "yellow fever." There were still plenty of oddballs left in my science and math classes, so I never lacked for friends when I looked for them. The problem was that I stopped looking for friends after my mom died, and once I drifted out of the social mainstream, friends stopped looking for me. For the last year of high school I was home-schooled via computer and made a handful of online friends. No questions, no complications. But also fewer and fewer shared posts, texts and instant messages. Sometimes my chats went silent for days.

Now, months of daily Aikido practice have leaned out my face and corded and broadened my neck. Most of my dark-brown hair hangs jaggedly in a pixie cut – it's been a year or more since it's been styled by a professional. All I need is a pair of scissors and mirror for "dojo styling." Just below my bangs and above my right eye is a puckered red line: Six stitches from getting hit with a wooden sword. It happened in advanced weapons class my first week in the dojo, while I was practicing with Thierry. Sensei was standing behind me, and I was trying to impress her with my power and quick reflexes. They both were pushing me to my limit in a partner practice with the *bok-ken*, the wooden sword used in Aikido weapons. A *bokken* isn't as dangerous as a live katana blade, of course, but it can still crush bone and rip skin. Especially when used full-force against an arrogant and inexperienced opponent.

"Faster! Cut stronger, Cherry, faster!" Sensei shouted.

I sliced straight down toward Thierry's skull with a straight cut called a *shomen* from above my head. Thierry, weapon in the same overhead position, stepped back, pulled his hip back and slammed his bokken into mine at top speed. He's the dojo expert at *kiriotoshi*, a bokken cutting practice that neutralizes an overhead strike. I'd been pushing myself to attack more aggressively every time, despite fear so intense my stomach hurt. I wanted to show Sensei I had what it takes.

This time, my attack was fierce, all my fear and rage channeled into a wild overhead slashing. Thierry's eyes widened before he swiveled his hip back and countered with a mighty blow. My attack was effectively neutralized, but my *ma-ai*, or distance, was off – too close for too long – and I failed to absorb Thierry's energy enough to avoid his strike. Forget the technical or spiritual excuses: I just messed up and got bashed in the head.

The tip of his bokken, tapered for maximum cutting speed, smacked against my temple just above my right eyebrow. At first I was just dazed, falling back on my ass to the mat. Blackness with some explosive yellow sparks ricocheted in my brain. Then warm tears started to flow down my cheekbones to puddle in my eye sockets, a gush that became a red scrim of blood once I opened my eyes.

Sensei took one look and declared that the traditional treatment for a superficial face wound – using the membrane on the inside of eggshell to seal it shut – would have to wait until I got stitches. We took a trip to the urgent-care center, Sensei looking grimly at the bill, my white uniform crusted with blood and salt from tears. It was all an embarrassing blur after that. Sensei's egg did its work well after my stitches came out, and the wound closed completely in a few weeks. It's an old Japanese martial arts tradition: The membrane from a fresh egg, carefully peeled away from the shell, is plastered onto a gaping but superficial head wound. The egg membrane pulls the skin closed as it dries.

Probing at the wound, I'm happy that the scar has faded a bit, but find myself hoping I'm left with some permanent mark to commemorate my first advanced weapons class. Will the scar stay jagged? Turn white or stay red? Keep its puckered edges? It will be a great story to tell my students someday. Tonight in the frigid bathroom, the scar is the only thing that looks alive on my face.

After a few more minutes checking for zits and enlarged pores in the mirror, I pack the rags back into the bucket, wash my hands well and push my way through the balky door and back into the hallway. Just as I turn toward the dojo, a slim figure bounds up the stairs and skids to sharp stop in front of me: Dar, the guy from the elevator last night.

"Hey, Art of Peace girl!"

"That's me. Doing some cleaning right now."

Looking like a complete mess. Smelling like dirty feet

and bleach.

"Right. I can see that. Those bathrooms are surprisingly clean, considering the state of this building." He gestures toward the light fixture hanging all wonky above him.

"Our Aikido school takes care of these bathrooms. You should see the ones on the second floor. The ladies in the main office clean the first floor, but all the others are disgusting, except this one. We clean it at least three times a day. OK, maybe once a day, if we remember."

I'm babbling. Dar's bundled in a puffy jacket, scarf, hat and boots. He's also carrying a bag of some kind. As I look closer, it seems to be a kind of long backpack with a sleeping bag attached. Another building overnighter? And only a few dozen yards down the hallway.

Dar notices my glance. His features tighten a bit, but then he breaks out into one of those stellar smiles.

"Hey, you still offering some green tea? I want to learn more about the martial path as it's practiced in the inner city."

"Sure. I don't have some tea made right now, but I can boil water make some really quick. Not boil, but heat to just a little below boiling for the best brewing. And I've got some cool Japanese cookies flavored with pickled plum – you've got to try them. Not like *pickle* pickles, but sweet and sour and salty. Trust me, they're really good!"

Babbling again. I force myself to shut up, and turn to let us both into the dojo. He places his backpack carefully against the wall by the shoe rack.

Heat lingers in the space thanks to the recent class so it's still a bit warmer than the hallway, and I see my guest relax and loosen his scarf. The clouds outside mute the light and help hide the dojo's worn interior – I like to think the gray glow makes it look more minimalist than shabby. Dar loosens his coat and takes off his shoes at the rack before I can ask him. His eyes range around the space, and I think I see some appreciation there. I gesture toward the lounge area and he takes a seat and settles in, flipping through an Aikido book as I fumble with the tea supplies. I fill the electric kettle from the water cooler and silently pray that I've cleaned the scum off the bottom of the teapot recently. My babbling starts up again as we wait for the water to heat up.

"So earlier you said you didn't have a phone. Have you taken a no-tech pledge? Me and my dad only write to each other on paper. Tech seems to get in the way of my traditional training here, but I'm surprised that you're doing it."

Dar looks up with a bemused smile.

"It's kind of a new lifestyle thing, but I make my money on tech, so I guess I'm still in recovery. Tech and various energy projects. Don't make me explain: It's all really boring and technical."

He goes back to the book. Do I look too stupid to deserve an explanation? I'm a bit insulted, but focus on pouring hot water over the tea leaves and counting out precisely 90 seconds of brewing time. Then a quick pour into the insulated pitcher so it won't cool down too fast. Then two servings poured into the most Japanese-looking cups I can find in the storage cabinet.

We sip the tea in silence, steam furling from the celadon porcelain. It's come out just right, grassy and herbal and just a little bit bitter. It will get stronger as it sits in the pitcher, slowly cooling and turning sharp and funky by bedtime. The dregs go great with toothpaste although I've got to cut back on green tea late at night. I pass Dar the box of plum cookies, each round individually wrapped and spiked with MSG. I'm sure he'll like them until he finds out the secret to their full flavor.

His dark eyes are roaming around the room as we snack, lingering on the ceiling and my array of buckets and dishpans designed to collect water dripping from the ducts. It's not really obvious in this light, but water-stains stripe the walls on all sides.

I guess any more conversation will need encouragement from me.

"What do you know about Aikido? Have you ever practiced?"

Dar laughs and flexes his biceps. "No exercise for me, please! I'm all about spending every moment of waking life as a brain in a box. But what about you? Why spend all this time studying Aikido? Don't you... have other interests?" he asks.

"Like why don't I study or help the homeless or cure cancer or something, you're saying? I get asked that a lot."

"I'm not trying to give you hard time or anything."

"No, it's good for me to think it through and explain myself from time to time. I do want to make a difference in the world, but I think I can best do that by practicing Aikido, if that makes any sense. Every time I work with someone on the Aikido mat, it's like I'm confronting human nature. Humans have this violent side, and this peaceful side. In Aikido, we take the violent energy and make it peaceful."

Dar laughs and twists his arms up like a pretzel.

"Hey, I've seen videos of Aikido, and it doesn't look too peaceful to me. People getting tossed around and their arms bent back!"

"Right, you see that, but what you don't see is that the person getting tossed around started it first. They attack with violence, and the Aikido person takes that violence and turns it into something that neutralizes the attack, but doesn't hurt the attacker. At least that's how it's supposed to work."

"Aren't all martial arts like that in some ways? Why not practice Karate or Judo or something and become an action star?"

"Actually, most popular martial arts are about dominating and hurting someone. Aikido's philosophy is non-violence. If you want to get really deep, Aikido is also about fighting the violence in yourself. You may want to hurt someone who attacks you, but you're trained to always take care of them and make sure they aren't damaged."

I can't help but blush a bit at this nice speech. After all, I've been getting in trouble a lot in the dojo lately for pushing my Aikido techniques a bit too far and hurting my partners.

Time to re-read some Aikido philosophy.

"Wow, it sounds really interesting, if contradictory. But other martial artists are always criticizing Aikido for not working in real fights. Don't you want to win in a street fight?"

Dar throws a quick punch at my face. It's not a real one, but I react automatically and deflect the blow, then tag his face with a light slap.

He laughs too loud, holding up his hands in surrender.

"Whoa, I stand corrected! That stings."

I'm embarrassed that I lost my cool, but Dar doesn't seem angry. I decide to ignore the fact that I've just slapped a dojo visitor in the face. Sensei doesn't need to know.

"No, you're right. There's a lot out there about how Aikido doesn't work in real fights. But no single martial art makes you an invincible warrior. Aikido is more about fighting yourself and human nature, and making you a better person.

"But if you get good enough at Aikido, you'll be able to defend yourself. Better yet, you'll be able to stay away from street fights for good. The senior students tell me that they are much calmer and more confident, so street thugs stay away. For me, I don't think about street thugs as much as learning how to control my emotions. Fear, anger, frustration – all that."

This is getting a bit personal, so I change the subject.

"You must be getting sick of talking about Aikido. So what about you? You're with that new power company that Sensei was telling me about? She sounded really impressed about what you guys are doing."

Dar's face snaps around to mine and his eyes seem to sharpen their focus to laser points.

"You could say we're a power company. Could say we're a tech company. Not really easy to explain the whole thing. Wow, look at the time."

He's not looking at a watch or anything, and my retro alarm clock is hidden behind the box of cookies. What did I do wrong? Did Sensei let some secret slip? Wouldn't be the first time.

"Thanks for the tea, really. Got to go."

There's a few awkward beats. I think he's forgotten my name.

"Cherry, that's my name. It's the translation of Sakura, which means 'cherry blossom' in Japanese. My mom wanted me to be girly and flowery – too bad for her!"

"Of course, Sakura. Cherry. See you around. Thanks again for the rescue from the elevator last night. I'll stop by again for tea, I promise."

"Great! Bye."

The door swings shut with just enough force to fall short of a slam.

What just happened? All that talk about martial arts then I said the wrong thing and he just shut down.

Another squeal as the door swings open again.

"Nice name, really. My name – Dar – is short for Darabh. Means 'one who has conquered the sky' in Sanskrit."

"Yeah, you told me last night. Your name, I mean, not what it means. That's interesting."

He stands at the door and that smile erupts again. It almost seems like he's ready to come back in, but the silence lengthens and he turns away toward his end of the hallway. He closes the door more softly this time.

✳ ✳ ✳

Dar's visit was strange, but a welcome distraction. Now my sweat has dried, and my uniform is growing heavy and throwing off waves of stink as the cold gust of air he let in from the hallway blasts through the dojo.

The dirty uniform goes into a straw basket under Sensei's desk: Thierry has offered to take the dirty laundry home every few days. My underthings go into another basket for later washing in the kitchen sink on an afternoon off. With Thierry's help and a little scrubbing, I should be OK on clothes for the week.

Sensei has also left some of her old uniforms that need sewing repairs in case I run low. She showed me the sewing supplies and some needle techniques – that's another project for my down time.

In fresh clothes, I collapse into Sensei's cushy office chair then wrap myself in blankets. Too spent to read or write, I pull the chair to the window and look out. A dry towel I grab off the shelf serves as a kind of head wrap, insulating me from the drafts that blow in through the window frame. Outside the sun seems to redden with shame in the late afternoon, slipping behind distant hills at it sets fire to satellite dishes and sneakers tied to electric wires. There've been brief intervals of hail and snow flurries off and on all day, but now the sky is clear.

It may be a crumbling hulk, but the dojo building is high enough up to give me a panorama of the surrounding city. Upon taking in this view, a visitor from Japan might ask, 'When did the tsunami hit?'" It does kind of look like a giant tidal wave has leveled the neighborhood. Like most industrial cities of the last century, it's a wreck. The building next door looks like it was picked up then dropped from a great height, walls buckling and every window agape in starbursts of broken glass. A tattered tarp hundreds of feet long covers the biggest holes in the roof; smaller holes open to the sky like the burrows of some massive, civilization-eating rat. A coating of snow frosts the decay without adding an ounce of charm. To left, another former factory has decayed to a skeleton, only steel beams and concrete floors left to catch the last rays of the day.

Just beyond are some spindly trees that have recolonized a toxic dumping area. Now they are ice-caked skeletons that look unlikely to survive into spring. To the right are once-middle-class homes, now sagging and shabby, their porches and rooflines buckling, brightened only by the occasional swags of police tape. Frozen snowdrifts, sprinkled with trash, glitter as the setting sun hits them.

Of course there are nicer neighborhoods out of sight to the left, and some impressive office towers and church spires backlit on the horizon at the center of town. But rot has taken hold and spread in this neighborhood, and won't easily be dislodged. This part of town has cheap rent, and cheap rent is how Sensei can keep the dojo going even with the economic crash. It's also why a slightly out-of-her-depth, half-Japanese 17-year-old can camp out here in the building unnoticed and unbothered.

Sensei led me through the building on my first full day as a trainee, perhaps hoping to scare me into a quick trip home. After all, a traditional Aikido teacher is supposed to turn away an aspiring student at least three times before accepting him as a trainee. And it was always a him, at least until recently. Rejection and discouragement at the start make for a student who can brave the rejection and discouragement to come later.

Discouraged was how I felt on my first glimpse of the building housing the dojo. From the outside, the structure looks like it's been dragged behind a car – covered in scab-like concrete patches over cracks that had been gaping to the elements. None of the tenants on the first two floors stay in the building past sundown, Sensei said, and those relatively big spenders are the only ones who matter to the landlord.

Once up on the fifth floor and inside the dojo, Sensei got me up on a stepladder to read the labels on the panels above the windows. "Warning: Asbestos. Do not puncture or cut." The panels were visibly crumbling at the edges beneath some clear sealant that Sensei had sprayed on.

"Be careful cleaning up around here," she warned.

Asbestos keeps fires from spreading, but gets into your lungs and gives you cancer or something, and it hasn't been used in buildings for decades. Great, a broken building and toxic waste, too. Toxic waste that's crumbling into the air right above my bed.

Feeling adventurous, Sensei next took me to the floor below the dojo, untouched since the 1970s and coated in dust and cluttered with broken office furniture. A hole through the concrete near the front of the dojo that once held a pipe offers a peephole down into that floor – gray and sad during the day, shadowy and shifting at night. The thought that someone or something down below might someday pop its head up had me creeped out from the first week I trained here. As soon as I decided to move in, I found a piece of scrap wood to cover the hole and anchored it with lots of duct tape. Sensei didn't say anything, but the wood stayed in place. After all, that hole lets the heat out, right?

Our next stop on the tour was the roof, more hospitable three months ago when the weather was warmer. Sensei shoved open a door at the top of some stairs to reveal a stretch of tarpaper and gravel. Walk a few steps and you get a close-up view of the only new thing for miles around: a shiny wireless transmission tower. That's how the landlord survives with a mostly empty building, by renting out the roof for the tower, Sensei explained. But everyone in the building has to pay the price, she added. The signal emitted by the tower disrupts all incoming and outgoing transmissions not already blocked the metal in the walls, not that I care.

More and more I find myself adjusting to life without quick answers and streams of data, big free spaces opening up in my mind that I'm not too anxious to clutter. The other day between classes, I discovered that I had been looking out the window for nearly an hour, watching a bird peck at something on the ledge. Mornings before class I spend minutes just lying on my bed, reliving fights with my stepmother or trying to remember details about my mother. I've got no idea about what's happening outside the building or even exactly what kind of weather is coming, but living without technology has become more of an adventure than an ordeal.

Sensei said that those of us who live completely without tech are clustered on the fifth floor, probably because the transmission tower interference is stronger up here. There's Werner down the hall, the bald artist who I see now and then washing his brushes in the utility sink. On the other side of the fifth floor lobby is the space of Emma Wong, a Tai Chi teacher who spends long hours in her school lately due to some kind of bad situation at home. She's not all that much older than me, but gives me no end of attitude because I practice a "brutish and warlike" art like Aikido. She's not exactly friendly but hasn't kicked me out the handful of times that I've dropped by her unit, and I know we could be friends. This week might be a good time to get to know her better. A young guy who practices the Brazilian art of Capoeira has a space down the hall from her, but I try to avoid him for reasons I'll explain later.

Two floors below the dojo is another empty floor used by cops for "urban assault training." Sensei and I explored it together my first week here on a lark. Walls smeared with paintball spatter and floors littered with old mattresses, the third floor has been my preferred escape on days when I can't bear to look at the dojo's four walls anymore. It feels more like a party house than an abandoned ruin, and I love reading the filthy graffiti left by cops on the wall.

The second floor, where Jean-Baptiste has his company, is the only space that resembles any kind of regular commercial building as it's been fixed up relatively recently. There's a mysterious import/export company in the middle of the floor with papered-over windows and a sealed door. People come and go from that floor at all hours, Sensei says. I've been conducting my own sporadic surveillance of the parking lot in the hopes of discovering something interesting, but all I see is people with packages coming in and out now and then. I haven't seen anyone in the last few weeks, so maybe they're taking a break for the winter.

Shai, the building manager, has an office on the first floor in the front. He holds court there during business hours, attended by two West Indian assistants who double as the cleaning staff. Lionel from Jamaica does the building's maintenance – such as it is – filling potholes and getting abandoned cars towed to the lot next door. On the other side of the first floor is a closed-down rock-climbing gym, watched over full-time by a guy called Brah. I've only met him once, but Sensei wants me to check on him next week and make sure he's opening his food deliveries. I guess he's a little absent-minded.

The building feels impossibly big and crowded right now at the end of the day as cars buzz in the lot and voices echo in the stairwells. But night is coming, and most of the cars are going to leave soon. If the acid metal band doesn't shake the walls with its practice around 11, I'll be left alone here in the dojo to face the darkness.

What – or who – will be waiting for me?

＊ ＊ ＊

"Hey, keep it down! Lift, don't push!"

Nothing is guaranteed to wake me up faster than people whispering outside my bedroom – or my dojo. That's how I first knew something was wrong with my mom: urgent whispers outside my bedroom door.

Tonight I must have fallen asleep while doing research for my tengu project, as the desk light is on and I'm stretched out on the futon still in its couch form. By amassing a mound of blankets, coats and uniforms to keep warm while reading, I created such a comfortable cocoon that I must have drifted off. A glance at the clock shows it's 1:24 am.

Could that be Dar shuffling around late at night again? Emma the Tai Chi teacher might be camping out tonight, or Jean-Baptiste. But he's downstairs and she's on the other side of the building. These voices are coming from right outside my door.

My eyes adjust to the dimness beyond the desk with help from the bright moon outside the windows. Best not switch anything else on in case someone scary is about. I ease my feet into slippers then carefully lift myself off the futon frame to minimize creaking. I creep my way to the expanse of wall to the right of the shoe rack, where one of the many bolt-holes in the cinderblock allows a view of the hallway outside.

The emergency bulb by the bathrooms highlights several dark figures hoisting what looks like a couch or a long object of some kind. As they shuffle past my door to the lobby, I recognize Dar as he shushes the others with a free hand. Something about the way they are moving makes me think they don't want to be noticed, so I tiptoe back to my desk. With the way the desk lamp is angled, it's unlikely they could see the light from the hallway, so I crouch down and keep still until the sounds fade to nothing.

Why move something so big so late at night? Why risk getting stuck in the frozen freight elevator again? Or did they take that huge thing by hand up the stairs?

What is my new friend trying to hide?

CHAPTER THREE

Sunday

L ike a tiny hammer rapping on my skull.
    Drip, drip, drip.
DRIP DRIP DRIP.

My eyes open into blackness but my pupils soon adjust to take in some gray, pre-dawn light. I ease down my sleeping bag and the cold air hits me like a stinging slap across the face. I pull it back up.

There's a leak somewhere, louder than usual. Strange that anything would be flowing in this cold.

Drip, drip, gurgle.

What the hell? That sounded like it was coming from right next to me. Sensei deliberately set up her office and the lounge – also known as my sleeping area – far from any known leaks. What could possibly be dripping?

And what did I have for dinner again? Something smells like rotten meat in here. Could that stink be leftovers gone bad?

Gurgle, gurgle, giggle.

Giggle?

My sluggish brain stirs to life: That's not water gurgling, it's someone laughing. The crazy swordsman from the other day? Dar? A stalker student? One of the band guys playing a prank after a late jam? Who the hell would sneak into someone

54

else's space in the middle of the night? Why can't I get a decent night's sleep around here?

All these thoughts rush through my head as cower in my sleeping bag, trying to shrink into the futon frame without attracting attention. Scariest of all: Maybe someone's broken in to rob the dojo without knowing that I'm here. Memories rush into my brain: The cops downstairs at home in California, my dad's face collapsing as he talks about what happened. My mom's body left in a bloody heap by a gangbanger with a gun and a shaky trigger finger.

A thump brings me back to the cold dojo, right now. Then my bed shudders as if something heavy has landed on it.

Something *has* landed on it, and is next to my left leg. Feels like the size and weight of cat – or a giant rat or spider of some kind. My terror spikes and I can't help but pull back the sleeping bag to take a look.

Wide-open eyes quickly bring my tormentor into focus.

A giant spider would have been better.

What's sitting on my bed looks like some kind of nightmarish mashup of a frog, a turtle and a crazy old man. It's greenish-gray in the dim light, squat and froggy with beaky features, big eyes and scaly arms erupting out of some kind of armor or shell. The eyes – shining and freakishly huge – catch mine, and my panic subsides a bit. It almost looks friendly, whatever it is. And it looks kind of familiar.

It shuffles across the bed a few inches toward me, and something wet and slimy lands on my cheek. Is it spitting at me? Steam is rising from to the top of the thing's head, where something glitters as it moves.

Another shuffle and it's almost within reach, scuttling across the mattress between my body and the edge of the frame. The creature is the size of a big cat, so I should be able to fight if off if it tries something nasty. Right now, it just seems to be checking me out.

An abrupt croak makes me jump and I slide up against the wall to get away from the thing if it decides to bite. Another croak and it seems to shake a bit, like a wet dog. To my surprise, Japanese words seem to sound themselves out of the swampy croak.

"Mushi-atsui, ne?"

"Mushi-atsui, ne?" it repeats, louder this time. I know those words, but they don't make sense in the moment.

Mushi-atsui…Ok, now the meaning comes. I've said that phrase a million times to relatives in the summer and in Japanese class back home. Translation: "Hot and humid, isn't it?"

Huh?

The equivalent of "Whew, hot day," that phrase is one of the most common uttered in the Japanese language, a tutor at home once told me. My ancestral homeland's unbearable summer heat causes asphalt to melt and old people to drop dead on the streets, she said. In California, we used it on hot and humid days in class, even though a "humid" day back home is still bone dry compared to Japan. Sensei told stories of having to wring out her uniform after sweaty practice sessions during Tokyo's summers and uttering "hot and humid, isn't it," incessantly for months.

But why is this frog-monster talking about summer weather when it's probably below freezing in the dojo right now? Why is it making delusional small talk while sitting on my bed?

"Hot and humid, isn't it?" it repeats in Japanese, this time convulsing in what seems to be an exaggerated shiver. "So hot!" Lucky for me, his Japanese is as simple and direct as a child's. Now he explodes into gurgle that splatters into what can only be a laugh. Is this creature making a joke? Sitting on my bed in the middle of the night playing out the concept of sarcasm?

"Hot and humid?" The shiny beaked face is inches from mine, and the stench of its breath is almost unbearable. Like something dead washed up on a beach and left to rot. Something dead and fishy and froggy. Left there for weeks.

"HOT AND HUMID?" More liquid splashes on my face as the thing raises its voice.

I can't help myself: My Japanese lessons and perhaps my genes compel me to politely echo questions like this with the standard response.

"*So, desu ne!*"

Translation: "Yes, so it is." Said in the polite form, with my voice high and girly like an anime character. This phrase serves as a generic response to any question you don't understand or don't want to answer either way. I used those words constantly in my meetings with visiting Japanese relatives after my mom's funeral, and they complimented my dad on my good manners.

"So it is," I repeat.

The thing giggles again and seems to hop around a bit on the futon. A few more warmish globs of something splatter against my face. Seems like there's something liquid on the top of its head that splashes when it moves. Where have I seen that before?

"What…what's your name?" I sputter out the phrase, trying to throw in as much polite Japanese as I can.

The creature spins in place, then croaks back at me with a blast of stinking spray.

"I am Kappa! Nice to meet you!"

Right – now I know where I've seen this particular froggy face. My reading in on Japanese demons like the tengu has lots of info on the kappa, a true celebrity from ancient folklore. They're famous for being somewhat cute, stinky and living around water. While swimming in Japan, kids are told to watch out for a *kappa* swimming underneath: They're known for trying to pull you under and drown you. A *kappa* might also try to pull your intestines out of your rear end. Yes, they're known for lurking underneath swimmers and yanking your guts out of your butt. Only in Japan, really.

That particular disgusting fact stood out from my reading. What kind of culture am I descended from? Why such a disgusting and creepy creature? Why can't we have leprechauns and fairy godmothers? I guess it's really no worse than vampires or werewolves, if you think about it. Vampires must have bad breath, too.

As the Japanese demon sits on my bed in the flesh, I mentally scroll through my recently learned knowledge on the kappa. Do I ask it to grant me wishes? Feed it something? What am I supposed to do now? Seems easiest to just stick with the Japanese introduction niceties. My spinning brain kicks out some Japanese small talk, in polite form, or course.

"Hello, I'm Cherry. Nice to meet you. Um, what business brings you here to our dojo, Kappa-san?"

Oops, was I supposed to call him Kappa-*sama* – the title for an honored customer or demigod – to show respect? Or Kappa Sensei – the title for a teacher or doctor? The Japanese language is loaded with ways to insult someone without meaning to. This particular demon's nasty streak is legendary.

It doesn't seem to matter.

"HERROOO!" Again a few seconds to translate in my brain. Could it be "Hello," as translated through a Japanese brain? It bellows again, this time waving its webbed paw at me.

Forget about the niceties of formal Japanese, this kappa knows some English.

More dancing around, more splashing.

"Heroo! Herroo!"

That splashing: I remember from my reading that kappas are supposed to have a dent on their heads full of water. If the water drains out, they lose their power, so people used to challenge them to wrestling matches. Perhaps if the creature turns away I can give it a little shove off the futon. But I need it to get a bit closer.

"Hello! Would you like to do some Aikido practice with me over there?" I gesture toward the mat.

That seems to quiet the kappa down a bit. It turns its triangular skull toward the front of the dojo in the direction of the mat then turns back and stares at me for a bit longer. My nose doesn't seem to be capable of getting used to the stink – it hits in renewed waves of rotten seaweed and four-day-old roadkill every time the *kappa* shifts its boxy body.

"Can you stand closer to the edge here? The smell..."

"Yes, I like to stink! Smells great to me. You are lucky, Cherry-san. Have you met Akaname? He's another *yokai* who sneaks into your bathtub at night and licks the dirty slime off the sides. He smells so bad! I smell like wind in the pines compared to him."

Yokai – monsters and demons from Japanese folklore. The crazy man from the night before and this smelly thing could both qualify as yokai, I guess. The monsters are famous and are featured in lots of Japanese comics and movies, but people haven't actually believed in them in centuries.

So what have I been eating or breathing to make yokai appear in this dojo, during this week that I'm here alone? Am I brain-damaged? Something in the air vents? Is my imagination running wild?

Without warning, the kappa scrambles down to the foot of the futon then drops out of sight, followed by a squishy plop from the direction of the floor. With a sound like someone running with wet feet, he waddles out of sight into the mat area. More giggles and gulps echo into the darkness then fade gradually into silence. Nothing but the stench remains, nearly visible as a gassy cloud around my bedding.

Should I get up and see if he's done any damage? Mop up any puddles or light some incense to freshen things up? As my fear fades away and the cold air starts to numb my exposed neck and hands, the idea of leaving my sleeping bag becomes unthinkable. I shift down into the warm depths, pull a blanket over my face and try to let sleep overtake me.

The yokai, and whatever it is that's bringing them into my life, will have to wait until morning.

❈ ❈ ❈

My first thought on waking up: Yay, it's Sunday, my day

off.

My second thought is that I must have pooped my pants. A lingering stink seems to float over my sleeping bag, but quick sniff under the covers reveals it's not coming from me. Memories of my *kappa* visit flood back, to be quickly dismissed as another bad dream. I fight to push back doubts about my sanity and worry about what's in the air in the building to focus on the day ahead.

First things first: My body check. I stretch out in the sleeping bag, feeling my joints pop and my spine unfurl. Today's soreness level: moderate. My left shoulder, which I landed on badly two weeks ago, is aching but seems to have regained a full range of motion. The thigh pull from two months ago – tight but no pain. My mood: pretty good, considering the nightmares.

Ready to die today?

Sensei advised that I keep track of my physical and mental health, so I started keeping inventory on a spreadsheet back at home a year ago. Now that I'm here, I'm going to have to keep track in my head because my lack of access to technology. Too cold in the morning to write by hand.

Ready to die today?

That last question I came up with myself after reading lots of stuff about the samurai "Way of the Warrior." A warrior has to be ready to die at any moment, to let go of fear. This morning, fear is competing with curiosity about my visitors of the last two nights. Then there's Dar, another puzzle.

But the sun is out, if shaded every minute or so by clouds. It's Sunday, my day off. No classes, only a few light chores, no visitors from outside asking me questions. The brooding winter light flooding the dojo has nudged me awake just after 8 am, but I theoretically could have slept until noon.

The snow starts just as I finish my first cleaning of the day, a wipe-down of the *kamiza* and all shelves with a fresh rag. First everything gets taken off the kamiza shelf: the picture of Aikido's founder, a bowl of sand for sticks of incense, the mirror, cup of water and dish of salt. I learned all about the meanings of these things when I first became an official Aikido trainee. The mirror is a sacred object in Japan representing the world as it is. The water and salt are daily offerings to the Shinto *kami*, or gods, and represent purification. There would usually also be grains of rice on a kamiza, Sensei said, but we've had problems with mice in the dojo in the past, so we leave that out. Incense gets lit when anyone dies or to pay respect to someone who has died. We put a picture of the founder of Aikido, O-Sensei or "Great Teacher," front and center to show him respect for creating our art.

Although I did this cleaning routine first thing yesterday, dust has recoated every surface overnight. That dust is causing my nightmares, no doubt. After carefully wiping down the kamiza, I take my rag to the window ledges, each swipe painting a swath of grime onto the cotton. I try not to breathe in any nightmare powder that might be sprinkled in the dirt.

Outside, the sky opens up seemingly with the flip of a switch: nothing, then the air alive with movement. The first flakes are heavy and sooty against the dull gray, spiraling downward. Then the fall separates out into tiny particles floating every which way, flowing together only with the occasional gust of wind that shakes the trees below. The students in class yesterday had mentioned something about snow squalls coming ahead of a big storm next week. Storms mean canceled classes, and more time alone here. Not sure that's a good thing right now.

I keep my eyes off the floor all morning, willing myself to dismiss last night's happenings as a dream. But when my cleaning routine nears its end – a final mopping of the concrete – I squat down next to my bed to take a closer look. Visible all over the floor are splotches of what looks like spilled green tea, dried up and crusty. That's what must have been dripping, a knocked-over teacup! It was a dream, after all. No teacups in sight so I must have picked it up and put it away in my sleep, right?

Before swiping with my rag, I run my finger through the greenish scum. Smells like the piece of fish that fell behind our stove at home last summer and wasn't discovered for a week. Low tide and road kill. My brain searches for explanations. Green tea sometimes smells fishy if you let it sit too long. That was some funky batch of green tea I had last night! That has to be the answer.

With cleaning done and my brain buzzing with impossible thoughts, I finish my chores and get ready for my planned Sunday workout: stair-climbing in the building. Eight circuits and I'll reward myself with a heaping serving of rice porridge, which I set to stew in the cooker. A few bowls of that and those lingering nightmares will disappear.

"Rice porridge" sounds like a punishment, but the way Sensei taught me to make it, it's the best meal possible on an off day. First rinse off your brown rice with cold water in the bathroom sink until the water runs clear. Swish it around and eventually, agonizingly slowly, the starch gets washed off and stops clouding up the rinse water. It takes about 20 fills of a teacup to get the water clear, I discover. My hands are numb by then. Sensei says the best thing is to set up the rice to soak before evening class and let it sit overnight – no chance of fermenting or sprouting with the dojo temperature after class hovering around 35. Last night I fell asleep before washing the rice, so I'll have to make do.

The rice water finally runs clear. You then add more water and set the rice cooker on the "porridge" setting. An hour or so later you mix in more water get wonderfully warming, flavorful stew with tender grains in a soupy broth. Add some scallions, sesame salt and kimchi and it's the best Aikido brunch ever, according to my teacher's teacher. I try not to think about French toast or bagels.

A few limp scallions are hiding in the bottom of the dojo fridge, lucky for me, and I stocked up on kimchi before Sensei left. The sesame salt is kept in a tin on top of the fridge so it can be dumped in anything that needs some flavor. Some people also like crumbled seaweed on top, but I can't stand the fishy taste and slimy texture when it's mixed in. Fishy and slimy, just like the kappa last night.

I quickly shove my nose into the kimchi jar to clear my head. Garlic and chili fill my nostrils as I inhale quickly, but the fermented cabbage funk quickly takes over and brings my thoughts back to something unsettling again.

Time to break a sweat.

* * *

Ichi, ni, san, shi, go, roku, shichi, hachi, kyu, ju.

One, two, three, four, five, six, seven, eight, nine, ten.

Counting in Japanese is the first thing you learn in Aikido class as a kid, and I picked it up before I could even roll across the mat. Now I can't do anything training-related without the Japanese words ticking off in my head.

Ichi, ni...

San, shi...

*Go...go...*come on, go!

No, actually, I can't go.

Before I can stop myself, I slump against the stairwell wall, exhausted. I pull away quickly but not before my white uniform top gets smeared with dirt from the walls. It's only the fifth step on the second floor, but I've already done seven up-and-down circuits of the building's five flights of stairs and my thighs are giving out.

Sensei told me not to do stairs while she was gone: "All that pounding is bad for the knees. You'll feel it in your third decade of Aikido, I guarantee it." But I know I have to keep up my conditioning while she's gone, and the coming storms mean fewer classes, less vigorous practice.

No students, no class, no workout. No one around to keep me from going crazy.

I could taste the hot porridge waiting for me as I pounded up and down the five flights in my sneakers, doing my best to raise my knees and "be lively," as Sensei would say. My energy ran low on the last climb, thighs burning and puffs of steam rising from my aching lungs.

Now, if I can only drag myself up three more floors and get back to the dojo.

The pounding of my heart eases in time for me to hear another rhythmic thump – someone is coming down the stairs at a fast clip. I ease myself into the corner of the landing a bit so I'm not in the way.

A familiar face pops into view as the visitor rounds the corner.

"Hey, Cherry! How's it going, ninja girl?"

It's Dar, practically mummified in what looks like puffy ski pants and a jacket. He's on his way out, obviously.

Great, my face is shiny with sweat and my hair looks like hasn't been washed in days. It hasn't been washed in days, actually. Not to mention the eye bags from my nightmare last night and my dirty uniform. I could just say hi and keep going, but I've got to find out more about what Dar is up to. What was he moving the middle of the night? It's my duty to find out as guardian of the dojo.

"Hey, Dar. How's the power project going? Saw you moving something in last night."

He starts a bit. In the light from the window, I see that he's looking a bit worse for wear as well. His hair is lank and frizzy beneath his cap, and his eyes are sunken into wells of bruised-looking skin.

"Good, good, really good."

"Well, you look as tired as me. I'm making some rice porridge if you want some – it's kind of like oatmeal. But not sweet. Kind of salty, but in a good way…I'll be up there in a half hour or so if you're coming back."

"Sure, actually I'm just going to the basement to deal with a blown fuse."

"Great, see you up there. Number 503, remember? I'll leave the door open."

"Sure."

* * *

My sweaty clothes are stashed and I've lit incense to freshen up the place, three sticks of the strongest blend in the burner on the kamiza. Something still smells nasty in the dojo – I just hope that Dar doesn't notice. Got to get around to mopping up all that spilled tea.

An hour passes and I've almost given up hope that he'll stop by when a knock comes at the door. Dar's out of his outdoor gear and swathed in a fleece cape over sweatpants. He's carrying a box of something.

"Wow, smells great in here. Like fresh rice. I got these the other day downtown at the Chinese store, thought you might like them." Japanese cookies, the expensive ones that taste like shortbread.

"Thanks, that's great. We'll have them after brunch."

His eyes are darting around the space again.

"Want to look around? I guess I haven't given you the official tour."

"So, what exactly do you call this place? A practice hall? Gym?

"No, it's a dojo. Means "place of the way." We're pretty traditional in Aikido so it's a '*do*,' or way, instead of just a fighting system. Like Judo or Karate-do. We're all martial paths, not just fun and games. Like more about improving yourself than just kicking ass."

Why can't I learn to just answer a question? I think to myself.

"Does calling it a dojo mean it's more like a temple or religious place?"

"I guess you could say that. I actually did a research project on the idea of a dojo when I first got here and there's lots of stuff in the space from Japanese religion. My teacher asks me to research stuff and present it to the members as kind of an educational exercise. Beats school, right?"

Ugh, I can't believe I just said that. Now he's going to think I'm a stupid kid.

Luckily, Dar seems too interested in walking around the dojo to register my mistake. He studies the lists of techniques on the wall, and the Japanese calligraphy. He walks the length of the mat and pauses up front. I try not to freak out that he's still wearing his outside shoes. Wearing outside shoes in a sacred space like the dojo is pretty much a major crime in Japan.

"Is that an altar of some kind?" Dar gestures toward the *kamiza*.

"I guess you could call it that. We call it a kamiza, which means 'front seat' or 'seat of the gods.' Goffe Sensei – she's the main teacher here – doesn't put any Buddhas or anything on it but she still calls it the kamiza."

"So I guess you're kind of a monk or something in this religious experience of Aikido."

"An uchideshi, or 'inside training student,' actually, is what I'm called. No worshiping for me, just training and cleaning. Speaking of cleaning, can you take those shoes off and leave them up front? You'll track dirt around."

"Oops, sorry about that. We do that in my culture too, but I'm so distracted today."

"Really, no problem. It's just my job to say something."

I can't help myself. Japanese blood and years in dojos mean I have to speak up about the shoes. Wow, I've managed to make myself sound like a boring drudge with no sense of humor. Better shift the focus of this conversation.

Dar takes his shoes off and drifts toward the lounge area, studying the Aikido seminar posters along the back wall this time.

"So are you a physicist or something? Tell me about your work."

Dar pauses in mid-step, seems to think about my question a bit then catches sight of the steam rising from the rice cooker.

"I'm really hungry, is the brunch ready yet? Smells done

to me, but I only know Indian rice, not Japanese."

Subject changed, I busy myself with ladling out the porridge, nicely soupy and fragrant. Dar piles on the kimchi and seaweed, and even says yes to a pickled plum on the side. Intensely salty and sour, picked plums are great for when you want to wake up your stomach. I'm not always in the mood, to be honest. We each finish a big bowl of rice porridge, then dig in for seconds. I'll barely have enough to eat cold tomorrow morning. Tea and some of the cookies serve as dessert as the small talk peters out.

With the bowls stacked and tea cooling, Dar starts to talk.

"So all about me, huh? I'm an engineer. Well, that's my training, although I can't say I've gotten a paycheck for it. I was a student at the university for four years then did some post-grad stuff in a really interesting lab. Unfortunately, my own ideas were too interesting for the administration and they kicked me out last summer. Took my ID away and everything.

"Lucky for me I had copied some of the tech and 3D-printed some hardware at the student center so I could continue the experiments myself. Did some work with friends at home in Vermont but I needed a little more raw material out here, so I came back a few months ago. That's my story. Sorry you asked, right?

"No, I actually did some engineering in high school, a summer internship not far from Silicon Valley. Are you working in electrical or chemical?"

"Kind of electrical, kind of biomedical. Do you really want to hear about this stuff? I've put many a friend to sleep explaining my work."

"Totally, I'm interested. My dad thinks I'm going to study some kind of tech in college, so the more I can talk about the stuff, the fewer questions he's going to ask about when exactly I'm going to sign up."

"You're smart to stay away from higher education, Cherry. All the tech is becoming automated so you won't get a job. And exposure to those people will make you completely crazy."

"What are those people like?"

"For example, say you have a great idea like tapping into the collective consciousness as an energy source. They'll go nuts with all these made-up ethical problems and shut you down."

"Collective what?"

"The combined brain activity of the entire human race. In here – he points at his head. "It's all biochemical and other kinds of energy, it's going out all into the atmosphere, going to waste. What if you could tune into the frequency of every brain out there and channel that energy? It would be a uniquely human resource, and potentially endless. We've already done it with bacteria and even simple animals like jellyfish. My work was on human brain energy, but these idiots at the university are so short-sighted."

Dar jabs his fingers in the direction of the campus of the university, a few of its neo-gothic spires visible in the far distance. His face clouds over with a sullen rage, and I wonder if it's time to change the subject. My American curiosity beats back my Japanese politeness instincts, and I press him.

"Brain activity must happen at a very low level of energy, right? Or all our brain tissue and skulls would get cooked. How can that be a real energy source? Wouldn't making cold fusion or something work better?"

"My idea is to use nanoscale components in tune with the brain to amplify the energy and channel it into a usable, renewable form. Problem is, at this stage, I need a huge amount of plain old regular power and transmission capacity to make this happen. Stupid administrators at the university said they couldn't see the expense as justified. And this is after I nearly blew up the campus when my experiment worked just once, for a few seconds!"

"Wait, that was you? Last year with the big explosion and stuff? We even heard about that on the West Coast. My dad called Goffe Sensei here to make sure she was OK."

"That was me, all right. Don't believe what they were saying about 'dozens of injuries,' though. Just some whiners and jealous co-workers trying to get disability pay."

Dar stands up to take a mock bow, his face glowing with what can only be called pride. But only a minute later, what looks more like a storm cloud settles over his features. This is one intense and angry guy. But even Sensei says the university is mostly staffed by half-witted drones. His rage is probably justified.

"Didn't some people actually die in that explosion?"

"Only one guy, a lab tech who ignored all of my warnings to stay back. The university did a great job of blaming his death on my own actions, but he really shouldn't have been there in the first place. Even so, I do feel some guilt about that."

He doesn't look too guilty. Actually, he looks a little proud of himself.

"So is what you're doing down the hall going to blow this place up? Should I be worried?"

"No, of course not! I've made a lot of refinements to my equipment since then. I'm also tapping into a smaller power source – but getting more out of it thanks to my new work."

"The building's power grid?"

"Yes, that and our friends at City Security with their transmission tower on the roof. They built a nice modern generator for that, and it's just right for my needs. This building is perfect in so many ways. I can also get new raw material when I need it by sneaking into the university through the tunnels. There's an opening not even a mile away."

Dar leans closer at this point, and extends his arm toward me while looking into my eyes.

"I don't need to tell you that this is all our secret, right? My work could mean the entire world order could be disrupted – in a good way. A little borrowing of power sources and materials is such a small thing. I know I can trust you."

He gently closes his hand on my forearm and leans closer. He smells of burnt plastic and sandalwood.

"I, uh…right, our secret. Of course, it's not my business. Sensei says that the only way this building works is if we all mind our own business. Not too many questions, not too many answers."

"Smart woman, your Sensei."

Dar leans back, away from me, and something seems to clamp shut in his features.

"It's been nice talking to you, Cherry. I've got to get back to work, but we'll talk again soon. I forgot what it's like to meet someone who is intelligent but unspoiled by academia."

"Thanks – I guess? Well, stop by any time. I'm officially here on weekdays, but I sometimes come on weekends for extra projects. And sometimes I'm here pretty late."

He looks at the futon frame and the rice cooker still steaming on the desk. His eyebrows raise, and I know he's figured it all out.

"Right, I hear you. I'm in the same boat as of today. Thanks again for the porridge. See you soon."

* * *

The dojo door swings shut, and silence descends on the space, feeling emptier than ever in the pale winter light. I wander toward the window and look out on the snow-dusted landscape. It's only 2 p.m. or so, but the day already feels used up and the whitened limbs of the trees below look like they're sagging with exhaustion.

The futon frame is folded into a couch and most of my bedding is packed away, but my sleeping bag calls out to me from where it's stashed under Sensei's desk. I could just crash for a bit on the mat. But I know better than to bed down now, considering my lack of rest. Daydreaming will turn into a nap soon enough. A nap in the afternoon means I'll have to get myself up again for dinner, and the evening will stretch out into infinity. Better to busy myself now and then charge up on more green tea until an early bedtime.

Free time means more opportunity to hone my martial awareness. Sensei's voice echoes in my head, pushing me to intensify my Aikido training even on off days.

Slippers and socks come off and I walk over the weapons rack and pick up "the Axe" – a solid slab of white oak called a *suburito* that is used for building strength to wield the Japanese sword. The suburito has a flat surface along the top that serves as the *mune*, or back of the blade. The cutting surface itself is rounded off so the weapon is as heavy as possible, the better to build strong wrists. Those muscled wrists will be a sign of my discipline and questing mind, unspoiled by higher education.

I bow to the kamiza and get ready for practice. First I settle into "horse stance," legs wide, knees pointing out, toes gripping the clammy mat. Each movement will have me sinking into a deep squat, thighs parallel to the ground if I'm feeling ambitious. The left hand goes at the bottom of the handle portion of the *suburito*. The right hand goes above it, thumb up and placed so that when I look down, there is no wood visible between my wrists.

"Grab it like a live fish: Not too strong and not too weak. You don't want to crush the fish, nor do you want to let it swim away." That advice from Sensei, which came directly from her teacher, isn't much use when your forearms are tired from a hard week of Aikido and the axe seems to have gained weight from the afternoon's dampness. My knuckles seem locked and my wrists and elbows are already aching before my first cut.

"One cut, last cut." That's another snippet of wisdom from Sensei. It means you shouldn't swing the piece of wood around like it's *just* a piece of wood and let each movement blur into the next. Each cut should be the last cut, the death blow, the final move of a brutal duel to the death between you and a ninja assassin or a renegade samurai. Easier said than done.

Push with the heel of the left hand against the wood and let that movement bring the suburito up to *jodan* position – parallel to the floor, your left wrist on top of your head. Now the body drops, pulling the hands and, with them, the sword down in a slicing motion that cleaves your opponent in half from the crown of the skull to the navel.

I'm not sure how that's supposed to work in real life – does the person fall into two neat halves like in the anime films? If you stop at waist level like you're supposed to, do the two halves fall to each side as the body keels over backward? Or does it fall forward? Is one half of the brain so heavy that it pulls the corpse to the side, instead? Do the brains gush out on impact or do they stay inside their respective pieces of skull like halves of an avocado? Since you're cutting between the neck arteries, does that mean the blood just kind of flows out, or is there some spurting? And how does this work if you're cutting from the back of a horse? Why would you be cutting from the back of a horse?

There are probably some videos out there that answer these questions. Luckily, I can't search for them here. Forget about college if computer searches like "how to chop people in half with a sword" are tracked by admissions.

Monkey mind! So easy to get distracted when you're supposed to administering death blows.

Back to my "one cut" – probably twenty or thirty "one cuts" right now if I had been counting instead of daydreaming about spurting arteries. Push with the heel of the hand up, ratchet up the wrists, pull with the left hand down, blade swinging in a wide arc as if I'm about to hurl it across the room. I'm focused on counting, hoping to reach a thousand before the dojo cools down too much. One hundred, two hundred – now sweat is beading along my back and my arms are aching, elbows sharp points of pain. My knees are feeling the stance at five hundred, and the sweat on my forehead is sitting there getting cold as my body shifts up, down, up, down.

The blister I gave myself two days ago pops at seven hundred, and blood starts oozing along my hand, mixing with sweat to fall in pinkish drops to the mat. Sensei would approve, or would she call it a biohazard? Would she think I'm showing off?

The trickle of blood along my arm stops me at eight hundred cuts, along with the ticklish breeze from a wall crack just behind me. My uniform is damp and the draft is giving me a serious chill despite my hard work.

Better to spend some time sealing up that crack instead of creating more of a mess, my rational side says.

You are monkey-minded weakling who can't even finish a thousand cuts, my other rational side says. Stopping now means those ugly blisters will heal faster, the wimp in my head says.

Anyway, the crack in the wall has got to be fixed and raw blisters will need tape or they'll annoy me all next week in class. The Axe gets a swipe with a rag and is placed back on the rack, its handle dark with sweat and blood. My hand is still bleeding, so there's no use in getting started on dojo repairs. I sit on the couch and try to apply the perfect combination of bandage and tape to hide my latest war wound.

* * *

Minutes pass, ever so slowly. It's getting late and the sun isn't so much setting as the light is leaking away, draining the color from the trees and rooftops below the windows. Snow has fallen in fits and starts all day, and now the sky outside seems expectant, flash-frozen in anticipation of something more dramatic. An empty and desperate feeling fills me at the thought of darkness and the silence of an empty dojo. Not to mention the prospect of nightmares.

I sit with my emotions for a minute, trying to use the skills Sensei has taught me. I see myself as a mountain, standing tall above a stormy sea where my fear, anger and frustration boil up into waves. The mountain stands tall, unmoved by storm. My breath comes more slowly, each exhalation calming the waves, bit by bit. Then my nose starts itching and the waves start crashing again. The mountain cracks into pieces as I furiously rub my nose, then collapses into rubble. Enough, already.

Mindfulness is not going to work, so perhaps I need a human distraction. Time to visit the only person I can actually call a friend in the building, even if she has a pretty challenging personality. On go my winter kimono and my straw "hallway" sandals. Like a traditional Japanese home, the dojo has a complex system of inside, outside, hallway and bathroom footwear to ensure that nothing impure makes it over the threshold. Sensei yelled at me last week for wearing my bathroom shoes to walk her to the stairwell – seems I was tracking bathroom impurities into the lobby, where they could be picked up by hallway shoes and brought into the dojo or something like that. Whatever, I learned my lesson.

My hallway sandals swish slightly on the uneven concrete and I slip into ninja-walk mode, placing each foot lightly and deliberately to minimize noise as I cross the elevator lobby to the far side of the building. A silent approach is best over here, because I've had some incidents in the past, as I'll explain later.

Sifu Wong, also known as Emma, has a space on this end of the building, past some artists' studios and several practice spaces. The units on this side are the cheapest because of noise from the street and damage from some kind of blast in the 1970s before the ammunition testing facility shut down.

Emma's door is plastered with flyers for live music shows and lessons in all kinds of Chinese energy practices – Tai Chi, Qi Gong and Bagua. Even from the hallway I can feel warmth from the inside: Sensei said Emma once had a big-time job and spent lots of money for an industrial heater to keep her studio warm. The wood of the door is practically hot against my fist as I knock, softly at first and then a few sharp raps.

"Hello, anybody home?" She must be there if she has the heat turned up so much.

"Emma? It's Cherry from down the hall. From Aikido?"

Silence as I listen for movement behind the door. Nothing except a rustling across the way in another space, which is unmarked and has windows covered in black paper. Creepy, but likely just the wind.

The door opens with a whoosh of hot air and the scent of incense.

"What do you want?"

Emma could be five years older than me, or she could be fifteen years older than me. Her constant practice keeps her energy fierce and her face is always in some kind of scowl. Now she gleams with what must be sweat, and her jet-black hair stands straight up in a brush cut. She's about my height but skinny as a stick and vibrating with a kind of manic excitement. The Tai Chi shoes on her feet and the three-foot sword in her hand mean she's been practicing.

I try to think of a good reason for interrupting her.

"Got some soy sauce? I'm running low."

"What, just because I'm Chinese you think I have soy sauce? Do you want mu shu pork, too? Some kung pao chicken? White rice or brown? You are really killing me with these stereotypes. It's bad enough that you Aikido people are appropriating such an unrepentantly colonialist culture with a history of imperialist and genocidal aggression. Learn some Asian history before you bow down the Japanese."

Sensei briefed me before my first meeting with Emma: Don't react to anything she says. Don't get mad or offended. Think of it as *atemi*, the strike to the face that opens some Aikido techniques. She's looking for an opening to take you down. If you stand your ground, she'll respect you.

"Sorry, I really need the soy sauce. I'm making this organic kind of cup noodles and they taste like nothing. I thought you might have some soy sauce."

"Sounds tasty. Are you going to bring me some? It's not polite in Asia to talk about your food if you're not going to offer it to someone."

"Sure, I can bring some if you want...I can just heat up another cup."

"Forget it, I'd rather dig some termites out of the wall and flash-steam them in toilet water. How about ketchup? I've got some of that."

She turns away and leaves the door cracked – that's as good as a welcome mat when it comes to Emma.

Inside her space it's practically tropical, with steam clouding the windows. I slip off my shoes at the entrance and scuttle to the corner, where some cushions are set up as seating. My winter kimono comes off, and I already feel like I'm going to have to shed another layer in the heat. What a treat.

"So watch this form, and tell me what you think I'm doing."

Anything to stay longer in the warmth, I think to myself. Emma puts her sword down and walks to her bamboo-floored practice area. She stands for a minute then stretches her arms forward, her hands poised palm-up. One hand turns and floats upward as the other follows and traces an arc across her body at eye level. Then a flurry of arms and hands and feet as her torso rotates in space.

"So, what was I just doing? I'll give you a hint: It's more bad-ass than anything you violent barbarians do in Aikido. And I'm not telling some kind of bogus story about practicing an 'Art of Peace.' Any Tai Chi master could kick an Aikido master's butt on her worst day."

"Er, you're slapping someone across the face and then pulling on their nostrils?"

She lets out a snort.

"Not quite. It's the 'single whip' from Chen-style Tai Chi. I'm pulling out some silk and then whipping the daylights out of you. I'm trying to make the action so obvious that even a Californian like you can see it."

Emma's insults don't sting much: She's half-Asian, just like me, and grew up around here. Like me, she's never actually been to Asia, and she's also working out some issues with her martial arts. Sensei says she's very good, but she's had conflicts with other teachers in the area, which is why she's alone in our building and doesn't have too many students. Seems like a lot of our neighbors here in the building are either broke, in crisis or escaping from reality somehow.

I help myself to some tea from Emma's insulated carafe – identical to the one in our dojo. Some kind of dirt-tasting fermented brew hits my tongue like a mouthful of pond water. Emma does a few more rounds of forms as I feel my arms and legs thaw out. It's starting to almost feel too warm in here and I'm getting sleepy. Emma notices and stops her training, pulling a cushion up across from me and looking me in the eye.

"So what are you running away from being here in our martial arts palace on a Sunday? Parents too strict? Bad boyfriend? Lousy test scores?"

Ugh, not this again. Explaining myself to other people is worse than than explaining myself to myself, if that makes any sense.

"What are you, a guidance counselor? I'm training to be an Aikido teacher."

"Guidance counselor? What are you, 12 years old?" Emma pulls herself back a bit and frames my face with her fingers.

"Belinda said you're 19, but I'm not sure. Half-Asian or not, that's a baby face. Come on, how old are you really? A real 19-year-old wouldn't have gotten so defensive about a few life questions."

"What does it matter? I'm not running away from anything, really. Parents are fine. Parent is fine."

"One parent then."

"Yes, my dad. My mom died a while ago. We're fine, just the two of us. Kind of like roommates. Except for my stepmother, that is. He let me come out here on my own. I'm serious, I want to teach Aikido full-time. You seem to like the martial arts life, right?"

"I love the life, but I'm lucky that I have some savings from my professional days to live on. If a student pisses me off, I kick him or her right out. If I don't feel like teaching on Sundays, I don't have to. Speaking of that, I have a student coming soon. So take your soy sauce and go."

Emma rummages in a big cabinet by the window and pulls out a brown bottle. I get a glimpse of an entire shelf of condiments, and stacks of instant noodles as well. A pile of what could be bedding sits on the top of the cabinet. Could she be living here, too?

"Thanks, I appreciate it. Wow, and gluten-free, too!"

She gives me a wry smile and I feel like I've scored another friend point. The next eight days will go a lot faster if I have a place to warm up and chat right down the hall. Emma ushers me toward the door and shoves a bar of Korean chocolate into my hands on the way out. We exchange glances – this will get me through some tough spots.

"So watch yourself out there on the way back to your space. You've got a young admirer on this side of the building."

My heart sinks. "That guy. Does he know that I'm staying here?"

"No, he doesn't know that. And you don't know that I'm staying here, either. Or that your admirer has lived here full-time for six months. Or that Jean-Baptiste and a few others are staying on the second floor."

"Wow, this is turning out to be a pretty crowded place. I thought it would be like a mountain monastery. All alone except for the mice and vultures."

"Remember, the landlord – that guy Shai – doesn't care as long as you don't use too much hot water. He even stays here himself sometimes. Hard times and all."

"Why are *you* living here? I thought you were rich."

"Not exactly. But I wouldn't be here if my roommate weren't going through some changes. Hormonal stuff, if you know what I mean."

"I guess." I giggle a bit.

"How old are you again? I would swear you're not even sixteen, the way you react to some stuff."

"Seem like it might be time for you to get some glasses, *Oba-san*! That's Japanese for a nosy old granny."

"Smartass. Watch your step out there. Oh, and if you see anything…strange around here, don't feel like you can't come talk to me."

Emma's eyes are boring into me, but I'm not quite ready to admit to my nightmares yet. What if it's more evidence that I'm too much of a little kid to be staying here?

"Right. Er, sure."

That was weird. Is Emma having some unusual nightmares, too?

* * *

My chat with Emma has me thinking about a lot of things, so despite her advice I'm a bit distracted as I head back down the hall to the dojo. I walk kind of loudly, and I don't check the doorways for shadows that move.

"Uh! What the..." An abrupt, powerful force slams into my back, emptying my lungs and sending me staggering forward. For a split second I think I've been shot, then a familiar voice explodes into my ear.

"Got you again, Samurai Girl! You sound like a herd of water buffaloes coming down this hallway. Got some milk for me, buffalo girl? Those stupid cows are taking over my rain forest!"

Rage quickly replaces fear, and I duck and pivot as fast as I can in an Aikido *tenkan* motion, swinging my arm in the direction of the voice, but at knee level. I know my attacker will expect a punch to the face, so I hope to surprise him for a change. No such luck. he hops up in a quick back walkover, leaving my arm to smash at empty air.

Barata is his name, and he's been sneaking up on me in the hallway for weeks, trying to prove something about how I lack martial awareness – the ability to sense someone sneaking up on me. He may be right. Barata has been studying the Brazilian martial art of Capoeira since he was a fetus or something, and he has it over me in reflexes, at least.

I slump back against wall, limp with frustration.

"I told you not to do that to me again, Barata! Next time

I'm going to do something I regret, and I may not come over empty-handed. How are you going to flip away from a sword cut to your skull?"

Barata just laughs and sprints back down the hall to his space.

Jerk. Barata isn't even his real name, it's his *appelido*, or Brazilian martial arts name. His real name is Ramon or something like that, 100 percent American with a Brazilian grandfather or two. He tells me that slaves in Brazil in the last century invented Capoeira to make their fighting techniques look like dancing; they gave each other nicknames to keep their identities secret. I'd be impressed by Barata's art and his skills if he wasn't so damned annoying.

Very fitting that Barata means "cockroach" in Brazilian Portuguese. He says he's proud of it, and he won't answer to Ramon. We had a few conversations before he decided that he needed to test my Aikido skills every time we meet, so I've been trying not to get snuck up on in the hallways. I'm off my game today.

Anyway, what is Barata doing here on a Sunday if he's not living here? Emma said he's been here six months. Sensei said he gave private lessons on weeknights and I wouldn't see him much when she went away. Now it seems he's added weekends. And did I see a towel around his neck? Emma's right, he's my neighbor in the building this week. Great, this place is turning out to be more like a crowded dorm than a place for silent contemplation of my future.

My back also stings where Barata kicked it and I'm getting hungry again. Some cup noodles with soy sauce sounds pretty good right now, and I may need to dip into Emma's gift as well as the emergency chocolate stash.

I drag my aching, annoyed form back to the darkness of the dojo.

This is going to be a long week.

CHAPTER FOUR

Monday

B ANG!
Gunshot? Backfire? – That sounded pretty close.
BANG! BANG!

My eyes snap open: It is pitch dark. My sleep-addled brain runs down the checklist: No sudden pains, check. Head down, check. Body below the concrete window ledge and out of the line of fire, check.

It's not so unusual to be startled by loud noises in this neighborhood. It's usually an old car backfiring, but sometimes the ever-present sirens wail closer and closer. In summer, Sensei says she'll pass sidewalks around here on a weekly basis tangled up with tape: "POLICE LINE DO NOT CROSS." Someone fresh out of jail, usually, beefing with his old business associates.

Now the wait for the sirens, the only way to know for sure.

It's dark and I feel like I've woken up from a years-long coma, head clouded with dreams. Despite my plan last night to study Japanese ghost stories for exactly two hours after dinner, then read Aikido history books for an hour, I drifted off minutes after eating my cup noodles. A book called *Terrifying Tales of Old Japan* is splayed on top of my sleeping bag; my headlamp light has died and fallen down my face and the strap is now digging into my cheekbone. I decided it was too cold to sit up with the table lamp.

Silence inside the dojo for now, except for the scraping of branches against the windows, high-pitched and insistent. Something like a cool mist passes over my face, a feeling like a cloud of tiny droplets hitting my skin. Broken glass from bullet holes?

Wait a minute – the dojo is on the fifth floor, well above the tops of surrounding trees. That sound can't be branches. And bullets fired on the street likely couldn't reach the windows this high and at the back of the building, much less sound like they're that close.

Not again.

I listen closely and turn my head slightly: The scraping seems to be coming from the windows opposite my bed, the second row of panes about ten feet from the floor. Inch by inch I sit up, waiting for any hint that my problems are from actual humans this time and I'll have to duck. Then I turn my head all the way to see what's going on outside.

Nothing remotely human about this.

A column of white and black is swirling outside the dojo windows, waves of motion extending across the glass expanse in a blur of movement. On closer look, the waves resolve into a female shape in a flowing kimono that hangs well below what would be feet on a human.

There is a woman floating five floors above the ground outside my window. Not possible, but I can't help but take a closer look. Twisting coils of white extend out from the figure on all sides, what looks like a heavy ribbons of snow blown by a strong wind. Whatever that thing is, it's raking what look like claws across the windows, making that rattling, scratching sound. Not angry like the first demon, or disgusting like the second. This thing is just really creepy.

Gaping black holes open in the creature's face as the scratching turns to scrabbling with long black fingernails. A few bangs explode as it beats on the glass with bone-white fists –

those were the sounds like gunshots that woke me up. I shrink from the horror in the windows even as the name of the specter comes to me, along with a shiver of recognition. I read all about this ghost last night for my research: Yuki-Onna.

The story goes that a beautiful traveler in rural Japan once died in a snowstorm and came back to life as a kimono-clad demon: Yuki-Onna, the "Snow Woman." She wanders the forests looking for revenge on those who left her to die. No forests here in the city, just a scared young girl in an Aikido dojo hoping the demon realizes her mistake and heads for the park a mile up the road. I try to send her a mental message: Hey lady, there are lots of trees up down the street, wrong turn!

No such luck. The shape whirls closer, presses itself against the glass and fixing a pair of crusty eye-holes on me. With a horrific screech like the opening of a rusted door, a voice erupts from a jagged hole at the bottom of the demon's skull.

"Please open the windows, younger sister. It's so cold."

My reading is still fresh in my mind, luckily. Say you're a woodcutter spending the night in a forest, and Yuki-Onna knocks on your door. Let her in and you'll be frozen to death in a single blast of her arctic breath. She might kill you – but decide to settle down with your friend as an especially gentle and pale-skinned wife. The key is the invitation: Don't ask her in and she can't come in, from what I remember. Glad I've done at least some of my research for my yokai project.

Knowing the demon's identity – and knowing that this encounter is certainly another nightmare – makes me brave. I edge closer to the window and curl my gloved hands into a megaphone.

"Be quiet! You'll wake up the whole neighborhood. You know I'm not going to let you in."

The demon writhes and moans, waving her arms and splattering sleet across the window like buckshot. Yuki-Onna's face presses tighter against the glass, leaving a lacy pattern of frost in the shape of a grinning skull.

A loud bang explodes from the hallway just then, pulling

my eyes to the dojo door. Another demon inside the building to keep the snow witch company? When I turn back to the window, Yuki-Onna and her clouds of snow have disappeared. A full moon now blasts the landscape with a harsh glare. No snow, no wind; nothing moves outside, and the demon's face-print on the glass fades quickly into nothingness. I sink back against the wall and my eyes fall to my sleeping bag.

On top of the dark fabric lie hundreds of tiny ice crystals, sparkling in the moonlight. I just sit there and let my heartbeat slow down, watching my breath steam in the darkness. By the time the last crystals on my sleeping bag evaporate, my breathing has returned to normal and I decide to find out what's going in the hallway. It can't get any scarier, can it?

Cracking open the dojo door, I'm greeted by a blast of icy air and a glimpse of a figure emerging from the men's room. My neighbor from down the hallway, Dar, in dark sweatpants, jacket and hoodie. Almost looks like what I wear to sleep in this building.

He starts, then strides up to the dojo door to greet me.

"Sorry, did I wake you up? I didn't mean to slam the door but it was sticking a little in the cold. What are you doing here so late?

"What are *you* doing here so late?"

He looks bemused, and takes a few steps back.

"Yeah, about that. Remember what your Sensei said about minding one's own business? This is one of those times, I guess. For both of us." He's smiling and looks generally amused with the situation, not angry or suspicious. For a second I think about inviting him in for some tea, to keep the demons away for a bit. But then a familiar stench starts wafting past me from the depths of the dojo: Old cigarettes, sweat and those pungent Japanese breath mints, Jintan.

Too late, Dar's already headed down the hall.

"Stay warm!" He calls back.

"Uh, you, too!"

With a sinking heart, I head back into the dojo. The night

is still young, the demon swordsman is waiting, and he's got plans for me.

"Hey, lazybones! Time to get to work! Pick up your sword!"

* * *

The attacker approaches from my right.

His face is blank but I see his arm tense – before he can draw I've smashed the end of my sword onto the back of his hand, stomping my foot as put all my force and weight into it. He falls back, stunned and yelping in pain.

On the recoil from my stomp I draw my sword, pivoting quickly as I sense another enemy behind and to the side. A quick thrust to the left rear and the second guy is dead, blood spurting and the space echoing with an unearthly howl of pain. I've pushed the razor-sharp tip of my blade into the gap between his padded obi sash and his breastplate, piercing his stomach and spilling his intestines in a sloppy gush.

The first guy has recovered and is charging me like a maddened bull – he gets an overhead cut from my sword before he even realizes that I've pivoted around with lightning speed. The two halves of his head pull apart in a gush of blood and brain.

Then a third guy gets cut in two from right rear as he rushes in to avenge his buddies. Last I turn to the left front as a slower thug, hesitating a bit, decides to pull his sword out in a rush. I turn to him, tucking my sword behind me at my side, presenting an irresistible and defenseless-looking target.

Attacker Number Four starts to raise his sword for the kill, but my cut gets there first, cleaving this time nearly to the waist. The smears of blood on all sides pull together into a vast crimson puddle on the dojo floor, steaming in the cold air, as the final breaths leave my four enemies. Fresh blood, hot iron, open bowels – the smells of victory.

I pause for a minute of reflection, contemplating the

briefness of life and inevitability of death. Then I shake the blood off my sword with a quick flick of the blade to the side and sheathe the gleaming steel. Four down, an entire building full of enemies to go.

"Wow, that was something! You were slashing like a maniac!"

A voice coming from the direction of door makes me jump and nearly cut my hand off with my sword, again unsheathed as I start another form. I pivot to see Jean-Baptiste, wrapped in his mummy-suit parka and holding a bag. I quickly sheathe my sword and take a closer look at the bag in his hands: I hope there's food in there.

I've been practicing sword forms all morning after no one showed up for the first class. Morning class is always small but the sheen of ice I saw on every surface outside when I woke up explained today's empty mat. From up here it looked as if the entire world had been coated with clear nail polish. Even with the ice I had to be ready for class, so I turned on the heater, put on my uniform and did my morning chores. With class time approaching, I put on my hakama, placed a cushion on the mat and eased myself into meditation posture, letting the profound silence of the building sink in.

It was still half-dark outside and the dojo was barely lit by a sallow glow from the horizon. The building creaked and shifted as the temperature rose in the space – perhaps 10 degrees at most, but enough to shock the cinderblock and asbestos to life. Meditating this early, before the monkey mind has time to start rampaging, is the only time I glimpse a bit of stillness and peace.

Stillness soon gave way to tiredness, then itchiness and hunger. What seemed like an hour later, I glanced at the wall clock, and only twenty minutes had passed. Time enough to figure out that no one was coming to practice this morning. I let myself simmer in disappointment and feelings of loneliness for a minute or two – then pulled out my sword and started fighting off enemies. It's an antique katana that Sensei lent me, more than 400 years old but sharp enough to hurt me if I get careless with my forms. A few near-misses when my thumb grazed the blade and I was fully awake.

For two hours now I've been working on a series of sword forms Sensei taught me a few weeks ago. Now I'm at No. 10, a good time to stop for a mid-morning snack. Reheated rice porridge doesn't seem appealing right now and I hope Jean-Baptiste has a better idea.

"Hi JB, sorry, didn't see you there when you came in. That form is called 'Four-direction Cut.' Imagine this: I'm walking along a street in Old Tokyo, minding my business, when four guys come at me from all sides with evil intentions. Lucky for me, they're all a bit out of sync so I can take them one by one, if I'm fast enough. Overhead smiting to the skull, slash to the gut, another skull, then cut a bad guy in half. Just a typical day for a samurai on the town."

"Cool. It looked very deadly."

I smell something tasty and I have to stop myself from drawing my sword and demanding that paper bag.

"So is anything open out there selling food? Bring something hot?"

"I've got some Jamaican patties if you're hungry. Still a bit warm from the fryer, from that place on Dixwell Avenue where they make it just like home. They cook for me no matter what the weather because they live upstairs. Fryer oil was already hot from breakfast."

"Sweet, JB, that's so great. I'm getting tired of eating the same thing every day even though I know it's the traditional way. So you drove in this weather? Looks scary out there."

"I walked. Needed some fresh air and it's actually bit warmer today."

"Walked all the way from home to here?"

"Um, actually, just walked from here to there and back. Didn't want to drive last night after working late so I crashed on the couch. Did Belinda tell you the score about me staying in the building?"

"You too? Including you and me, there are about a hundred people living in this building right now, it seems. I thought I'd be alone here all week." I've draped my hakama over a chair and thrown my winter kimono over my sweaty gi. It will do for now as I'm pretty warm from sword practice.

"I still can't believe Belinda left you here all by yourself. And in this weather… The rest of us at least have some experience camping out in these temperatures. You're a Californian!"

"Hey, we've got snow in California too. We can see it on the mountaintops on a clear day from the city. Or so I've heard. Anyway, Sensei didn't know this cold front was coming. If she knew how bad this would get she probably would have insisted I stay at Thierry's. But really, I'm keeping plenty warm and I like the chance to live the dojo life. People come every day for class and I've got plenty to read. Check out my subzero sleeping bag – I get too hot some nights, I swear!"

"Still, I wouldn't want to be a young girl staying here alone. Scary place, scary people – except for me, of course."

"Everyone I've met so far has been cool, especially you. The people aren't scary… Anyway, thanks again for the food."

I grab for food and we both settle into chairs in the lounge area. Sipping hot tea after scarfing down all but one of the beef patties, I decide to take my new neighbor into my confidence. My visitors from the past few nights are taking over my thoughts today.

"So, tell me JB. Is there anything… strange about this building?"

His hat off and parka half-unzipped, Jean-Baptiste had been relaxing on the couch and looked ready for a nap, his head lolled back and eyes half-closed. But when he hears my question, his lids snap open and he tilts his head toward me.

"What do you mean by strange?"

"Uh, strange in like ghosts. Like a haunted house."

He laughs, but his eyes are serious.

"Well, this building was used as an ammunition testing facility and I heard they built it over a place they hung witches in the Colonial days. Before that I'm sure it was a Native American graveyard, and now it's full of people who do strange things at strange hours. Other than that, it's like any other commercial space in the city."

"Seriously? A graveyard?"

"Probably, at some point. Listen, Aikido woman, there are graveyards and lynching grounds all over the place in these old towns. Everywhere around the world, trust me. Ghosts and demons all around us."

We sit and sip tea for a minute or two, thinking about ghosts.

"So what kind of ammunition did they make here? Was this some kind of military town?"

"The Winchester gun factory was right over there on the next block. Winchester started making rifles here in our city, 'the Gun that won the West.' Also guns for most of the wars of the two centuries. So much death, blood, justice and injustice, made here in this place."

We sit in companionable silence, munching cookies, thinking of life and death. Now might be the time to bring up my night visitors for real.

"So with all these guns made here and those burial grounds, do people talk about ghosts or spirits of the dead showing up here in this building?"

"What the hell are you talking about, Cherry? Actual ghosts?"

An awkward silence descends. Jean-Baptiste shifts his body even farther forward, his forehead furrowed in thought.

"Cherry, have you seen anything in here? You can tell me, you know. I won't think you're crazy."

I'm about to spill when the dojo door screeches open.

"Hey, anyone home? I smell something good in here."

Dar's head pokes in, but his face freezes when he sees Jean-Baptiste.

"Dar, hi! We just finished some Jamaican beef patties but there's half of one left if you're interested. Really tasty and still a little bit warm. Jean-Baptiste, meet Dar. He works down the hall."

Dar is already on his way out the door.

"Sorry, no meat for me. But I did want to show you something, so I'll stop by later. Sorry to interrupt."

Dar ducks out and eases the door shut before Jean-Baptiste can finish his response.

"Nice to meet you... So who is that guy?"

"Another person staying here overnight this week. Guy who's doing some tech work down the hall, that small room under the transmitter. Nice engineer named Dar. Very polite and he knows the deal about the building, about people staying here."

I don't know why I added that detail about the transmitter, and suddenly I'm not sure that it's a good idea to tell Jean-Baptiste about my nightmares. After all, I started seeing demons right after Dar fired up his experiments – could they be related? I don't want my new friend to get in trouble for such a minor inconvenience. After all, what is the worst that has happened? A few blisters from midnight sword practice, ice on my sleeping bag, a few sleepless nights. Better keep my strange dreams to myself.

"Thanks for the patties. JB. I've really got to get going with reading these books for my presentation on Japanese folklore for Sensei next week. Should be half done by now but I've been spending so much time daydreaming and chatting."

Jean-Baptiste gets the hint and zips up his jacket. "Right, that's an impressive pile of reading you've got there. If you want to talk about anything, you know where I am. I promised Belinda that I'd watch over you so don't hesitate to come down and talk. You can even set up your bed in the spare office down there – it's a separate space with a deadbolt lock and a space heater and everything. I'm a few feet away on the other side of the waiting room so no ghosts can get by without me hearing."

"Ha, funny. Thanks for the offer, really. So far so good up here on the top floor. Toughening me up and all."

"Take care, Cherry."

"Bye Jean-Baptiste, thanks again for keeping me company."

* * *

Changed into warm clothes and with the darkness deeping outside, I decide to really get some reading done this time.

A pile of books, bound in the dull brown library covers issued by the university, sits stacked on top of some shelving. Sensei said that every other week or so she'll be leaving me an assignment, something she cooked up with my dad to keep my study skills sharp. We went to the library together last week to stock up on material for this week. My first month at the dojo, I presented on the history of Aikido. A month later, sword-making. Now these crazy Japanese fairy tales. Sensei has me write up the information in an entertaining form to present to the members at our social nights. They get to drink beer and ask questions as I spew out my research. My first one was rough but I'm getting better, and this latest assignment had pretty fun. Who knew the Japanese had such crazy imaginations?

Looking at the scuffed book covers, I try to convince myself that the research is what is filling my head with demons and ghosts. My imagination seems to be more vivid in this building, so that's why the demons are knocking on the windows and keeping me up nights with cleaning and sword practice. These creatures have to be in my head, right? Maybe something in the toxic fumes people say fill the building is making my reading seem to come to life.

I rub my hand against my face and nearly let out a scream – my palm is raw and oozing blood from the sides of a bandage. Memories of last night flood back: After meeting Dar in the hall, the Demon Swordmaster made me do hundreds of cuts with a wooden sword, screaming at my poor form for what seemed like hours. The torment stopped only at the first hints of dawn glowing at the horizon, just before I collapsed. For a nightmare, that guy has a loud voice. And my hands are pretty painful. Sleep-swordwork? Who ever heard of such a thing?

Concentration on my reading just isn't happening right now, so I decide to reheat some stew leftover from last week and try again to do my homework after dinner. Reading may be firing up my brain and hurting my hands, but it's got to be done.

✽ ✽ ✽

"Wow, that smells familiar. Something Japanese?"

It's Dar again, this time opening the door and stepping right into the dojo without knocking. Like he belongs in here.

"Sorry to just barge in, but I saw your light and smelled food."

"Japanese leftovers, yeah. How did you guess? Sorry, does the stink bother you?"

"Not at all, I just recognize that smell. Is it some kind of soup?

"Oden – just boiled vegetables and tofu. The radish and seaweed can give off a powerful funk sometimes. Sensei made a big pot of it just before she left; she says it's very warming and purifying for the blood. The skunky smell is daikon radish, full of sulfur compounds that smell like farts. The whole thing keeps forever in the fridge and I'm just reheating it now."

"Oh, I remember that stuff. Don't they keep vats of that simmering in the convenience stores over there in Japan?

"I think Sensei said something about that, but I wouldn't know. You've been to Japan?"

"Yep, two years studying at the technical university north of Tokyo. Long, cold two years in a cheap apartment with no central heating. Lots of oden stew from the convenience store and ramen noodles in the winter."

"Nice, I'm surprised you survived that much MSG."

"MSG, ghee, Velveeta, every culture has its unhealthy indulgences."

"You want a bowl of oden? Or did you reach your lifetime limit of daikon and seaweed? I wouldn't blame you if you said no. Sensei wants me to eat stuff like this all week so I can improve my ukemi."

"U-what?"

"Ukemi – falling skills. In Aikido we like to throw people down, but you have to learn how to fall first. Fall so you don't break anything, like a bone or your skull. I can take ukemi pretty well, but Sensei says my falls have to be livelier or something. Oden and vegetables make you lighter, she says. Pizza and ice cream make you land like a ton of bricks."

"So this stinky stuff will help me fall down? Nice."

Dar sits with his bowl and slurps noisily as he scoops up chunks of radish and tofu, dabbing them with strong mustard to kick up the flavor. Sensei would approve. He seems pretty relaxed, so I take a chance on another nosy question.

"How's the collective unconscious thing doing down there? Powering stuff up?"

He turns to me with a smile. "We've been experimenting all night for the past few days. That's partly why I'm here. Late night is the best time to do what we're doing on the sly. Coming really close to something significant. We're tapping into a kind of energy that extends way beyond my expectations. You could even say it approaches the ultimate energy."

His voice has gotten louder, and his eyes burn with something other than environmental fervor. Something like fury. Something like madness.

We're both quiet for a bit, and he seems to collect himself.

"It's really boring stuff, but we think it has potential to make big money. We just want to research on the down-low for a while until some bugs are worked out."

"Who is we? Are you guys post-docs or something?"

"Really it's just me, but I do have some former colleagues who help with materials. You'd be amazed how easy it is to get people to help you do something when they know that will change the world."

That crazy glare again. I'm not sure this guy is completely sane. I'm not sure I like the idea that's he's making the dojo his second home, now that I think of it.

"What do you think of the oden? Authentically bland and funky?"

"Really good, actually. You could sell this stuff."

"Right, I'll do big business next to the pizzerias in town. 'Forget white clam pie, Get your tofu and radish stew!'"

"Well, thanks for the hot meal. See you around. Heard about the snowstorm coming?

"Heard a little. Is it going to be a big deal?"

"'Storm of the Century,' or so they're saying. Hope you've got enough food to last you a few days. I'm stocking up on instant ramen. My favorite spicy Korean stuff."

"I've got tons of that! The freezer in here is full of stews and I've also got lots of rice and pickles, more than enough for two. Come by anytime if you're bored with your ramen diet."

I can't believe I'm saying that, after seeing this guy's scary side. I guess a crazy human is better company than the crazy nonhumans I've been spending time with lately.

"Appreciate the invitation. I'd invite you over to our space but it's jammed with equipment and samples of brain tissue – not very appetizing surroundings."

"Brain tissue? Is that legal?"

"Let's not go there. Let's just say the donors of the tissue wanted their brains to be used for science, and that's what we're doing. It's actually not even tissue, more like brain dust. We got it from Alzheimer's patients – full of metals and compounds useful for our research. Nothing that's going to make you sick or something."

"So how do you get energy from brain dust?"

"You really are a curious ninja, aren't you?"

I don't appreciate the patronizing tone, but Dar's mood has lightened and I'm not so worried about him right now. Keeping it light and positive is the key. Sure enough, he settles himself into a cross-legged position to explain his project.

"This building is pretty unique, you know. These walls are two feet thick with enough metal reinforcement to block satellite and heat-seeking technology, as you probably know." Dar is definitely in a talkative mood.

"Well I know about the metal walls because none of us can get signals from anywhere but inside the building, and no one's phones work."

"I noticed that, makes it tough to run a business, I imagine."

"Most of us here aren't businesses in the traditional sense." I sound like I actually know something, when all I do is listen to Sensei gossip about our neighbors.

"What do you mean?"

"No naming names, but some people here are laundering money for someone, living off trust funds, selling stolen stuff. Very few actual legal profit-making enterprises. That's what Sensei tells me."

"Sensei? Is that your master?"

"More like teacher, it's a term of respect. Goffe Sensei has so much more experience in Aikido than me that it would rude to call her by her first name. Does that make sense?"

"I guess."

"So I agree that this building is definitely off the grid. And no one asks too many questions or gets in each other's business. Sensei says that the only thing that gets the landlord worked up is hot water use and bugs – a few cockroaches are OK but don't let it get out of hand. Take your pizza boxes out to the dumpster now and then."

"Good to know."

His oden finished, Dar gets up and stretches, then walks around the dojo space. I ease myself up and follow, planning to offer a guided tour. He stops at the kamiza up front, and to my embarrassment, drags a finger across the scarred wooden shelf. He holds up a finger ashy with dust. Damn, I cut short my morning cleaning today, too tired to finish. Dar closes his fingers in a pinch, trapping the dust.

"How old is the wood on this altar?" he asks, squatting down to take a closer look.

"Hundreds of years old, I think. Sensei found it at a thrift store in the middle of nowhere – they sold it to her as a side table for keys and stuff. Turns out it's some kind of valuable antique from China."

"You'd be amazed how much information is stored in this wood. Actually, any material from something old and in contact with the collective unconscious. Like, for example, your grandma has an old Bible. Once our technology goes full-speed, we can summon a character like Jesus from that Bible and bring his energy back into the world. All we need is some resonance from a human who knows the stories."

Old things. Old stories. Energy from the mind bringing things to life. Things like – demons? It makes so much sense. I'm still a bit wary of bringing up the subject of my night visitors. Better let him think I haven't met his "energy source" up close until I figure out how to ask the question without sounding crazy.

"OK, so you channel things from human culture and brain dust? How does that make energy, exactly? What happens if you use material from another place, or even another planet?"

"We need the combination of something culturally relevant and an adjacent mind to tap into the source. The human mind allows the energy to take physical form."

"So here you'd get Jesus or Buddha. So in another galaxy they'd be like silicon crab gods?"

"Try hexene throat eels."

"For real? How do you know?"

"Let's just say I hacked my biometric badge to collect some samples at that university observatory on the hill. You really don't want to know the details."

So it's likely that Dar's experiments are the source of the demons that have been infesting the dojo, and my dreams. But if they're just manifestations of the collective unconscious, they can't really hurt me, right? Only six more days here alone. Six more days... I'm about to ask more questions when Dar seems to sprint toward the door and grab his shoes.

"Got to go, I've got to rest up and prep for tonight's work. You are making my long days here much more interesting, Cherry."

"Sure you have to go? Why not take an evening off? Class is at 6 and I could show you some Aikido moves."

"Some other time. You better hit those books!"

My eyes swing back to the pile of unopened books on the desk. The last thing I want to do right now is my research, which could end up summoning up some other horror from Japanese folktales, from what I've been hearing. Dar's got his shoes on and the door open before I can put together a sentence.

"*Oyasumi nasai.*"

"*Oyasumi nasai!*" In Japanese, the "good-night" sounds even more final.

❋ ❋ ❋

"So who do you think this scary demon is? Some kind of samurai warrior?"

Emma gives me a skeptical look. I've dropped in during her practice again but she said she'd been working on a Chen Tai Chi form for hours and welcomed the break. I burst right out with the story – a demon swordmaster has been keeping me up at night and it might be fault of the new guy down the hall.

"A samurai is a warrior – that's like saying 'soldier soldier,'' by the way. I'm not sure, but this demon is really obsessed with teaching me to clean. He also had me do five thousand cuts last night."

"Five thousand cuts of what? Cheese? Does he have you committing hara-kiri or something?"

"No, don't be stupid. Suburi cuts – cutting with a wooden sword to improve your downward killing blows. He's some kind of demon taskmaster. But he also hits me with this stick like a monk."

"What the hell kind of monk hits you with a stick?"

Perhaps Emma wasn't the best choice to talk to about the strange goings-on around the dojo. I'm getting sick of explaining everything and dealing with her attitude.

"Zen priests do that when you're falling asleep during meditation. It's supposed to both wake you up and help you realize that there is no separation between you and the universe."

"Huh? Only the Japanese would think up something like that. Crazy bunch."

I'm so tired and so annoyed by Emma's attitude I can't help myself: I reach across and give her a light slap in the face. Her deflection comes a split second too late, but her counterattack lands like an explosion – a dead-on punch to my gut.

We're both too well-trained to yell or cry out but Emma's face glows crimson and I can feel a tear slip across my cheek and run into my nose.

"Nice surprise slap, but I could have burst your spleen if I really wanted to. Why did you do that, by the way?"

"That was an illustration of why Zen monks hit you with a stick. When someone smacks you, all the crap goes out of your head. Were you worried about your roommate problems just now? Guess I could have explained it a little better."

"Definitely. Don't think that just because I do a lot of Cloud Hands doesn't mean I also don't do the Spleen Buster. Remember, I'm Chen style. Our Tai Chi kicks ass."

"Got it. I won't do that again, I promise. I'm just so tired and my whole body hurts. This swordsman guy is a maniac with the stick thing and the sword thing. I've heard of a guy like this somewhere. My brain just feels like rice porridge right now. I don't know what I'm supposed to do."

Emma shakes out her fist, stands up and walks toward her window. She's covered the glass with a heavy velvet curtain, but something is shimmering and winking over in the far corner of her space, as if a patch of moonlight has broken through. I peer closer and see an oddly shaped crystal sculpture against the wall, layers of some kind of plastic or glass stacked up and sparkling and glinting like they're under a strobe light. It wasn't there yesterday.

Emma sees me looking at the object and catches my eye. I can't tell what she's thinking, but she looks a little scared, for once. As we lock eyes, a smell something like an ocean breeze also wafts toward me, seemingly from the direction of the sculpture. A little fishier and fouler, and that could be Kappa's smell. Emma pushes me toward to the door, not very gently.

"You need to go home and take a nap before your evening classes. You're starting to get delusional with lack of sleep. Put something over your windows and just set the alarm for five."

"Take a nap? You should see the dust bunnies in the corner of the dojo. Not to mention the sand that people track in from the parking lot is all over the place. I've got at least three hours of cleaning before the evening crew shows up. And we're supposed to have some social time tonight so I have to make rice and miso soup."

"Your life really sucks, Cherry. Only someone Japanese would pay to do this much menial labor."

"Half-Japanese, remember."

"So you're only half-stupid."

"Tesshu! That's who I'm thinking of. Remember when I had to do that presentation on great swordsmen of Japanese history? This guy Tesshu was a Zen monk and swordsman and was supposed to be a real hard-ass. Only problem is that he died about two hundred years ago."

"Right. Makes perfect sense. A two-hundred-year-old swordmaster is haunting our building because some guy is playing crazy genius down the hall. You really need some sleep, sister."

* * *

"Yo, *kohai!* Pick your head up and check your senior's glass right now! This is no time for a nap – your *sempai* needs another round of tea!"

I lift my head and open my eyes. A grassy smell – spilled green tea that has seeped into the collar of my *samue*, the blue uniform I wear when helping Sensei entertain students after class. Only this time Sensei's away, it's got to be close to 10 p.m., and the students won't leave.

"Did I tell you about the time I puked into the train tracks at Ginza Station, Cherry San?"

"Not recently, Ellie Sempai."

"Ha! No really. I'm pretty sure I've only told you the G-rated version. Well, we started drinking right after my morning shift at this Indian restaurant right down the street from my company. I had myself lots of rice and then a big bowl of chickpeas in spinach, if you can visualize that mess."

Ellie is a great sempai, or senior student, helping me in every class she attends with subtle, wordless hints on how to make my techniques better. She never tells when she can show, at least on the mat. But after class, she seems to overcompensate with a flood of words, often stories from her four years working at a newspaper and practicing Aikido in Tokyo. The stories are great, but I've got another hour of cleaning to do after everyone leaves and another hour of other chores before morning class tomorrow. Not to mention my reports and the fact that I'm sleep-deprived from the night before – and the night before that.

Ellie looks over and seems to finally notice my sagging lids and slumped shoulders.

"Ah, our poor uchideshi is training hard and needs her sleep. Did you see her blisters?"

Everyone at the table nods approvingly. My fingers, swathed in bloodstained bandages, testify to my dedication to practicing my sword cuts. What the members don't know is that the vigorous practice over the last few nights wasn't my idea.

"Let's help her clean up and then get our butts home!"

I don't really want the students to leave, but in some strange way I'm also looking forward to the expected visit from a demon tonight. After all, are the demons really that much different from the motley crew who show up to train Aikido every day? Kappa's a bit like Ellie, talkative and full of stories and jokes. The Swordmaster shares a lot of traits with Sensei, ordering me around and pushing me to my limits.

Yuki-Onna, the ghostly Snow Woman, could be a twin of the ghostly "snow man" who comes to morning class once a month or so. He's a youngish guy, pale and withdrawn, and Sensei told me he's in treatment at the university for some serious mental issues. The Snow Man seems to come alive only after the hardest falls, when his blank face fractures into something like a smile. He gives me the creeps but Sensei says Aikido helps him connect to the world.

We've got our little constellation of demons here in the dojo, not so different from my visitors of the past few days. So as much as I wanted earlier to take Ellie aside and tell her about my nightmares, I find myself focusing on my cleaning and making small talk.

Footsteps from the last student going down the staircase are still echoing in the hallway when I hear a crash behind me followed by a throaty gurgle. Kappa's back, and he has knocked over the cleaning bucket and is now splashing and giggling and making a mess. He promised he'd tell me all the gossip from his village in Japan tonight, after he shows me how he can fart along to regional folk songs.

Forget about sleep. My night has just begun.

CHAPTER FIVE

Tuesday

T he dojo shimmers with moonlight broken up into a million tiny shards. I find myself gently easing out of sleep sometime after finally drifting off, not quite awake, not quite asleep. I'm floating in a bubble of calm and peace although I know something supernatural is about to happen. Above me on the dojo ceiling the light dances and quivers without quite opening up the shadows of the space. I find myself squirming out of my sleeping bag and setting my feet on the floor.

A pulse of stronger light draws me to the window. The black hulk of the wrecked building below sets off sheets and ribbons and gusts of snow, seemingly glowing from within. The bare trees stand still, but currents of air quicken the flurries into a river of white.

Could be a few minutes, could be an hour. I stand there, entranced, until movement pulls my eyes to the pitted surface of the glass in front of me.

Someone is standing behind me.

Someone with something shiny in his hand.

I turn my head a bit to get a better angle on the reflection. A face comes into focus – intense blue eyes burning at the center of holes in a ski mask. A ratty denim vest that shows off tattooed sleeves. Anger wells up as a bitter taste in my mouth.

It's my mom's killer, right here in the dojo with me, with a knife that's moving toward me at impossible speed. I try to turn but it's like we're in two different time zones. I'm just starting to move as the knife flashes toward me.

Now I feel something icy at my throat, and terror and rage envelope me. Roaring fills my ears and blackness seems to push against the back of my eyes as I start to pass out. It can't end like this. He killed my mom; he can't be killing me.

Then something swirling emerges out of the blackness outside, drawing my eyes forward even as the metal blade starts to bite into my flesh. The darkness between the snow flurries clumps together and swells, taking the form of something majestic and terrible.

Massive wings extend to block the moonlight across all of the windows, and a jagged mouth opens wide as it rushes toward me. Something like an eagle, something like a dog, something like a lion – the creature looks like nothing I've ever seen or even imagined. It's so huge the dojo can't begin to contain even its wingspan. A massive head crashes through the windows in a shrieking roar and lunges my attacker. Toothed jaws close with a juicy crunch and the limp, tattooed body is shaken like a cat toy.

A pair of monster claws then close over the gangbanger's torso and with a whoosh of cold air, the creature and my mom's killer are gone. Glass tinkles to the concrete as I slump forward into blackness.

❊ ❊ ❊

I'm flying.

Literally flying through the air, wind in my hair, arms and legs high off the ground. Flying in a sort-of superman pose, arms straight in front of me. I try to stretch the moment out – up so high, weightless and free. But the mat rushes up too fast, my body pivots in midair and my back and side hit the mat with a resounding thud. The dojo seems to shake around me. For a few seconds all is quiet, and my legs tingle from the impact. Then a voice booms out from behind me.

"That was great! Excellent height you got there with that extra hip twist at the end." Thierry walks over to Walt, the guy who just tossed me four feet in the air, then claps him on the back.

"What is that called again, Thierry Sempai?" Walt is beaming and doesn't even look down to check if I'm still alive. I lie on the mat in heap, unhurt but not ready to get up yet.

"*Sutemi waza*, or sacrifice throw. The idea is that you sacrifice your standing posture to launch your attacker across the room. Your weight dropping down kind of slingshots the attacker and sends them airborne. Cherry took a pretty good fall but more advanced students fall like a feather."

Thanks a lot, Thierry. You try falling like a feather after staying up all night with demonic visitors. I try not to grimace as I ease myself up from the mat. My whole body feels like it's been thrown off a roof.

"That was so cool. Why don't we do sutemi waza more often?" Walt has five years of experience in Aikido and is stepping up his practice in preparation for his black-belt test.

"First of all, sutemi waza is not on your test. Second, if something goes wrong you can pull the attacker right on top of you and you both crack ribs. Or you throw too hard or in the wrong direction and she ends up with a broken femur or something. I've seen it – a guy landed standing up but not quite straight. Bone was poking out of his thigh muscle like an alien probe, all yellow and slimy."

"OK, I get it. No more description necessary."

"Want to try it again?"

I've got to pipe up at this point. It's only half-past seven in the morning and my whole body is vibrating from a bone-shaking class. According to Sensei, a very wise senior Aikido student once said that the first roll of the morning should be a jelly roll, as in a pastry. Certainly not the high-velocity throws and falls

I've been subjected to in the past hour. Enough is enough.

"Er, isn't it time to wrap up, Thierry? I can make some tea."

Not that I want everyone to leave just now, I just want to stop being tossed around like a rag doll.

Between my nightmare about my mom's killer last night and visits from the winged beast, Kappa and the Swordmaster, I'm exhausted but eager to talk out what's been going on around here the last few days. Thierry's got to have noticed that something's up: My eyes are like black pits and my hands are raw under layers of athletic tape that have turned pinkish with blood seepage. The blisters are the fault of a thousand sword cuts two days ago, two thousand the night before last and what seemed like five thousand last night.

A bitter taste of panic still lingers in my mouth after last night's vision, although of course the windows were intact this morning and I was snug in my bed at sunrise. No feathers, no bloodstains, no tattooed corpse with claw marks. A search of my reference books turned up something like what I saw outside in descriptions of different kinds of tengu, the bird demon from Japanese folklore. I'd been reading about the tengu for my project, but the cartoony pictures in my books were nothing like the beast from last night. "The appearance of a tengu often signals the approach of war," according to my book.

Great, that's all I need right now. For some reason the Tengu visited the dojo last night to take revenge on the gang-banger who decided to rob a tax office in L.A. six years ago and shoot my mom. I'm so tired today, but seeing that scumbag brought to justice by a warlike bird-beast has me coasting on some kind of emotional high. I'm jittery and jumping around the mat when I'm not paralyzed with exhaustion.

Walt and Ellie say their goodbyes and rush off to start their workdays, leaving Thierry and me in awkward silence as we finish the cleaning chores. Glare from fresh snow on nearby rooftops bounces off the walls, making the dojo almost unbearably bright. Standing still for the first time all morning, I find myself squinting and wishing I could crawl back into the futon and hide under the covers in the dark. Thierry takes his time hanging up the mat rags then turns toward me with a look of concern.

"How's it going here, Cherry? You look really tired. Having trouble sleeping on the futon mattress? I'm sure it's cold in here when the heater is shut off. It's totally understandable that you're struggling and I *insist* that you stay with us tonight. Matt is making chickpea patties and potatoes and we were going to watch some old samurai movies."

I turn away to scrub the corners of the dojo a bit and take my time in answering. Do I really want to spend another night here? An answer bubbles up in my mind, seemingly out of nowhere.

"No, I'll stay. And that's a cheap shot! You know I love samurai movies. You also know that I promised Sensei I would stay here and watch the dojo. I gave my word and I intend to keep it. I want to show her that I'm serious and ready for training at the next level. I'm a bit tired but I'm getting used to the cold and all the late-night noises in here. I'll get more sleep tonight, I promise."

Thierry gestures for me to put away my rags and cleaner and sit down on the couch. He pours some tea from the kettle and pulls out a plastic container from his Aikido bag. I'm finding my determination wavering in the face of homemade chocolate-chip cookies and the thought of a real dinner. He leans in and starts the pitch.

"I understand the whole 'warrior alone' thing, trust me. That was me about a decade ago when I first fell in love with Aikido. But you look like you've aged ten years in the last week, Cherry. You've got these major bags under your eyes and your skin looks terrible. When was the last time you washed your hair? I don't want to be mean but staying in this building would be tough for someone even twice your age. The cold, the creepy people, this spooky old building."

"Spooky how? I mean have you heard anything weird

about this building, like it might have some ghosts?"

"Ghosts? Haunted? As in haunted house? Don't be ridiculous. It's just spooky in that it's mostly deserted and falling apart. Doesn't need any ghosts to creep me out."

Thierry sips carefully at his tea and takes a hard look at me, his face wreathed by steam.

"What exactly are hearing in here at night? Are you seeing ghosts or something? Are people creeping around after dark?"

"Not ghosts, more like demons. To be honest, I think there are some demons in this dojo."

Thierry sets his teacup down on the table with a bang and looks at me with worry in his eyes.

"Demons? By demons you're talking in the abstract Buddhist sense, right? Like your own fears and emotions confronting you?"

Now I'm looking confused.

"What are you talking about?"

"The demons in Zen, when we sit there and meditate. Demons come up in your mind when you sit Zazen, don't they?"

"That Zen meditation we're doing can call up demons? Sensei didn't say anything about that! It would have been nice to have a warning. Could have saved me some nightmares."

"Not literal demons, with fire and horns and all that. In Zen we think of demons in the psychological sense – parts of your personality that torment you and take you off your path. Like when Buddha battled with Mara. Remember the scene in that movie I sent you?"

"I don't remember that part. Anyway, I hadn't really done much meditation before I got here. Just a little bit at home to get ready for training with Sensei. I kept getting distracted by my cat so it was only like five minutes here and there. But I did watch the movie, I promise."

"Well, I'm disappointed you didn't take the practice more seriously. Mara was the demon who appeared to Buddha when he was really close to enlightenment. It appeared in the form of beautiful women and tried to seduce him – remember that scene with the music and dancing in the movie?"

"The sexy part? Wow, I didn't realize that was a demon. Looked like fun."

"We don't think of Mara as a literal demon. Mara is a symbol for all of Buddha's passions and desires that kept him suffering."

I'm getting confused with all this philosophical talk, and I'm hoping Thierry will move on to another subject.

"So Mara wasn't like a real person, trying to feel him up while he was meditating?"

"Not at all. So are you having nightmares about demons? The ones with horns and all?"

"Not exactly horns – more like old Japanese sword-masters making me clean the shoe rack and keeping me up all night with cutting practice."

"Let me get this straight: You're having nightmares that Japanese demons are making you do sword practice? And do work around the dojo? I hate to say this, but those aren't demons, those are your responsibilities."

"Not in the middle of the night! I actually think they're nightmares. Could be hallucinations from mouse poop or something else in the air in this building. Whatever they are, they are making me do sword cuts for real – you saw my blisters. That demon makes me clean the dojo for hours. More hours than I'm supposed to. Another one keeps me up all night telling jokes and stories. Then the other night this snow-witch demon tried to freeze me to death, and last night there was this giant bird-man who could have been the Crow Tengu."

Thierry leans back in his chair and rubs his temples.

"Wow, Cherry. I really think you need to pack up your stuff and come home with me right now. This sounds like you're having some kind of psychological crisis. Do you have any proof that these things are real?"

"Not like physical evidence, but I'm not sure it's all in my head, Thierry. There's some weird stuff going on in this building and I want to find out more. Yes, I'm tired. But you saw me in class – I can still train and I'm not really scared, just curious. I can handle it. I just wanted to see if you knew about anything happening before in this building. Has Sensei said anything?"

"Now that I think of it, she did say her teacher got her up nights sometimes to do sword cuts. But the guy was just fierce on the mat, not a literal demon of some kind. And this was when she was living with other students in her teacher's house so it's not so strange there would be training in off hours.

"You really need to come home with me tonight. My shift at the hospital ends at midnight so I'll come by here after that and pick you up. No arguments!"

Thierry picks up his teacup and turns to watch the snow flurries dancing in the wind outside, his face tense with worry. I decide not to argue and sit there, fighting to stay awake and prove him wrong about lack of sleep making me crazy.

Could the demons somehow be the product of my own mind? The grinding routine of training every day and chores could be pushing me a little over the edge. Hours of cleaning in the dojo in daylight hours has also yet to yield a single piece of clear physical evidence of my nighttime visitors except some strange stains and smells.

Yes, the dojo was unusually clean. Yes, there were some scratches on the windows. But those could be gravel from the parking lot or acid rain seeping down from the roof. There are always green stains and funky smells around after a "visit" from Kappa, but the tiny teacups we use after morning class do splash easily and green tea can get funky. Sweaty humans and gas-causing food like daikon radish can also add a certain aroma to the dojo, demons or no demons.

Either way, Thierry is determined to get me out of here.

Great, now I'll never know the truth about Dar's experiments. Even as I described the demon visits to Thierry I could feel that what I was saying was true: I'm not scared. My curiosity about the goings-on in the building and Dar is stronger than my fear.

But then there are my blisters, and the sounds of the

Swordmaster's shouts that ring in my ears even now.

I'm ready to die today.

I have to face these demons, whether they're psychological disturbances or not. Especially if they're psychological disturbances.

So what do I do about my sempai's plans to take me out of here after tonight's class?

❅ ❅ ❅

After Thierry leaves, my mind is racing, so I focus on getting my morning chores done, starting with cleaning the kamiza at the front of the dojo. I've skipped this task a few times in the past few days, so maybe I'm making someone angry.

I walk the front of the mat with my special cleaning materials, a rag that's only used for the kamiza and some gentle cleaner. First I bow to the front from the waist, somewhere between 15 and 30 degrees with my eyes forward. But I'm not bowing hello or goodbye to anyone – I'm paying homage to a shelf with a picture on it. Someone watching might think I'm crazy. Better not go there.

Even without flowers, the kamiza is a complicated task and demands my full attention. First, all the objects on each shelf have to be taken down and placed carefully on the mat. Then the gnarled cherry wood has to be wiped down with some mixture of stinky oils that smears away the dust and brings out the sheen. Then the water in the litttle cup has to be switched out – yesterday's dumped in a bucket and replaced with a fresh pour. The cup of water represents something important about purity in Japanese culture, but deep-down I think Sensei has it up there to make my life difficult. Then each item has to be dusted and polished, then placed back on the shelf exactly where it was before.

Last, another bow to the shelf. Yes, there's no one here watching, but I'm not crazy, I promise.

This is supposed to be repeated before and after morning and noon class, then again tonight for evening classes. Right now the routine is comforting somehow as my brain whirls with thoughts of Dar, demons and my upcoming eviction from the dojo.

* * *

One minute I'm standing, the next minute I'm hitting the ground hard, my legs swept from under me.

"Nice, now do it again. Faster this time."

Quan had a snow day at his high school and his mom dropped him off for noon class. Now he's taking me down with one fluid swipe of his heel and I'm falling harder each time as he hits the perfect angle of foot against knee. That last fall actually made my whole right side tingle, and not in a pleasant way.

It's just me and Quan for this noon class, not too surprising considering the flurries and talk of a huge storm tonight. Everyone's out stocking up on food and batteries, Quan's mom said. Quan and I have been doing free practice the entire hour, trying different defenses from different attacks and working up a sweat. The sun is still bright outside and the dojo feels surprisingly cozy, even as ice crystals form on the inside of the top row of windows. Getting up and down constantly for an hour warms you right up.

"Ok, good job. Let's call it a day."

Pulling myself up from the last leg sweep, I turn to see Quan facing the right corner of the dojo, his body stiff and tense all of a sudden.

"Quan? What is it?"

He stands as if paralyzed and doesn't respond. I take a few steps toward what he's looking at and glimpse a brief flash of blue moving freakishly fast.

Oh no, not now.

Quan stays still, horror in his eyes.

"What is it? What do you see?"

His smooth, dark face is immobile and his eyes are glistening.

"Quan, what is it? Was it a frog or a crazy-looking old man? I should probably tell you that there's been some weird stuff going on around here."

"I can't be. He can't be here. He's been in jail for years."

"Who are you talking about?"

"That cop, did you see him?"

"Cop? No cops in this building today. Haven't seen any around here since they found the body in the back lot last month. Certainly no cops in the dojo. It's kind of dark in here – you must have seen some shadows."

I force a laugh, trying to dispel the chill that seems to have fallen over the dojo like a frigid shroud.

"No shadow. No ghosts. That was a cop, one cop that I know. The cop that shot my brother. He was standing right there in the corner."

"How can that be? Didn't he go to jail for life? No cops in here, Quan, I promise."

"I know what I saw."

I can't really argue with him – I've seen some unexplainable things myself this week. We stand like that for a minute or two more. I've got no words of comfort, either, as memories of last night's tattooed killer flood my brain. Finally, I break the spell with a clap to end the class – the best thing for Quan's peace of mind would be to get him out of this place.

Quan is shaking but he follows along with the routine of bowing to me to finish our practice, then formally bowing to get off the mat. He avoids my eyes as we clean the mat and the space.

Cops are everywhere in this neighborhood, so could one have possibly snuck in here undetected and peeked in the side door at the front of the dojo? We don't usually use that door but I haven't checked to make sure it's locked recently. Cops usually are sure to call the landlord and announce themselves loudly as they walk through these half-dark halls, so I doubt it. There's only one obvious answer: Quan's seeing the same things that I've been seeing in the last few days.

"Do you think about that cop a lot, Quan? Can you talk about it?"

He's sitting now on a bench at the edge of the mat, sweat beading his face and steaming slightly in the cold. I've never seen him look this lost.

"Sure I think about it. He killed my brother in cold blood, just because he didn't get his cut of drug money. He's a real monster and I never thought I'd see him free in my lifetime, anyone's lifetime."

A real monster... just like the other monsters that have been infesting this building. Could it be related?

"Quan, I have to tell you something. There have been a lot of weird things going on in the building in the past few days. People have been seeing all sorts of things, nightmares and monsters and demon-type of things. I'm not sure it's all real or some kind of mass craziness. Invisible rays or chemicals left over from the ammunition testing from the last century. I'm looking into it and I'm going to make it stop."

My voice sounds strong, but I really don't know what I'm talking about.

How exactly does one stop a demon infestation?

❊ ❊ ❊

The blood surges from the wound, pooling into a gleaming crimson bubble, perfect and smooth. Then, before I can react, the bubble bulges and the crimson starts rushing down my thumb to my wrist, heading for the whiteness below. Too late, I jerk my hand back as the blood beads on the cotton.

Damn, the thirsty fibers of the gi pants I'm wearing soak up the blood before I can blot it. A splotch of red spreads on the snowy cloth. Nice – it's right in the crotch area. As if being a woman in Aikido wasn't tough enough.

Evening class is hours away and I've done all the cleaning I can stand, so I move on to sewing up torn uniform pants. The needle that I'm sewing with is sharp but almost too big to push through the cotton. The stabbing motion I used to punch through the fabric has left me with a hole in my finger.

Sewing up gi pants is one of my least favorite uchideshi chores, but skipping it means I have to do more of my absolute least favorite chore – laundry. Sensei left me with a stack of pants with tears in the knees and seat that I've been steadily returning to service. If I keep up with the pace of one pair of pants fixed every other day, I won't need to do my laundry until she gets back.

An Aikido uniform, called a gi, consists of a pair of pants and a kimono-style top in white cotton. The pants are relatively thin and get sweaty fast, especially if worn under the black hakama pants that denote a senior student. As an uchideshi trainee I get to wear the hakama, which comes in very handy at times of the month where white pants are a liability. I only got my period a few years ago and my body loves to surprise me. Thank god for the hakama.

The top part of the gi is made from heavier-weight cotton to stand up to shoulder and collar grabs. When the weather was warmer, I discovered that a sweaty gi top, if left to air out, stops smelling in a few days once the sweat oxidizes. It has to be hung up in the sun and left for at least a day – two wearings in 24 hours results in an unpleasant odor not unlike the smell of a gerbil cage. Three wearings in 24 hours results in a cat-pee smell that can be detected at least a few feet away. Must be a pheromone thing. In general, students won't complain to Sensei about someone in a smelly gi until four or more wearings, I've discovered. Even then, a wrinkled nose is as bad as it gets, usually. But with Sensei away and demons visiting, I'm sweating more and feeling more self-conscious so I have to plan carefully to ensure I smell OK until she gets back.

Now if I can get these pants fixed without stabbing myself

again, I'm golden.

I spit generously onto an uninjured finger and dab the saliva on the bloodstain – another bit of Aikido lore passed down from Sensei. The enzymes in spit break down the blood cells and fade the crimson to brown, then a yellowish smear. A quick rinse in the bathroom sink and the blood will be gone. Only a couple more hours and another gallon or so of blood and spit and this pair of pants will be perfectly stitched.

"Hey got some green tea?"

Dar has cracked the door, his face more open than it was at the end of last time he visited. I nod and he slips off his shoes and strides to the windows.

It's an hour before evening class but the sun has already slipped behind the skyline, sending up shock waves of vivid gold and orange. The sky is so wide and bright still it's hard to believe the city will soon be as dark as if wrapped in black cloth. Grayish piles of cloud are massing on the horizon.

Dar gestures at the skyline.

"Wow, do those colors in the sunset mean a storm is coming? I keep hearing about a major blizzard and the air in the stairwell smelled like snow earlier. Whatever that means."

"I'm not sure. I'm from California, but seems like something is building up out there. The students have been talking about it, the few that showed up today."

Unsettled and anxious, I've been watching the brightness drain from the sky for hours. I don't want the night to come. I put my sewing to the side and steal a glance at the mirror on Sensei's desk – my hair looks unwashed and my face is bumpy and shiny.

"Check this out: You can see part of the campus if you lean to this side."

Even as I edge up next to Dar at the window I can smell stale sweat wafting up from inside my layers of fleece: a blend of gerbil cage and cat pee. Should have changed my sports bra after noon class.

"It's so amazing to me that this neighborhood, which

looks like the aftermath of a nuclear war, is only a bit more than a mile from the university. They sit there in their million-dollar buildings, marinating in money and arrogance as the city around them decays."

"Right."

It's all I can think of to say. Today Dar is sending off a strong burnt smell, this time of metal with sandalwood.

"See that building there next the cemetery? With all the windows?" He gestures off in the distance, then leans in very close to align our heads. He bumps up against my shoulder.

"Sort of – is it that bluish one?"

"Experimental biophysics central. If I had a star-destroyer base, I'd blow that place to bits. More evil people there than any place in the world. Now that I've got what I need for my work, the whole building and all its petty bureaucrats should vanish off the face of the earth."

"Didn't someone already try that in the last century? My mom told me years ago there was some kind of bombing in that building before she got here and she met the survivors. The Unibomber was trying to kill a computer science professor."

"He takes a hard look at me. You're from a university family? I never would have guessed. Thought they were all entitled rich brats."

"Not quite. My mom did taxes, so we weren't poor but it's not like we had our own plane or anything."

"So what are you…"

"What am I doing here? Why aren't I at a bank or doing relief work and getting awards? Not all of us university legacies want to go down the same path as our parents. My mom's path ended up her getting killed."

Awkward silence for a few seconds. The last thing I want to do right now is tell my mom's story. I tend to cry even now when I get to the part where she lay there bleeding after the robbery for three hours until someone found her.

Time to change the subject. "So speaking of killing, didn't a guy just get chopped up or something down there on campus recently? The students were talking about it at noon class."

"Could be. There are lots of people who deserve being chopped up down there. I wouldn't worry about it over here. You're in a fortress in this building and lots of people are looking after you, seems to me. I see all these people coming and going at your dojo all times of the day and night."

"Does that include you – looking after me? I can take care of myself, you know."

"Hey, I just visit you because I like the conversation and the ambiance in your little Japanese monastic cell here. Your situation intrigues me."

He's still looking out the window when the dojo door creaks open. The first student for evening Aikido class, pulling off a parka and snow boots as he sings out a greeting. Rommel, a voice teacher at the university, is leading the class tonight and we could be doing anything and everything before the final bell rings.

The conclusion to my intense conversation with Dar will have to wait until later.

✳ ✳ ✳

"Strike forward, brain that attacker! Cherry, your angle is too flat – you're just annoying the guy. Remember, he's laid siege to your master's castle and intends to pillage and murder your entire family!"

We've just started evening class, and the blood and gore is already flowing. All the pillaging talk might be disturbing if not for Rommel's pink, babyish features and his frequent wisecracks. He's trying to make swinging a wooden staff more interesting, but I'm not in the mood for rivers of blood tonight. A handful of us are striking forward with the jo, a weapon that is used in Aikido practice to develop awareness of distance, timing and force. Swinging a four-foot white oak stick helps us learn how to more effectively hit and deflect with our three-foot arms, from what I understand.

All I know is that today my jo feels like a clunky shaft of ice that doesn't want to obey any of my body's commands. I stand with my right foot forward in the Aikido stance, my left foot behind me at an angle with my hips nearly square to the front. Shifting the weight from foot to foot while rotating the wrist in a figure-eight pattern is supposed to generate an explosive cutting motion, "martial baton-twirling" as Rommel likes to say.

Instead, my jo is wobbling and weaving and even has the nerve to smack me on the cheekbone when I try to crank up the speed. No serious injury, but this class can't get any worse for me tonight.

We switch feet then practice a series of attacks: swinging at an angle at the temple, thrusting to the midsection and then whipping the jo downward from the center to pulverize the top of the head. Visualizing the impact as I let my arms unspool and extend, my mood improves. We pair up to practice a partner form, then change partners to hone a tricky defense.

"Circle of doom!" Rommel chirps, then we pair up again to practice the defense, a hand strike called *makiotoshi* or "rolling drop." As my partner thrusts to my midsection, I lift my jo then roll it down the length of partner's weapon, pushing it aside as I release all of my force onto his hands. If he's quick, he'll just get a tap. Unfortunately, my partner this time is Rommel and he returns my thrust with an explosive whack to my knuckles that vibrates through my whole body.

"*Itai!*" I can't help but call out "it hurts" in Japanese as I drop the jo. No blood, but a purplish swelling hints at the bruise to come.

Rommel studies his handiwork, gives me a long look, and then pulls me off the mat and over to the first-aid kit. He activates an instant ice-pack with a practiced twist and slaps it onto my hand none too gently.

"Your attack wasn't committed that time and you were wide open to the counter, Cherry. You need to be more connected through the whole movement."

My eyes tear up a bit. I can't show Rommel that I'm tired and miserable right now. After all, I need to convince Thierry later tonight that I can tough it out in the dojo until Sensei gets back. Thierry might also check in with Rommel on how I did in the first class.

"Cherry, I've been hearing that you're...overdoing things with Sensei away. Is that why you're not connected tonight?" Rommel's baby face is too close right now. Here it comes. The senior students have been talking to each other and they're all trying to get me to interrupt my uchideshi training. Time to create an opening so I can stay here.

"I do have some blisters but they're getting better, I promise. This whole uchideshi experience is intense but I'm starting to really get into the rhythm of daily practice. A few more days and I'll have all I need for an excellent college admissions essay."

Rommel works at the university and knows how important those essays are. Should be a good angle of attack.

"OK, If you're sure. We don't want any angry parents in here again, like with the kid this summer. You weren't here, but we had an uchideshi from the next state over who was supposed to stay for a few months and he only lasted three days. We came in for evening class and he had left a letter and all the uniforms that Sensei lent him in a dirty pile.

"'You are too bossy to be a true Aikido master and you make me work too hard,' or something like that. Bunch of bull, if you ask me. But his parents were really mad and yelled at Sensei for about an hour in the hallway while we were trying to do a class. Guy was 19 like you but not tough enough for uchideshi life. Nothing wrong with that. It's really not for everyone."

"I like getting bossed around and working hard, I promise! It's just taking a little time to get used to the cold in here at night. Plus all the weird building noises that sound like ghosts sometimes! It's not exactly scary, more like distracting. I'll get used to it."

"Good, I'm glad we won't be hearing from your dad. Now get back out there and show me some nice makiotoshi!"

Rommel is smiling. Attack deflected. My hands have feeling in them again even as the bruise on my knuckle darkens to deep purple.

Now to convince Thierry.

* * *

Great, another leak in this crappy building.

That's the thought going through my head as I ninja-walk along the hallway to Emma's side of the building and spot something strange up ahead.

What Aikido kids know as "ninja-walking" involves hugging a wall with your back and bringing one leg across the other while never picking your feet up off of the floor. It's actually called *yoko-ashi* according to my research – good for sneaking through narrow hallways at the daimyo's castle and dense forests infested with enemies. Ninja-walking is what we call it in children's class: Sensei says that kids respond better if you use words they see in their phone games.

Evening class ended a little early to due to the snow, which erupted out of the darkness midway through the hour of jo practice. First a few flakes against the windows, then curtains of white in a matter of minutes. When the wind picked up and started to hurl flurries against the glass with an audible clatter, Rommel had us bow out to end class.

The roads might keep Thierry from his mission to move me out of the dojo later tonight, but I can't be sure. So I'm headed to Emma's space to get her advice on how to convince him to let me stay. She might even be talked into coming down the hall with me to assure him that she'll keep an eye on me and make sure I don't succumb to demon-haunted delusions.

My legs are getting tired from the ninja-walking, but if I side-step just right and minimize shuffling sounds, Barata the

Capoeira nutjob won't hear me coming. Better yet, he won't be waiting to spring out of any of the empty rooms along the hall to sweep my legs. As I pass the bathrooms, the only sound is a gentle swishing of my straw sandals on concrete and the crackle of my left knee joint.

No Barata, no noises from behind his door.

Up ahead the ribbon of something shiny comes into focus, snaking across the hall right near Emma's space. Closer up I see it's a stream of water, running out from under her door and along the concrete, flowing a little sluggishly in the cold.

Funny, Emma's always boasted that her dojo was bone-dry. She loves to remind me that Sensei was the sucker for renting a space on the side of the building with the power transmitter and the big puddle that collects on the roof after any rainstorm that makes for lots of leaks.

So where does water leak from on this side of the building?

"Emma? Emma, are you there?"

Her unit door is papered over with fresh notices about introductory Tai Chi classes. Women's class. Kid's class. Over 50. Over 80. I peel aside a "Tai Chi for New Moms" poster and press my ear to the scarred wood. It's warm, but I don't hear a thing.

Could she have left before the snowstorm hit and her water cooler tipped over? A few seconds later I catch a definite sound from behind the door. Could that be Emma making that weird slurping sound? She's never been a big ramen noodle fan. I knock, as loud as I can with frozen knuckles. The slurping abruptly stops, followed by a clatter like a tray full of plastic cups falling off a shelf. A few swishes and squeals and more plasticky clattering and tinkling. What the hell is going on?

"Emma, it's me, Cherry. Are you alright in there?"

Her voice comes back right away this time, much higher and squeakier than usual.

"Cherry! Wait, I'll be right there. Give me a minute."

The door cracks open and Emma's face pokes through. She looks tired but OK.

"Sorry, didn't mean to keep you waiting. No problems here, just doing some cleaning."

"What's with the water under the door and the noises? Is someone there with you?"

On closer inspection, Emma seems dusted with iridescent glitter, with a few big droplets of what looks like oil in her hair.

"Are you having some kind of party in here? What's with the glitter?"

"It's a ... I broke some stuff. Glitter-like stuff, like plastic walls."

"What?"

"Listen, I'll tell you about it later. It's not a big deal, but weird stuff has been happening in here. I'm not in danger, but I can't explain right now, OK?"

"Actually, there's been some weird stuff happening in the Aikido dojo as well! We need to talk about it but Thierry might try to kidnap me tonight and take me home. I can't leave here now – I need your help."

"Cherry, I'm sorry – not now."

My eye catches movement below me at the base of the door, near the hinge. The water leaking into the hall seems to be flowing back into Emma's space in some kind of reverse flood. As I watch in amazement, the edge of the puddle slides back up the hall and slips under the door. It's almost as if it's some kind of huge, slow-moving tentacle.

Emma looks down at the track in the grime left by the retreating ooze then gives me a look of embarrassment, of not quite fear.

"Sorry, now really isn't a good time."

Several loud clacks and tinkling crashes come from behind her. The scent of low tide surges in from the darkness and hits me with a familiar blast of funk. Not quite a Kappa pond-scum stink, more like a hot day at the beach.

"You sure you're OK in there?"

"I can handle it. We'll talk in the morning."

"If you say so. Hopefully I'll still be here!"

Emma's got a demon, I'm sure of it.

On my way back to the dojo I hear a sudden shuffling behind me and pivot before I can even process the sound. At the end of the hallway where it turns in to the stairwell I catch glimpse of a shadowy figure shuffling haltingly out of sight.

Could be Barata, but last time I checked, he had two legs.

Whoever this was wore a red cap, had shiny black skin and was wearing only a ragged pair of shorts. Strangest of all, he definitely had only one leg but moved with an otherworldly grace.

My surprise quickly gives way to curiosity, and the clear conviction that this was another demon. Not from Japanese culture, but a demon nonetheless.

What a relief – I'm not the only one.

But the relief soon gave way to a new kind of fear: The demons are now roaming free in the hallways. I don't even know what to call the other ones; they're not in my books.

And where was that one-legged guy headed, anyhow?

❉ ❉ ❉

I'm awake! So sorry, Sensei!

I push off my quilt and sit up in a split second, ready to take a tongue-lashing for sleeping through the alarm again. As the chill of the dojo starts chewing through my layers of clothing, I realize that it's still pitch-dark outside. A glance at my alarm – 3 am, two hours before I officially have get up. The sharp rapping sound – which sounded so like the swordmaster striking my futon frame with a wooden sword – sounds again from the window, followed by a rattling wail. Then another wail from the higher row of windows.

To my relief, it appears to be natural. Gusts of wind from the raging snowstorm outside.

Yes, I'm still in the dojo, thanks to that snowstorm. Thierry couldn't make it to the building after his shift. He sent me the message through Jean-Baptiste, who dropped by around dinner time with some steaming oxtail stew he had reheated on his hot plate. The storm forced him to stay over in building tonight, too. Thierry promised to come back tomorrow or as soon as the roads were clear and take me home.

So here I am, spending another night alone in the dojo. No demons so far, just roaring, relentless wind. Either hail or snow or ice has fallen almost every day since Sensei left for Japan, but this is a serious storm.

I pull the sleeping bag and quilt around me and lean against the wall, trying to warm myself through sheer will. "Cold is the mind-killer. Cold is the little death that brings total obliteration." Lines from my favorite books and anime series seem to pop into my head all the time lately. Characters from fiction seem to be speaking to me and filling the many silences in my day, if not my waking nightmares.

Tears start running down my face, warm tracks across a chilled expanse of cheek and chin. I feel so far from my family, far from the few friends I've made at home, far from any warmth at all. My shoulders hurt, my hands are raw from sword cuts and cleaning and an inflamed zit is making my nose hurt. What am I doing here?

I hear Sensei's voice.

"Do you really think you belong here? I'm wondering if you have what it takes. You are so casual about your practice – this is life or death here. This is not some enriching activity that you write about for a college essay. This is about your life, your spirit, and making the world a better place through reconciling the universe. Do you see that, or are you just some kind of silly kid looking to waste my time?"

Sensei's words stung worse than any blow from a sword or twist to the wrist. She had come to the dojo just minutes before noon class a few weeks ago, delayed by a police blockade down the street. She had walked across blood-washed pavement to get here, and I had nodded off on the couch. I was supposed to get an early start on cleaning but the dojo was still dirty from a packed morning class. I didn't even wake up until Sensei hit the couch frame with a bokken. Several more students arrived just as she roused me, so the lecture came later, after we cleaned up and I had dozed bleary-eyed through a half-hour or so of tea and socializing.

The door had barely shut when Sensei started in. My only saving grace was that I didn't cry right then, only later.

"I'm not a babysitter, you know. You are too young to do this program, but I made an exception because of your mom and because you wrote me such a great letter. Was that all bull? Did you even write that letter?"

"I wrote it, Sensei, and I really want to be here. I'm not casual about my training, I promise. I just can't get to sleep at night sometimes and my dad always says when I nap I sleep like a dead body. I didn't mean to do it."

"You should be ready to get up at any time. Sleeping like a dead body will make you a dead body in some cases. Do you think the samurai got a lot of deep sleep? My teacher used to travel with his teacher and he was expected to get up in the middle of the night to open the bathroom door *before* his teacher got there. His teacher was an old man and had to go multiple times a night. He didn't sleep through the night for years!"

I try not to roll my eyes. Does she really expect me to hold the bathroom door for her?

"Don't worry, Cherry. I don't need you to hold the bathroom door for me. That's just a metaphor for the kind of dedication you need for this job. As an uchideshi, you have the future of Aikido in your hands, and you need to take the role very seriously. Perhaps you're just too young for this. Do you have a return ticket to California yet?"

"Please, Sensei, I promise, it won't happen again. I'll open the bathroom door for you."

She cracks a bit of a smile.

"No need for that quite yet, thank you. I really don't want to have to give you this talk again. And I never want to catch you slacking off again. Smarten up."

Replaying that conversation in my head makes me cry harder. Now is the time I have to show Sensei that I'm different, that I'm ready to become a full-on Aikido student.

Outside, another burst of snowflakes hits the windows. The building groans in the wind, glass rattling in the window frames. Pops and cracks explode from the ceiling beams. Strong but not hurricane-force winds, I would guess. After a particularly powerful gust knocks loose a sprinkle of grit from the pipe above my futon, I pull the covers over my head.

This night will be over soon, I tell myself.

This night will be over soon.

CHAPTER SIX

Wednesday

S creams from the street wake me up what seems about ten minutes. I had finally dozed off amid the noise of the snowstorm.

I flip down the top of the sleeping bag – only a tired haze of streetlight is filtering into the space from the void outside. The howling starts up again: cats fighting outside or some stray dog in pain, I can't tell. Sounds far away, sounds like it's not my business. Or could that be the storm, ready to tear the roof off and kill us all? The far-off screeching continues, but something else starts getting my attention: I have to pee.

I lie there for a few minutes watching my breath steam in the cold and trying to figure out how badly I have to go to the bathroom. Pretty bad, it turns out. Damn that last cup of green tea before bed. I ease down the sleeping bag, unwrap my scarf and shuffle double-socked feet under the bed to find my slippers.

My leg is extended backwards under the frame, toe just touching the slipper, when an icy band clamps around my angle and gives a strong jerk.

Years of falling practice cause my arms to come forward just as my body flies off the bed and I slam into the floor. A second later with the arms, and I would have hit face-first. The thin foam mat on the floor is little protection: My frozen nose was barely an inch from getting completely flattened. But my forearms have absorbed the impact – no injuries. Years of training not to swear in the dojo space go out the window, however.

"What the…!"

As my arms tingle from the impact, my senses awake to the fact that something is still around my ankle. So cold it's hot, if that makes sense. Wide like the top of a running sock, or clamped fingers…Could Kappa be capable of such a nasty trick?

"Who's there? Kappa, this is too much!"

A hissing sound comes from under the bed, and the cuff tightens. I brace my arms against the floor and attempt to kick my foot free, but what feels like a thick rope pulls against my leg and yanks me a bit further under the bed.

Louder hissing this time, that resolves itself into slurred Japanese words.

"Sakura San, Sakura San."

Never has my name sounded so much like the hissing of a giant snake. That's not Kappa, with his friendly gurgling. Or the swordmaster's angry shout. What the hell is under the bed? Only one answer to that this week: another demon who needs to be dealt with. Just when I thought I was going to have a peaceful night.

"Hello, my name is Sakura, but you can call me Cherry. Can I help you?"

Angry hissing at higher volume fills the space, though the rope seems to slip away from my ankle. I push myself onto my knees then crawl back onto the futon, tucking all my limbs under the sleeping bag. I'm scared, but for some reason I assume that the intruder won't bother me now that I'm covered up.

The hissing fades a bit, replaced by a slithering sound that escalates then fades as the thing moves to the front of my dojo. My eyes have adjusted a bit to the light, so I carefully turn my head to the front of the space, searching out the source of the hissing.

Something impossibly big and impossibly shaped looms

out of the dimness, a blob with black rags hanging from it on the end of what looks like a giant rope. The snaky shape is twisting in midair, the rags whipping around amid the clacking of wood.

No, those aren't rags – it's hair.

That's not wood clacking – it's teeth.

And that's no rope – it's a neck that's got to be twenty feet long, ending in a woman's head. A woman who looks really pissed off. Of course, it's the demon that has to be the creepiest one of all.

Rokurokubi.

Rokurokubi is the creature who caught my eye from the first in my reading about Japanese folk tales: A female demon with a long neck that is human by day and a freakish drinker of blood by night. She's known for her anger – a rage so heated it literally boils water.

In one version of this story I read, Rokurokubi gets so angry that the water boiled on the hibachi stove when no fire was lit – rats also dropped dead in the alleys outside. Her greatest joy was to unfurl her incredibly long neck and scare the life out of mortals she suspected of sinning against the Buddhist law, or so the stories go.

Come to think of it, there are a lot of angry women in Japanese folklore. Yuki-Onna, the woman abandoned in the snow, freezes men to death. Rokurokubi boils water and kills people. Angry frog demons and bird-men, too.

Judging from my memories of my mom, some Japanese women do have that side to them: Calm and cheerful most of the time, erupting into rage at others. My mom's temper contributed to her death, the police said. She started yelling at the guy who was trying to rob her, and then the gun went off. They're blaming the victim, I said at the time. But who knows, if she had just handed over the $34 she had in her purse, she might be alive today.

Looking right now at Rokurokubi's twisted, sneering face, I can see how an angry woman with a mane of wild black hair could make you jumpy. And if you're stupid enough to rob a tax office, being jumpy can get someone killed.

The demon twists around in the air and howls in front of the kamiza, then swings itself around in an abrupt pivot. With one sweep of its hideous neck, the sacred objects and portrait of Aikido's founder are swept to the floor in a clatter of broken glass and wood.

The thing ducks its head lower to the shelves below and appears to bite at something: It's clamped down with its teeth on the stack of sutra books that we use for meditation. The demon wags its head around a bit and then opens its mouth to scream again: The sutra books plop down on the kamiza in the spot O-Sensei's picture once stood.

The unearthly howls rise in volume as the thing coils itself tighter and then slithers with uncanny speed toward the edge of the mat. It's headed right toward the futon where I'm cowering. Drool coats its chin and the screams are unbearable – I pull the sleeping bag above my head, pretty sure it won't help much.

A powerful shove and I've sprawled to the floor again, this time banging a knee hard against the concrete. I curl into fetal position, letting out my own howl of agony, and wait for the pain to subside. As I press against my kneecap to check for a fracture I realize it's quiet again in the dojo. A few more seconds pass and I pull the sleeping bag off my head. Something wet and warm drips onto my forehead from above.

Something wet, warm and incredibly stinky.

"Are you OK, Cherry San?"

"Kappa?"

"She's gone, that crazy woman."

The dojo seems a bit lighter now as I scan the space – no long-necked monster. Only Kappa, glowing muddy green and grinning in the half-dawn.

"See what happens when you get angry, Cherry-San? You don't want to be like that scary woman."

"No life lessons right now, please! I think I broke my knee."

130

Kappa tips his froggy face over the edge of the futon and peers down at my exposed joint. Another splatter of pond scum hits my face.

"Hmm, it hurts, right?"

He extends a knobby arm then clamps his shockingly warm and slimy hand to my knee. I start to recoil but the warmth seems to spread through my body, healing as it goes. Now the knee feels a little achy, but the sharp pain is gone. Even my elbow, which has been bothering me for months and got knocked hard just now on the concrete, feels a bit better.

"Thanks, Kappa. Thank you for taking care of me."

"Don't be so angry, Cherry-San!"

He plops down to the floor and scuttles off out of sight behind the shoe rack.

Silence once again descends on the space, and I pull myself onto the futon and burrow in the bedding, still stinking of frog demon. I'm alive, my knee feels better and the sun will rise soon. I let my eyes adjust to the light and turn toward the window.

The sky glows pinkish gray, blurred a little in places by gusts of snow. As my ears empty of Rokurokubi's screams, the roar of snowplow trucks filters in from the streets outside. The machines' grinding and groaning could be the howls of some prehistoric creatures in a death match. Now it's just me and the plows and an empty dojo. A feeling of dread settles into my gut.

What will this day bring, now that the demons are popping out all over the place?

❆ ❆ ❆

The pain slices through my forearm, then razors up to my shoulder before zapping me between the eyes.

"Wow! That was a good one. I won't be able to write in the logbook for weeks!"

Quan beams, his wrist arching a few degrees more as he

131

applies yonkyo, one of Aikido's most painful nerve pinches.

"Ow, stop! Didn't you hear me tap out?

"Sorry, Cherry Sempai! I got carried away."

Quan walked to class today – turns out there was more wind than snow last night and the sidewalks were clear except for a few drifts and splatter from plow trucks. It's just him and me for noon class again, although I'm expecting more for evening. The roads are still icy, though, so I'm safe from Thierry's concern for now and can focus on the demon situation.

Not that I couldn't use Thierry's help: Rokurokubi's visit this morning left me with a swollen knee and a bruise in the shape of a skeletal hand circling my ankle. Kappa took away the pain but something bad definitely happened last night.

What greeted me this morning in the hallway also left me with a burning determination: These demon visits have got to stop.

A few hours ago, when I finally limped off to the bathroom after figuring out that my leg hadn't been broken, I opened to door to something weird. Sounds of splashing and crackling came from one end of the building. That one-legged demon I saw before by Barata's space hopped through the lobby as I stood there with an audible cackle.

From the other end of the building, near Dar's lab, intense bursts of a harsh light flickered and flashed, with a sound like amplified static. Burnt plastic and metallic smells mingled in the air along with a heavy stink that blended smoked meat and charred grass.

From my spot just outside the bathroom door, I could hear unearthly howling floating up from the floors below. It's daylight, but demons seem to be everywhere. Seems like all of us here in the building right now are dealing with the same problem – we're all just too ashamed to admit it. Once Quan and I have finished our practice, I plan to visit everyone on this floor to organize some kind of action. I can see Sensei's face come alive with admiration as she hears of my leadership qualities.

I'm spacing out when someone grabs my wrist and jabs

a knuckle into my forearm again for another jolt of pain. The Swordmaster? No, just Quan, who can't get enough of the nerve pinches. Aikido's fourth teaching, *yonkyo*, consists of using your pointer finger's knuckle to squeeze your partner's carpal nerve. It feels like someone is stabbing a pencil into your forearm.

"Ok, that's enough yonkyo, Quan. Let's get the cleaning started. The paint's been flaking off the ceiling all over the place because of the storm and the cold –– let's get damp rags and wipe that off the mat and the concrete."

We get to work and the dojo is clean in no time. Perhaps I can squeeze in a nap this afternoon, after all. Just as Quan puts on his coat and shoes to head home, a face appears at the door. I'm startled to see Shai, the building manager, who mostly sticks to the first floor. Sensei took me down to his office last week to introduce me as her deputy while she was in Japan.

"If he sees your face once, he won't question why you're here at all hours, trust me," Sensei said. "He's a nice guy, just doesn't want to know too much about the idol-worshiping stuff we're doing in here. He's never even set foot in the dojo."

Great, Shai's taking his first look at the dojo today, while Sensei's away. Hope he doesn't ask too many questions about how I got to the building today, the morning after a big snow-storm.

Shai could be 30, or he could be 50. I'm bad at telling people's ages, especially when they're bundled up in East Coast winter clothes. Shai's old-fashioned suit and clunky shoes make him seem old, but his eyes sparkle and the parts of his face that aren't bearded look smooth.

He takes a few steps inside. Quan gives me a look but I smile at him and signal that it's OK for him to go home.

"Take care out there, Quan. Make sure the plow trucks can see you when they cross the road. Jump on a snowbank if they get too close."

For someone who grew up in California, I've learned quickly how to stay alive in the snow zone, thanks to advice from the dojo members.

"Bye Cherry Sempai. Take care in here."

Shai edges past the threshold when Quan leaves then looks at the shoe rack, but doesn't make a move toward taking off his boots.

"So, eh, what exactly is that you do in here? Some kind of yoga or something?" Shai pulls at his beard and fiddles with his yarmulke a bit. He's been the building manager for years, Sensei said, but still seems mystified by what's going on within his walls.

"It's called Aikido, and it's nothing like yoga, really. We throw each other around and pinch each other's nerves. Sometimes we twist each other's arms up like pretzels."

"Yeah, right. Funny. So that chanting and stuff you guys yell at each other in Chinese is some kind of praying?"

Sneaky bastard, he's been listening outside the door.

"It's Japanese, not Chinese. We thank each other in Japanese and do some chanting sometimes. The chants aren't worshiping, just kind of explaining Buddhist ideas so we can meditate. I guess that's kind of religious, but we're not praying to anyone."

"Like chanting the scriptures in Christian church?" He looks a little relieved. Perhaps calling our chants "scriptures" makes them seem a little less foreign.

"I guess. But I'm not a priest or monk or anything. It's more like the pledge of allegiance. Or telling an old story."

"Yeah, whatever. So just make sure your boss gets me the full amount for the electricity this month. You guys are keeping the lights on all day and night."

Uh-oh. Is Shai busting me for staying over the dojo? Do the broken-looking video cameras on the landings in the stairwells actually work?

"Sorry, I'll make the sure the students turn them off when they leave."

Shai stands in the doorway, shuffling his feet in his dirt-caked boots and fiddling with his facial hair. Why doesn't he leave? What does he want?

"Er, do you want to look around in here? Check for leaks or something? You're going to have to take off your shoes and hat, though. No hats in the dojo."

"It's not a hat, it's a yarmulke. I'm not taking it off. I don't want to get fungus from those floors on my feet, either."

"You can keep the hat on, then, and your socks. No fungus in here – we bleach it every day."

Another awkward silence. Shai takes a few steps into the dojo and fiddles with his shoelaces a bit. Great, now I'm going to have to play tour guide when I should be mobilizing the tenants to stop a demon infestation.

He stands up and looks me straight in the eye.

"So, anything weird going on with that new guy down in 540? The Indian guy with the machine shop? His electric bill is through the roof. Plus he's causing some issue with the transmission tower. You Aikido people OK with him as a neighbor?"

"Him? You mean Dar? Oh, he's a great guy. Very nice and helpful, good neighbor. Sensei says that too and she'll be back next week. She can tell you more about him." I better give her a full rundown as soon as her plane lands.

"Funny, I could swear I saw you chatting with him like an old buddy on the stairs the other day."

Some of those cameras must work.

"Well we're friendly neighbors, but I don't ask about his business. His name is Dar, by the way."

"Dar? Well, whatever. I'm sure he's a nice person."

Shai stands there for what seems like 20 minutes, fiddling with his keychain and humming. I'm not sure what to do, so I pick up a rag and pretend to dust Sensei's desk. Finally, after what seems like weeks, he blurts out a question.

"Speaking of new guys, are you getting some … unusual visitors in your studio in the last few days?"

Better play it cool. I don't want to give away too much if he's just trying to get me to admit to staying over.

"Visitors? I'm not sure what you mean? We only allow visitors who contact Sensei first, and she's away. No new people at all in the last week."

Another century of fiddling and humming as move my dusting to the cabinet. Turns out there is plenty of dust there to push around.

"Not people, something else. Like in our religion we have old story about a rabbi who made a monster out of clay and he came to life. The clay man came to life and started running around and fighting people."

Shai's face turns a bunch of different colors at once as I gawk at him – pink, red, ghostly pale. Is this guy crazy? Or is he asking about demons? I'm trying to figure out how I can bring up the subject without mentioning my overnights in the dojo. Better play it cool. Anything I say might get us all in trouble.

"Haven't seen a clay man in here recently. I'll keep an eye out and let you know if I see him."

We lock eyes for a few more seconds of awkward silence.

Shai leans against the shoe rack, pulls off a boot and gives me a hard look. He's no fool, this guy, despite his "see-no-evil" style of building management. He's probably seeing right through my tired eyes and the blisters on my hands.

He pulls off his other boot but keeps his socks on. He hops across the concrete with wide leaps – trying to minimize his contact with foot fungus, I presume. He flops onto a chair in the lounge and pulls his feet up to form a surprisingly limber lotus position. I put down my cleaning rags and walk over to hear what he has to say.

"Shocked I can sit like this? I know from yoga, missy. Let me tell you a story, Miss Karate Kid. Perhaps you can help with my problem, then. This entire building has a serious problem.

"So I'm in my office two nights ago – had to stay late to make sure the parking lot was plowed properly. Got a cot back there and a space heater in case I'm too tired to drive home, and this was one of those nights. Yeah, don't look so shocked. It's not like nobody ever stays overnight around here."

He gives me an intense look then cracks a smile. Our secret is safe, I guess.

"So I'm heating up some soup from home in the micro-wave when my office starts shaking like it's an earthquake or something. This isn't Vermont! No volcanoes and earthquakes, thank you! So I'm getting ready to run for my life when the supply closet door opens up real slow and all this crap starts flying out. Crap like dust and chunks of dirt and stuff. Then I see something dark and crumbly push out and reach around for the door-knob. It's a hand, a human hand, a huge hand made out of dirt!

"Wow." I pour myself a cup of cold tea and settle in for Shai's story. I guess I'm lucky my demons only smell bad. Imagine the amount of cleaning I'd have to do every day if Kappa was made of dirt!

Shai mops his forehead and continues. "I take a look inside because I can't believe my eyes and there's this huge man made of out dirt inside the closet, just shaking all this crap onto my copy paper and receipt books. He's like a bodybuilder size with a big round head and a slit for a mouth. I know this guy, I've seen him somewhere."

"Did he try to grab you?"

"No, just stood there and made piles of dirt everywhere. Let me finish what I'm telling you! So I move in a little closer to this guy and I see something white hanging out of his mouth and I remember the story.

"The Jews were getting clobbered in Prague in the Old Country a few centuries ago and one rabbi made this clay man, called a golem. The golem kicked some gentile ass until he kind of went rogue and the Jews had to shut him down. To power up the golem, you need some paper with the name of Adonai, like your Buddha, written on it. Stick that paper in the golem's mouth, and he kicks ass for you. Take the paper out, and he falls in a pile of dirt."

"So did you take the paper?"

"Wait, let me finish the story. So I grab the paper really quick, and sure enough the entire seven-foot monster falls into a big pile of dirt. We're talking two, three feet of disgusting brown stuff. Such a relief, but I'm too tired to clean up the mess just then so I go back to sleep. When I wake up, the pile is gone but there's this big dirty mark on the door by the handle. Like a handprint."

"Could be a dream, right? Did you eat a bunch of pizza the night before? Or drink too much Red Bull?"

"Right, I was thinking it was probably a dream. But what about that dirt? That's not coming from me. I keep a very clean office."

Shai grabs a cookie from the box I left on the table and takes a bite, then grabs the box to check the ingredients. He goes back to munching and gives me another intense look.

"You've got a green handprint on your side door, you know that? I was up here earlier and saw lots of weird stuff. Slime outside the Chinese girl's space, big pile of fur outside that photographer's unit."

"I thought that guy was gone."

"He hasn't paid rent in months. I thought he'd been busted by the FBI or something but that doesn't explain the animal hair I saw there a few minutes ago. He used to crash here all the time."

Ugh, I don't want to think about it. A big hairy animal that close to the dojo?

Shai shuffles a bit to get a better lotus posture and stares at me expectantly. Yes, telling him the truth about the demons means I'll have to tell him I've been staying overnight in the building. He might also find out about the rest of the sleepover tenants. But it seems like he's already got a pretty good idea of the situation. He must have figured out that many of us don't head "home" at the end of the workday. I've got to make sure he's not just dreaming, first.

"So any other sightings of this dirt monster?"

"Nothing, except this. Today I go into that closet to get some copy paper and I'm pulling at a brand-new box and the thing won't open. I pull and tug and yank and this thing and then – woof! It opens all of a sudden and I'm flying into the wall. Instead of paper, inside it's packed with dirt. I mean packed like cement. And on top is this paper."

He pulls a crumpled square out of an inside pocket of his overcoat. The heat's been off for a while so he kept it on during the entire visit. On the square are some angular markings, slashes and squares in a grid pattern.

"Is it some kind of code?"

"Code? That's Hebrew, silly. Can't you read even a bit of Hebrew? Only 22 letters in the Hebrew alphabet, not like your thousands in Chinese. I can read books a thousand years old with that alphabet!"

"Japanese, not Chinese. Sorry, I'll try to learn some Hebrew in my spare time. In the meanwhile, what does that paper mean?"

"Never mind, it's the name of the creator, and it's what you need to activate the golem. I sure didn't write that, and I sure didn't fill a box with dirt in my supply closet. Something serious is going on in this building."

We sit there for a few minutes as Shai polishes off the cookies. I pour him some cold green tea from the pot and we sit there a bit longer. I decide to trust him and tell him some of the story.

"I know that something is going on, and I've seen some stuff in the past few days that makes me think I'm not the only one. We all need to sit down and figure this out. How to stop this craziness. A few people on this floor made it to the building this morning so we'll at least have four or five if we get together."

Shai gives me a skeptical look.

"Wow, my tenants are tough – coming in and taking care of their businesses after a snowstorm. Do me a favor: Make sure the guy on the first floor comes too. He's around all the time but I'm not sure he knows about everyone else who's been camping out here."

Shai pops his legs forward and smiles. He seems to know that he's running a low-rent apartment house in addition to a commercial building.

"How about four o'clock or so – will that work or do you

need to get home for prayers or something?"

"That will work fine. I can do my prayers right here. Don't you worry about me."

"Thanks, Shai. See you at 4 then. I'll try to get everyone to show up, including Dar."

"I really want to talk to that guy, so do your best. Stay safe and take care, Miss Karate Kid."

"Aikido kid!"

❋ ❋ ❋

The guy on the first floor? Shai must be talking about Brah, who trains in the closed rock climbing gym at the back of the building. Sensei introduced us a few weeks ago in case I ever got locked out early in the morning. She said Brah practices his climbing at all kinds of weird hours and camps out at the gym for months at a time due to shaky finances. He seemed like a nice guy, if a big spacy. I can't believe he's living down there in that huge empty space when it's this cold in the building. But I've got nothing planned for the afternoon and I'm sick of cleaning, so I might as well venture downstairs and try to enlist another ally. I bundle up and put my outside shoes on for the first time in days.

The stairway is extra dim today and the lights seem reluctant to switch on so I take my time, listening for strange sounds. Only far-off dripping, likely melting snow. Floor by floor, I creep down as quietly as I can, listening at each landing. Finally I reach the ground floor, walk down the hall and push open the unmarked door to the rock-climbing space that's always unlocked.

"Brah! Brah? You there?"

As I step through the door, my voice echoes in the dark doorway then gets lost in the ductwork. The ceilings are extra high in this part of the building, an old delivery bay. Tons of lead and gunpowder must have passed through these halls back in the day when the gun factories were running full-steam. Light from windows high up reveal walls covered with textured slabs and surfaces marked with brightly colored handholds.

The rock gym has been officially closed for months and cobwebs shiver on the holds close to the ground as a steady breeze blows through the space. For some reason it's a bit warmer down here, likely because the other half of this floor has heat most of the time for the renovated offices.

"Brah? Hey, Brah, can you hear me? It's Cherry from up-stairs. Shai said you were around this week and he wants me to talk to you about something!"

"Yo, sister! A voice booms out of a doorway behind me and I jerk back, nearly knocking myself out on a dusty outcrop-ping.

"Geez, Brah. Don't sneak up on me like that. What are you, a ninja?"

"Yes, that's me sister, ninja-master-climber-god!"

Brah calls everyone remotely female "Sister," and we all call him Brah because he refers to everyone remotely male as "Brah" or "Bro." No one remembers his real name. He's been in the building almost as long as Sensei, starting at the rock gym as soon as it opened.

The rock-gym owner told Sensei one night after a few beers that Brah had hit his head one too many times after fall-ing. His climbing skills are intact but his short-term memory is completely shot. The owner had to cash his paycheck for him and take him food shopping to keep him alive.

When the gym closed down last year after the owner had tax troubles, Brah kept teaching privately in the shuttered space as he waited for new owners to come in. Six months on and he's still alone down here most of the day: practicing his holds, doing pushups and camping out in one of the back offices after his car got repossessed. The former owner still buys him food and asked Sensei to check on him now and then and make sure his grocery deliveries are getting opened. She asked me to visit him at least once while she's in Japan. Brah seemed like a nice guy, so I agreed.

Due to all the excitement of the last few days, I completely forgot about my promise. I feel a sharper pang of guilt as I glimpse two unopened delivery boxes sitting by the doors to the old gym offices, one seeping some kind of brownish fluid.

"Brah, buddy, have you been eating? What's this with your boxes here."

"Sister, I've been focusing on getting my weight down and I'm extra disciplined and fierce! Anyway, those boxes don't smell so good!"

"That's what happens when you don't open them, dude. Probably some killer avocados in there. It's cold in here but you have to put that stuff in the fridge for real."

Talking to Brah has me dusting off a California "surfer dude/reality star" speech patterns, although I've never surfed and always avoided "dudes" or reality in any form.

"Healthy fats! Good for the joints. Wow, thinking about avocados makes me so hungry right now!"

"Let's take this stuff into the staff room and see if we can salvage anything."

"Sounds like a plan, Sister!"

After picking through the rotten fruit and veggies in the box, we fish out some energy bars and packets of oatmeal only dampened by the slime. I heat up some water in Bra's microwave and we sit down to an afternoon snack. As I gnaw on an energy bar and after he wolfs down his oats, Brah starts talking.

"So, like, this dude was down here last night climbing my walls!"

"Last night? What time last night?"

Brah gestures at the microwave, the only thing in the space that seems to be plugged in.

"Don't know, sister, I haven't figured out how to fix the clock on this thing since that storm a few weeks back. Always 12:12 down here in my world! So I guess it was about 12:12 plus two hours or so – moon falling fast and stars fading out. This dude was here with these wicked long fingernails and he was pulling his scary ass up my walls with those nails! Screeching and scratching and howling something terrible. Freddie Krueger right here!"

"Who?"

"Freddie Krueger, that guy from the horror movies."

"I don't really stream those movies. Is he some kind of… demon?"

"Oh yeah, so scary that dude. My babysitter used to make me watch those movies on her phone when I was a kid to keep me quiet. Freddie is like a serial killer who wears gloves with long razors on them. He attacks you in your dreams! That Freddie was in my dreams so many times when I was a kid. Haven't seen him in years but there he was right here at 12:12 last night! Only he wasn't a dream, I don't think."

"Wow, weird."

I stir up another packet of oatmeal for him and we eat in silence. Brah doesn't seem too upset, and he soon launches into a mind-numbingly technical story about his last ascent of a local rock formation called Sleeping Giant. As he goes on about pitons and crevasses, I try to figure out his crazy "dream." It makes sense, I guess. Brah doesn't really have a culture and doesn't own anything but some rock shoes and an ab roller. The only demon he could summon through Dar's power device on the fifth floor was something from his childhood.

"Brah, you've got to go over to Shai's office in a couple of hours. We're all getting together. Like 12:12 daytime plus three hours or so. We're getting together to talk about these dreams we've all been having. You're not the only one. All of us are seeing monsters and demons and we need to figure out why and what to do about it. It's at 4 p.m. Can you do that?"

"Cool! Excellent! I'll be there. Boss Man's old watch is around somewhere so I'll find that and be there on time!"

"Great, Brah. Thanks for the snack and I'll see you later."

As I say good-bye I notice something else amid the cobwebs on the far climbing wall, a slab marked "Beginners." There, between two holds near the ceiling, are a bunch of scratch marks – two sets of five that run from the ceiling down about six feet. Who could get up that high with ten knives to do that? Why do something so destructive and ugly?

It's as if a crazy dude with razors for fingernails was clawing at the wall.

The marks look fresh.

✳ ✳ ✳

All afternoon I've been traipsing all over the building. Everyone's home and ready to do something about the demons. The only one who didn't answer my knocks was Dar.

Jean-Baptiste is scared out of his mind and ready for action. Barata the Brazilian pest answered the door on my first knock and didn't even try to kick me in the head once before agreeing to come downstairs at 4 pm.

Emma is enthusiastic when I finally muster the courage to visit her unit. No weird leaks this time, but she does keep the door mostly closed and I can't see what's going on behind her. I tell her my story, describing Kappa and my other demons in full as I shiver in the hallway.

After a few minutes of listening to all the disgusting details, Emma glances back and sighs, then erupts with an answer to my unsaid question.

"Clam monster, in case you're wondering."

"Clam what?"

"It's from Chinese folklore. I had a book of Taoist poetry in here and somehow the 'clam monsters over the eastern sea' came to life. I thought it was a dream for a few nights and then the biggest monster started building spit castles."

"Spit what?"

"Spit castles. It takes its spit and creates these towers out of plasticky stuff. You were looking at one the other day in my space. Only the clam thing is so big and clumsy that it's always knocking the towers down and it keeps me up all night. I'm ready for whatever is going on around here to stop!"

"Does it hurt you or make you clean or do a bunch of sword cuts?"

"No, it just builds spit castles. Lucky me! So glad I was born Chinese."

"Well, it's certainly inconvenient, but I think our Asian demons are kind of cool compared to the others in the building."

"Yeah, it's nice to see some Asian monsters around for a change. And Barata's got this cool Brazilian demon with one leg who smokes a pipe."

"I saw that guy in the hall the other day! Is he dangerous?"

"Just a prankster, from what I understand. That's what's so refreshing, not all of our demons are really that evil. Like your little frog-man, who just seems like an annoying frat boy who farts fishy smells."

"Yeah, Kappa's not so bad. Those farts are starting to smell almost good, actually. Although he does try now and then to grab my intestines from out of my butthole."

"Never mind, then. But that's a step up from the same old vampires and witches in all the books you read in school. Like aren't we globalized now? So glad we're getting beyond those tired European stories."

"Not sure a giant oozing clam monster is much of an improvement, if you get right down to it."

"Good point. Well let me clean up last night's spit castle and get ready for our meeting. See you down there."

✳ ✳ ✳

"OK, where do we start?"

We're all sitting in Shai's outer office, cups of lukewarm tea in hand and Japanese milk candy on the table in the middle. Emma, Jean-Baptiste, Barata, Shai, Brah and me.

Everyone jumps a bit at an abrupt crash – Emma had

pulled a big shard of clam-monster spit out of her hair and tossed it on the floor.

"Sorry guys. And sorry about the fishy smell too."

I get a whiff of something foul, but it's coming from me. The lower part of me, specifically. Got to confess.

"Actually, that's probably me. Kappa puked on my feet a bit ago. I tried to clean it up, but the smell doesn't go away."

"Kappa?" Jean-Baptiste gives me quizzical look.

"Kind of like a cross between a frat boy and frog. Always trying to pull my intestines out of my butt. He was trying to do an Aikido roll and got sick, threw up something brown on my socks."

"Wow, I thought I had it bad." Barata says, grabbing a piece of candy and unwrapping it in a hurry. My visitor just tries to trip me in the middle of Capoeira practice."

Jean-Baptiste pulls his coat tighter around him and erupts, startling everyone.

"I have it bad! Worse than anyone! Papa Legba won't let me sleep a wink and my work is really suffering. Some venture capitalists are due in my lab next month and I won't have a thing to show them! This is affecting my livelihood and my work."

"Your work?" Emma shouts. "Your freaking work? I've got a clam monster building spit castles in my space! I can't even get to the bathroom most days!"

I can't help myself.

"What about my Swordsman? Any day now he's going to get sick of disciplining me and just cut my head off! My life is in danger!"

"Stop whining, everyone!" Barata shouts. "We have more serious things to worry about. I heard this horrible screeching from the far end of the building this morning. Did anyone else hear that?"

"That screeching would be from right over there." Shai stands up and gestures toward his inner office. "Did you also hear a kind of booming noise from this floor early this morning, real early? Those were my bookshelves. And it wasn't me that knocked them over."

"Those huge things with all those tax books on them? Those must weigh a thousand pounds each. What, did you have a wild party?" Jean-Baptiste looks amused.

Shai stands up, peeks outside into the hallway, looks up and down and closes the door behind him. His eyes are even more bloodshot than usual, and I notice a bruise above his jawline. His hands are shaking.

"Cherry knows something about this, but you guys have to hear the whole story. Robbery, I am expecting in this neighborhood. Burglary, car theft, home invasions, yes. A creature from the Old Country, I don't expect!"

Jean-Baptiste looks at me, and I look at Emma and we all exhale. JB seems the most agitated of all of us and he breaks into Shai's story.

"Creature? Why don't you tell us about your creature, Mr. Landlord. Papa Legba is no creature, he stands between us all and God! He's got mighty powers and he won't let me get anything done in my lab."

Emma gets us back on track, hoping that Shai's story will be quick and allow us to focus on taking some kind of action.

"What do you mean by creature, Shai? I was thinking that whatever crazy dust that's floating around in this building wouldn't be getting all the way down here to your floor."

"I'll tell you what happened, right from the beginning."

❋ ❋ ❋

We've been talking for an hour and established that all of us staying overnight in the building have seen some crazy stuff, and the crazy stuff has been getting worse. But now I'm feeling that familiar itch I remember from my time in public school: Too much talk, no action. It's like I have to get up now and run around the room a few times or I'll explode.

Brah seems to read my mind and stands, stretching himself upward. He's so tall and his movement so abrupt that he punches through the ceiling tile. Chunks of ancient foam and brownish dust start raining down.

Shai starts yelling in what sounds like German.

We all jump a bit and Shai lunges out of his chair. Brah leaps up a foot or two and seems to hook his hands on a big metal pipe above the ceiling tile. He hangs there for a few seconds, swinging and smiling ear-to-ear, then pulls himself up so far he's only visible from the waist down.

"Hamster!" Brah's voice comes through muffled but triumphant. Must be some kind of climbing move.

Everyone laughs and the atmosphere chills a bit. Shai sits back down, annoyed. Brah has made his statement.

"So what do we do now?" Jean-Baptiste's long story about his terrifying visit from a Haitian spirit-being seems to have drained the fear out of him. He's all business, and ready to get everyone focused.

"Have we figured out whose fault this is?" Emma gives me a meaningful look as she speaks. We agreed while walking downstairs together earlier that something that Dar is doing seems to be causing the demon outbreak. There just hasn't been a chance to speak up. And I don't want to get Dar in trouble in case it's just a coincidence. I decide to explain things.

"I don't think we have figured it out. We don't want to blame someone unfairly. Yes, that new guy on my floor is doing something that seems related but I don't really understand what he's talking about when he explains his experiments. His name is Dar, by the way, and he used to work at the university. He's really nice, actually. I'm sure he doesn't want to cause anyone problems. Anyway, I can do some more research up on our floor. Why don't you guys ask around on your floors?

Jean-Baptiste knows Dar is up to something, and isn't buying my excuses.

"Um, Cherry, I think we all have an idea of which floor is the source of this craziness. And you yourself said that guy Dar next to the old photo studio is up to something weird. Since you know him, why don't you talk to him? Or talk to him again, because you seem to know him better than the rest of us."

Shai's had enough from his troublesome tenants.

"Talk? I think we need to do more than that! These creatures are causing damage and could end up hurting people! What if word gets out and the cops come in here with the city code enforcement? What are you guys going to do about that? My bosses in New York won't be happy."

Shai keeps an eye on Brah's swinging legs as he talks but then turns to me expectantly. Although I'm the youngest person in the room, everyone seems to think I should take care of this issue. Do they know that these creatures torment me all night long and I'm only 17? No, they think I'm 19 and and better start acting my fake age.

"OK, OK, I'll try again to talk to Dar. Nothing major has happened yet and we don't need to even talk about police right now. Just try to live with your demons for a bit and I'll get some answers. We can't do much more with the storms coming and all right now."

As I make my brave promise, I almost believe myself. I can make these creatures go away, and Dar is sure to listen to reason and shut down whatever he's doing when he hears about our problems. I can do this.

Something heavy and sticky flops against my neck and I feel a squirming shape wriggle itself out my hoodie and onto the shoulder of my winter kimono. Kappa has been in there listening the whole time, but he promised to keep quiet.

"Cherry-san can help you!"

Everyone stares at the froggy face of Kappa, then eases away and back into their chairs as his funky smell fills the room. He gurgles a bit and creases his face up into what could be a smile, pleased at being the center of attention.

"Wow, you Japanese are really messed up," Emma says, at last. "My monster is mostly quiet and doesn't smell nearly that bad!"

CHAPTER SEVEN

Thursday

The blade slashes down, brushing my ear and the side of my jaw before I can lift my own blade to block. Just in time, my sword deflects the attack before the other solid chunk of white oak can crash into my collarbone.

"*Baka!*"

The force of the impact sends me sprawling onto my side on the mat. My wooden sword twists out of my hand and clatters against the wall.

"Wake up, Cherry! You are so out of it this morning. Another mediocre practice like this and I'm going to have to call Goffe Sensei in Japan. A hundred cuts, right now. Dial back the right hand. Get those cuts straight!"

Never a kind word from Thierry in class. Never a compliment. Never even the slight grunt of appreciation he gives the other students when they get a form right.

Only "Wake up!" "Stay connected!" "Why are you so casual?" Smacks with the bokken to the knuckles and pokes with the jo to the bicep.

My bokken lies at the edge of the mat, its surface pocked with dozens of tiny craters where blows have dented the wood. The grip is warm and a bit sticky from sweat. The last thing in the world I want to do right now is pick it up and do more solo cutting practice – the Swordmaster demon has left my hands aching and raw, covered in tape. My anger overcomes my pain. I grab the bokken and start more cuts, mighty blows meant to cleave an opponent from the top of the head to the waist.

I hate Thierry right now with the heat of a thousand suns. Each of my bokken cuts become a smiting blow to the crown of his head, spraying brains and blood and splinters of bone across the mat. Oops, one hunk of brain just flew across the room and hit the window. Now it's sliding down the glass, oozing and wrinkly and pathetically soft – that's the piece of Thierry's brain that is always criticizing me. Lucky hit!

Thierry catches my eye.

"Are you cutting me in half right now, Cherry? I swear I can feel my scalp prickle every time you swing that thing. Much better form, by the way. I used to do the same thing myself when I was a junior – I must have chopped Sensei in half a million times. Helps with the aim. Here, give it your best shot!"

His head thrust forward as a lure, Thierry walks over to stand in front of me, his bokken at his side. I push the heel of my left hand into the hilt of my bokken and lift it up and over my head in a sudden rush of movement, cutting down with full strength toward his glistening forehead.

Thierry looks right at me as he lifts his blade then steals the force of my cut to propel his bokken around to his left shoulder as he shifts to the side. From there, he steps back, synchronizes his arms, right foot and hip a split-second later to deliver a slashing diagonal cut.

The blade slides through my spine precisely between the vertebrae, severing my spinal cord and lasering through inches of gristle. Blood spurts out of my neck as my severed head rolls across the mat, coming to a stop with my dead eyes open to the ceiling.

Only in my mind, of course. The edge of Thierry's wooden weapon is pressing against my neck just above my uniform collar. Not that it's any less humiliating that I've lost the fight.

"Wow, that felt good. Been a while since I cut a lazy

uchideshi's head off with a *kesa* cut. Perfect angle between the neck vertebrae, if I don't say so myself."

Standing there with the splintery edge of his sword digging into my neck, I have to agree.

"Yeah, thanks much for the quick death. So glad you made it to the dojo this morning, Thierry. With the weather, I was thinking you'd be relaxing at home."

My sempai slowly straightens himself up from his cutting posture and gives me another dirty look.

"Enough of this chit-chat on the mat! You can be sarcastic after we clean up."

It's just me and him this morning thanks the skull-cracking cold – another record blast of Arctic air from Canada, Thierry says.

The colder-than-usual dojo didn't really register until an irate Thierry yanked my sleeping bag down from off my face when he arrived just before morning class. The temperature drop must have knocked out the batteries on my alarm clock, I told him.

Now we're done with morning torture and we're cleaning up, pushing damp rags across the chilled expanse of the mat. Then some mopping with wet rags on the sub-zero wasteland that is the surrounding concrete floor, an effort quickly given up after we realize we're creating dirty slush, not picking up dirt.

We bundle up after putting everything away and sit in the lounge with some quickly cooling tea. Steam bathing my face, I prepare for my pitch: This uchideshi needs to stay a few more nights in the demon house. Thierry already told me before class to pack up my stuff and get ready to leave the dojo tonight. I can tell my weak performance this morning hasn't helped matters. He gulps down his tea and gets to the point.

"I was thinking about what you were telling me. You need to stay with us from now on, but it's not so surprising that you're seeing weird stuff in here at night. These demons you're talking about, is there anything like this in Japanese folktales that you know of? Aren't you working on a presentation for us about Japanese monsters and reading a bunch of books?"

"Not monsters, exactly. More like spirits, or gods involved in martial arts."

"Seriously? What kind of god makes you do bunny hops? Who would worship such a torturer?"

Usagi tobi, or bunny hops, are a practice Sensei imposes on those she deems are out of shape or need to be in better shape – everyone in the dojo, including her. Basically, the victim has to squat on the floor then leap straight up and land again in a squat. Repeat at least a dozen times. Brutal on the thighs and knees, even for a teenager, and the Swordmaster made me do a bunch of them last night.

"A demon must have invented bunny hops, true that. Even I'm not young enough to do them properly."

"Seriously, what kind of demons are there in Aikido? Are trying to tell me that you're engaged in some kind of good-and-evil struggle here? I know you've been angry and unmotivated since your mom's death. At least that what Sensei told me."

"She told you that?"

Thierry, to his credit, looks a little ashamed when admitting that he knows this personal information about me. I'm surprised and pissed that Sensei has talked to him about my mom and my mental state.

"Forget about psychological stuff for a minute, will you? This isn't about my 'unresolved anger.' We're talking real demons here."

"Real demons as in the devil?"

"I don't think they're evil spirits, if that's what you're asking. And it's not just me seeing them in this building. Emma – Shifu Wong who does Tai Chi down the hall – and Jean-Baptiste downstairs have them too, along with people on the first floor. Different people, different kinds of demons. They're all from Japanese folklore for me, that's true enough. There's been a Swordmaster and Kappa frog-man so far. Oh, and the lady with the long neck. And the snow ghost."

Thierry looks concerned, then amused, then concerned

again.

"Listen, Cherry. I'm willing to let you stay here again later in the week if you promise these fantasies aren't going to make you do anything stupid. If Jean-Baptiste and Emma are part of this, I'm willing to see at as some kind of abstract art project, I guess. Or group therapy."

"Getting to know those guys is really good for me, learning about other cultures and martial arts and stuff. They also have good jobs, or had good jobs at one point. We're kind of making a community. I'm learning leadership!"

"Right, whatever you say. A learning experience. So is there anything in your books about groups of monsters gathering in a specific place? Like an old factory?"

"Well I did read about these 'demon parades' in old-time Kyoto, where a hundred yokai used to march through the streets on summer nights. A yokai with a gourd for a head led the parade."

"Yokai? Aren't those just in anime shows?"

"No, that's the general Japanese word for monsters. There are hundreds – most of them kind of evil but there a few that give you good luck."

"Nice. Sounds like you've got a lot less than a hundred in the building, but we've got enough yokai at least for a quick march down Shelton Avenue."

We sit quietly for a few minutes, sipping tea. I can see that Thierry is struggling with the news of the demon infestation in the building, deciding on whether or not to take me out of here against my will. Staying silent and serious seems to be my best approach as he thinks it through. Maybe he'll start to see it as a scholarly project on my part.

"So do these demons tend to haunt old factories like this? Do the Japanese have haunted houses?"

"Not really, according to my research, Japanese ghosts tend to show up in remote cottages and temples. Though I did read something about an abandoned storehouse that got angry and ate a young girl alive. Nothing was left but her robe and her hair. The demon stripped and scalped her... not that my demons are violent at all, just really driven to get me to practice at all hours and clean the dojo."

That wasn't smart, talking about getting eaten by a building. Thierry is frowning again. Too much information. Just sit here and look serious but not crazy.

"Nice. Anything that keeps this place clean, I guess. But there's nothing in your books about old ammunition testing labs with dojos in them attracting demons? Or Aikido dojos and demons?"

"Not that I've come across. I'll keep reading. It's really an interesting intellectual exercise for me, with lots of cultural-identy aspects. I'll be definitely writing about this for a college essay in the next few months. This whole experience has made me think a lot about my future and going to college soon."

Bingo. Thierry slurps the last of his tea, pulls his coat tighter around his lean frame, and shakes his head.

"Cherry, you seem tired and distracted, but I can't force you to come home with me if don't want to. And I did talk to Jean-Baptiste on the way up to our floor and he swore that you're not the only one experiencing strange things in here lately. He seems to think you've got it under control and you've actually done good work getting the tenants together. You're not a kid and you seem pretty rational on most fronts. If I put myself in Belinda's place, I've got to err on the side of letting you tough this out.

"Last chance: We're having lasagna at home and we can watch *Sword of Doom* again tonight. Remember that 20-minute sword fight?"

"Nice try. Thanks, Thierry. I promise nothing bad will happen. We can watch *Sword of Doom* with Sensei when she gets back – I promise we'll act out the whole swordfight scene in your living room and we won't make holes in the wall this time."

"Whatever you say, Cherry. Get some rest."

I don't need encouragement. As soon as the door closes

behind Thierry, I wriggle back into my sleeping bag for a much-needed mid-morning nap.

✻ ✻ ✻

Cracking, then rustling and a throaty screech.

I wake up to what could be a spotlight or bright sun, but it's so cold in the dojo I feel a prickle of ice in my eyelashes and quickly shut my eyes. Don't be lazy! I tell myself. It must be time for noon class. I shake myself out of the toasty sleeping bag, swing my legs off the futon and brace my feet for the cold floor. But what woke me up was nothing so simple as people arriving for noon class – I've got a visitor.

The screech was the cabinet door – meditation cushions lie in a heap on the floor.

"It's the hour of the Rabbit, Sakura-San. Time to get up! We have much to do before nine strikes of the gong and the Horse Hour gallops up to greet us!"

A blur of kimono, hakama pants and mustache swirls before my eyes. The Swordmaster has decided to visit me during the day now, I guess.

Hour of the Rabbit, Horse … the Swordmaster uses the old time system used in ancient Japan, divisions in the days marked by signs of the Chinese zodiac. I flipped through one of my library books last night to review the chart: Sunrise is Hour of the Rabbit, marked by six strikes. Noon is hour of the Horse, sunset is Rooster, and midnight, Rat. It's bad enough that my clouded brain has to think in Japanese – now I'm thinking in time units not used in two hundred years.

Despite the rude awakening, I'm feeling rested. The Swordmaster didn't stay too long last night after I gave up on bunny hops, and Kappa left after detonating only two or three farts and leaving a stinky pile of something by the shoe rack. Thierry's class was intense but the mid-morning nap has restored my energy. If only the temperature hadn't plunged in here since last night.

Jean-Baptiste warned that today was supposed to be the coldest of the year and offered his spare office with the heater again. But I didn't want to miss the Swordmaster when he visited after midnight. I have a mission, frostbite be damned. I didn't have time to talk to him last night, but better late than never.

"Up, time for Zazen!" the Swordmaster barks and scoops up a cushion, then pushes me toward the cabinet.

Whew, that means I can stay wrapped up in my winter kimono and long underwear for a while. Starbursts of frost have formed in the corners of all the windows near the futon couch – a touch of my gloved hand confirms that the crystals are on the *inside* surface of the glass. The cup of water I left on Sensei's desk last night has a film of ice on it and alarming crackles and groans issue from the roof as the wind roars outside.

It's too cold to make tea, and the Swordmaster won't wait anyway. This is going to be the ultimate test of my martial spirit: Sitting still in subzero temperatures as a nasty demon lurks behind me, ready to smack me with a wooden stick.

I walk onto the mat then sink down to the cushion to take my posture. A fleece blanket from a chair gets draped across my lap and I wait for some warmth to travel up from my crossed legs and lower body. Shivers rock me on the cushion until the ultimate enemy of my meditation practice arrives: an itch inside my nose. My face feels numb at first. A few minutes pass and I start feeling like something has started digging into the skin right inside my left nostril and won't stop. It digs and drills and wriggles its way into some kind of crack in the skin and tortures me with an itching sensation that morphs into pain and then agony. Of course it's not an actual insect, just an unbearable, recurring itch that seems to arise every time I meditate. If I can just bring my shoulder forward to give the itchy spot a swipe.

"Namakemono!"

The blow comes from behind, from such close range that I can feel the wind from the swinging stick ruffle my hair. The *kei-*

saku, or "warning stick," hits me on a spot between the shoulder blade and spine, unleashing its energy into a powerful THWACK that pushes my torso forward against my knees. Sensei keeps a keisaku on the wall for our meditation sessions, but she doesn't use it very often. In hard-core Japanese monasteries, you get whacked with one if you look like you're dozing off or meditating badly, whatever that means. The stick doesn't exactly hurt, but the shock wakes me right up and cures the nose itch and shivers instantly.

Now is the time to ask for the Swordmaster's help with our demon infestation. But when I turn around, he's disappeared. Just as the door creaks open and first student arrives for noon class.

❋ ❋ ❋

Enemies surround me on all sides, ready to lunge in and take me down. I scan their faces and bodies for signs they're moving in for the kill, shifting my weight from foot to foot and keeping my face blank and my eyes moving. My noon class enemies today are Katie Sempai, Walt, Quan and the goofy beginner from the other day, Diego. Despite the cold, despite the snow yesterday, they decided to drag their butts up the stairs and practice Aikido today. Now they're all trying to attack me at once.

Of course it's not because they've all decided to gang up on me and beat me down: We're doing an exercise called *randori*, or "chaos taking," also known as a free-style with multiple attackers. In our style of Aikido *randori*, a student tries to take down attacker after attacker using the simplest, most direct techniques. Part of the practice is developing skill at Aikido movements, part of it is using the space and not getting trapped – most of it is not panicking when a bunch of people gather around you with a predatory look in their eyes.

Randori was Katie Sempai's idea: She has been leading the

class and trying to keep us all moving in the raw chill of the dojo today. We did high-energy throws for a half-hour, now she wants us to practice our skills against an angry mob. We did a bit of this practice back home, but I've never been comfortable with it. Something about being surrounded by enemies makes me forget all of my Aikido techniques.

Feeling pretty confident against the noon-class crew, I move toward Diego, figuring he'll take a while to recover from a fall and leave me plenty of time to take down the other three. Reaching out for his shoulders, I prompt him to raise his arms in self-defense, which I then easily hook with mine for a pivoting throw. Down goes Diego, with an impressive thump and grunt. Sure enough, he looks unhurt but seems like he's going to be on the ground for a while.

Next I turn to Walt, who doesn't hang back but immediately swings an angled *yokomen* strike toward my skull. Just in time, I enter and start to pivot again for another throw. Sadly, Walt is a bit quicker than I expected and he smacks me smartly on the shoulder as I step in. As I turn my hips to throw, I realize that I'm not in the right position for the technique and in fact have left an opening a mile wide for a counterattack. Like he has read my mind, Walt sucker-punches me in the gut, "showing me the opening." It's not a very hard punch, but it's hard enough to crumple me up a bit and make me really angry. I swing wildly at Walt from my position slightly behind him with an overhead strike, hoping to teach him a lesson.

Of course Walt sees my strike coming a mile away, swinging his body off the line with a *tenkan* turn and grabbing my arm as my strike misses. A quick pivot and wrist-twist on his part and I'm flat on my back. In the spirit of randori, Quan lunges forward and fake-kicks me while I'm down. Katie Sempai stands at the side of the mat, shaking her head.

Total randori fail. Total humiliating fail for someone who's supposed to be a teacher trainee. Total fail for someone with ten years in Aikido.

We try it again, and this time I keep moving, shifting from

one end of the mat to another as I counter overhead cuts with *atemi*, or strikes to the face. Each time an enemy moves in for the kill, I side-step and pop him in the nose, which prompts a big escape fall in response. My timing is better and I take down Diego and Walt again with no problem. But Quan mixes it up by grabbing my shoulders, and he's too close now for an effective face-strike, much to my annoyance. So I move in closer and try to hoist him up for a hip throw, but before I can position myself perfectly to set it up, Katie Sempai has grabbed my shoulders from behind, broken my balance and I'm down in a heap again.

"Keep your center, Cherry. You're letting your anger and frustration get in the way of the energy. Can you feel your ki stop flowing when stuff like Quan's attack happens? It's clear to me that you need to slow down and get out of your own head a little. Living here alone must be difficult, but you're very distracted. Remember, keep your center."

It is Sensei's voice and words that I'm hearing: Katie Sempai is repeating things I've heard countless times in the past few months. But it seems the more I hear words of wisdom, the less I understand them. From my position in a heap on the mat, it's all I can do not to sob in frustration.

❊ ❊ ❊

"Thank you for class, Katie Sempai."

My stomach feels like it's clawing its way out of my body I'm so hungry, and I'm hoping these few hardy souls who showed up for noon class today will hurry home. An hour with the heat turned on and a few bodies in motion has raised the temperature inside the dojo to tolerable levels, however, and the students seem to want to linger.

"By the way, the kamiza's looking a bit dusty," Katie says as she kneels to fold her hakama.

"Thanks, Sempai. I'll get right on it."

As the others chat and fold their hakamas, I pick up one

of the designated kamiza rags and try not to make a face. The senior members like to point out dirty spots in the dojo – lucky me. Uchideshi means "on-demand spot cleaner and indentured servant" in a traditional Aikido dojo, and everyone in this group seems to have picked up on that.

That kamiza has been wiped down by me at least three times already today – before and after each class. But a gust of wind from the hallway knocked some dust off the ceiling ducts a few minutes ago and I watched the motes hover in the air with dread as I swabbed the mat. The dust finally settled just as everyone got ready to leave, and Katie Sempai's trained eyes picked up the dullness on the wood up front. Now she thinks I'm slacking off. Quan hovers nearby ready to help but I point him to the dressing area to straighten things up. The kamiza is my job.

As I carefully remove every object on the shelf in preparation for cleaning yet again, an internal rant starts.

"Thanks, senior students. I appreciate your help but try to keep that 'mom' tone out of your voice when you point out my chores. After all, when *you* clean it's a welcome break from your professional jobs, a bit of mindful work to add to your practice. For me it's a daily grind and sometimes just too much for one person to handle without going nuts. You really want to help this uchideshi? Pick up a rag or broom yourself. Keep your mouth shut and just get it done."

Whew, that outburst of rage felt good, even if it was all in my head. Cussing out and insulting the senior members of a dojo in your head is a vital part of uchideshi life, Sensei said. She even promised that someday I could be part of an entire uchideshi posse when she sends me to train at one of the live-in Aikido dojos in Japan. Imagine the complaining and moaning we can do as a group. In multiple languages.

Sensei keeps talking about wanting to send me to Japan next year, but I'm not so sure. When I think about Japan I'm flooded with images from manga comic books and anime – vivid arcs of color and movement and lots of girls in short skirts with big eyes. Swords slash out of nowhere in bursts of angu-lar characters, leaving behind puddles of red. The way Katie Sempai describes it, Japan is crawling with British drunks and businessmen crowding into subway trains. She's lived there for work but never practiced Aikido seriously in Japan.

Goffe Sensei's version of Japan is populated with martial arts masters who require you to train in the hottest summer weather until you pee blood and force you to keep doing sword cuts even as the dojo building sways and lurches during an earthquake. "The sword teacher screamed that our cuts weren't straight, even as the tsunami sirens started going off… the water on the kamiza splashed all over and a chunk of concrete fell on the mat from the ceiling – he never even blinked!" Sensei loves telling that story. I've already heard it a few times – each version with new details – in my months here.

Sometimes I have dreams that I'm in Japan, and it always looks something like the big rest stops on the interstate high-ways in California: Sterile, packed with anonymous faces and slightly inhuman.

No point thinking too much about the future – right now I've got to clean and figure out how to survive the next few days.

* * *

The kamiza gleams and everybody is gone now. The after-noon break yawns ahead of me, hours before the flurry of activ-ity to get ready for evening class. Sensei warned me that this would be the hardest time of day, unscheduled and yet not long enough to truly relax or get decent sleep.

Before getting back into my sleeping bag, I force myself to walk over to the shoe rack and put on my outside shoes. A cold, steady breeze flows from one end of the hallway to another, and the spaces behind the locked doors are alive with whispering sounds from the gale outside. I knock on Dar's door but again, no answer. He might be out or busy – he seems to keep late hours so my mission to ask him about the demons will have to be on hold for now. Everything feels like it's on hold, and I'm exhausted and angry as I clomp back down the hall to the dojo.

"Watch for that attitude that can build up between classes for uchideshi, Cherry," Sensei said me in one of the many talks we had before she left. "You're tired, bored, sick of people and yet intensely lonely. Don't try to do anything that requires concentration – take a walk or do some odd jobs around the dojo. Don't just sit there and obsess about who annoyed you in the last class or which irritating students may show up for evening class."

Thanks for the pep talk, Sensei, but right now, it's not sinking in. And why are so many of your students so intensely annoying? Can't you do anything about that?

Today I'm particularly restless – feeling vaguely agitated, worried about my talk with Dar and full of anticipation for the reports from the other tenants on their negotiations with their demons. My muscles are sore and it's too cold to do the stairs today, so I decide to take on one of Sensei's long-term assignments: Building a new weapons rack in the relative warmth of the floor below.

Last week we cut the sides of the rack together in "the Aikido woodshop" downstairs, an office on the deserted fourth floor. Woodworking in the dojo space leaves sawdust everywhere and make the mat gritty for days, Sensei informed me. Better to pick an empty room nearby and take your project there. It's also significantly warmer on the fourth floor on days like today due to the extra insulation in the office suites.

The fourth floor of the building was some kind of administrative area in the gun factory days, but now all that is left is office after office full of broken desks, dusty cubicle dividers and stacks of rotting manuals. You have to take the stairs to get there and push through a door that feels locked but gives way with a well-placed shove. There are no tenants down there, so no chance of meeting any strange demons, right? That's what I tell myself as I gather up the tools from the cabinet that I need for the next step of the project. I add another layer of gloves on top of my hands, and set off for below.

The windowless stairwell glows a sickly green in the light from a high-up window. Motion detectors switch on with a clunk as I reach the fourth-floor landing, the sound of metal hitting bone. The aching cold eases a bit with every step downward. The fourth-floor door opens with a bark of protest, revealing a hallway lined with blank doors plastered with signs like "Accounts Receivable" and "Personnel Management." Dusty, 1960s-era wool fire blankets dangle like tattered flags from alcoves along the hall. All sound seems dampened down here due to the sealed windows and I can hear my own breath, raspy in the cold. I head to the first office on the right, just below the dojo. Sensei picked it out and we worked there last week, so I know there are no dead mice in here, and it seems safer somehow to be near the familiar. It was some kind of storeroom for old equipment.

Inside, I flick on the overhead neon lights and a dozen industrial fans loom up from the back wall, so coated with dust they resemble algae-covered shipwrecks. My tools get plunked onto a desk and I set up the piece of wood we had prepped and start hunting for a working outlet. Sensei marked the wood where she wants holes made with the hole-saw. Once the holes are drilled on both sides and the thing is put together, we'll have a new rack to store *jo,* or the wooden staffs used in Aikido practice. With a growl, the power tool lurches to life, wrenching my wrist as it rotates around the hole-saw blade. I let go and the tool sputters to a stop, leaving a chewed-looking scar in the plank. Ugh, another wasted piece of wood to be taken to the dumpster. This wasn't such a great idea.

Dojo cleaning is one thing, but my decision to tackle this project on my own was just stupid. Schools haven't offered wood-working classes for decades and my dad is more comfortable with algorithms than tools, so he never showed me anything. Waiting until Sensei gets back seems like the best move. I head over to the outlet to unplug the tool when my eye catches movement to my right, in the front corner of the space. A turn of my head and the movement comes into focus – the lazy spiral of something black and shiny slowly floating to the floor.

In the corner sits a head-high metal cube that I asked Sensei about a few weeks back. Featureless and iron-gray, the cube looks like an old-style elevator shaft or bank vault at first glance. But Sensei pointed out a rusted panel on the side and explained that it was some kind of power control center for the building, tucked away on an inner floor in case of explosion in the labs above. It's inside a shaft alongside the lobby that extends up to my floor. I had thought the boxy indentation on the wall was a supply closet at first.

I put the saw down and head toward the power box as if in a trance. The shiny thing on the floor shivers a bit in a draft: It's a feather – almost as long as my entire arm and much too big for any kind of bird I've ever seen. I squat down to take a closer look, careful to keep my eyes tilted toward the dark recess above. The feather is slick, glossy and still warm from the body of whatever recently shed it.

A rustling like the sound of hundreds of leaves in the wind erupts from above the power box and I brace myself for what's about to come.

War. This must mean war.

That's the first thought in my mind as I see the shadow above the breaker box unfold into an unmistakable form and hop down to tower above me. It's about twice the size of a big human, solidly built and powerful. Where the face would be, a ragged beak yawns open, topped by ink-drop black eyes. Claws as long as cement screws unfurl at the end of its blocky arms and legs. Its eyes rage with madness. It wants war, death, suffering.

I just read about this thing: It is an old-style *karasu tengu*, the "crow goblin" of Japanese folklore that tormented good Buddhists and acted as a messenger of war. The biggest, baddest and most feared of the Japanese demons, honored to this day by villagers in the countryside. Now the Tengu looms above me, its maddened eyes fixed on mine and its massive thighs tensing as it gathers itself to attack.

Before I can react, I'm knocked to the floor by the fast-moving if feather-cushioned demon, which hits me with what we call in Aikido a *tai-atari*, a body slam. I'm sprawled against the desk now, gasping with the wind knocked out of me. The demon stands to its full height above me. I raise one hand to protect myself – which the Tengu swiftly snags in its dripping beak.

My eyes clamp shut and I wait for the searing pain of the beak ripping my hand apart. The shrieking of the wind outside fills my ears and mutes my own screams, even as a crackling roar rises from the direction of the power box. The pressure on my hand releases. My eyes edge open to see the Tengu poised above me, its head turned toward the new sound.

A hiss erupts from the iron cube, then a stuttering moan as the bank of neon light above me flickers and then shuts off.

The stink of scorched metal and plastic fills the air as my eyes adjust to the dark space, now lit only by afternoon-dimmed daylight from outside. A ticking then a fading hiss are the only remaining sounds, followed by silence.

The Tengu is gone. A scattering of feathers and a livid red mark across my hand are all that remain.

* * *

Sensei will be furious.

That's the first thought going through my mind as I open my eyes and realize I've been napping again. Wrapped in my sleeping bag, stretched full length across the mat, lounging like a cat in a patch of sunlight.

"Treating the dojo, a sacred space, like a dorm room," I can hear her say.

An explosive bang from the shoe rack area has startled me out of an uneasy sleep and I dread the thought of another demon attack. Luckily, the completely swaddled figure is human, and familiar.

"Jean-Baptiste, is that you? Did you just slam the door?

He turns and walks quickly up to the edge of the mat, his dark face shining with sweat and steaming a little in the cold.

"Sorry, Cherry, really. Didn't mean to be so loud. I've just had enough Papa Legba in my space. He won't leave me alone!"

"Yeah, well I'm just recovering from being chewed on by a giant bird, and before that, a few whacks with a meditation stick by a demon swordmaster. The kind of whacks that are supposed to bring me closer to enlightenment, but it still hurt!"

"OK, sorry! We're all dealing with this craziness. What's going on with the plan to get the demons together?"

I think I just got the Swordmaster to take our side, but he only speaks in grunts so I'm not exactly sure. Either way, he's agreed to show up near the elevators at the Hour of the Dog."

"Hour of the what? Is there a dog demon in this building as well? Someone saw a huge furry beast in the stairwell earlier."

"Sorry, Hour of the Dog is the old Japanese word for around seven o'clock. I'll get the teacher to end Aikido class early tonight, if anyone shows up in this weather."

"Right, sounds good. Glad you're making progress."

Taking a seat on a bench near the edge of the mat, Jean-Baptiste slumps sideways.

"I just can't take this. Did you I tell you about the first time Papa Legba showed up?"

"Can you explain who he is again? I don't know much about your culture. That's not from voodoo, is it? I don't mean to be culturally insensitive or anything but my mind is on my Japanese pests these days."

"Thanks, I appreciate that. When people hear I'm Haitian, they assume all kinds of stupid stuff. But unfortunately, Papa Legba is part of voodoo. I guess this demon outbreak is all about reinforcing cultural stereotypes. I'm just glad I'm in good company."

"If you can call this good company." I hold up my hand, still swollen and red from the Tengu bite. "A giant crow goblin just bit my hand."

"Crow goblin? For real? That looks really painful, woman. I know you want to protect Dar, but he has to stop doing whatever he's doing down there because these things are starting to hurt people. Papa Legba keeps talking about killing Freddy Kruger and Shai told me just now that the Golem grabbed him and sprained his shoulder."

"Right, I'll talk to Dar as soon as I see him... He hasn't been answering his door and I haven't heard anyone go by in the hallway all day... when I'm awake. That old artist guy must be snowed in at home and the only people I've heard coming up the stairs all day are the maniacs who wanted to practice Aikido at lunchtime in this weather."

"So the sword guy is going to help you talk to Dar?"

"Not quite. I was just thinking that if we got some of the demons together, they might be able to keep things in control until I can get Dar to shut things down."

"Like a demon police force?"

"More like a peacekeeping force. The can work together to keep each other from hurting us humans. And I'm afraid that Dar might not be in control any more if the demons are showing up at all hours of the day and night. He only runs his machines at night, as far as I know. But there was some kind of power surge going on downstairs when the crow goblin bit me."

"Great. We may need to call in the Ghostbusters at this rate. So we're just waiting around until your sword guy shows up. Sounds like a plan, I guess. I don't have any other bright ideas."

Jean-Baptiste gives me a last exhausted look then heads for the dojo door.

"Walk me to the stairs, will you? I'm afraid of what you've got running around up here on the fifth floor."

"Thanks, JB. Leave a young girl alone with a floor full of demons. You're a real hero."

"I know you can handle it, Cherry. Me, I'm not a martial artist, just a guy trying to make a living in the bioengineering.

You professional warriors need to take care of this." We both laugh a little, but it sounds hollow.

Jean-Baptiste's anxious face disappears into the stairwell and the sound of his footsteps fades into a faraway patter as he heads to his office.

Drained now, I slump against the iron-gray blast door that divides the two halves of the fifth floor. The determination to take another nap is taking shape when I feel a firm grip clamp onto my left shoulder. My body reacts before my mind can process the grab – Sensei would be so proud. I pull my left shoulder forward even as I spin my right into the attacker, turning and slashing upward with the edge of my hand.

Nothing connects, nothing is there for me to counter-attack. Only Barata, standing now out of reach, a sardonic smile on his smooth boyish face. His limbs are nearly dancing with movement, even now. He's just too fast for me.

"Hi Cherry! Thought I'd say hello. It's really cool how you move almost in slow motion. Did your sensei teach you that or are you naturally that slow? It's like a special effect or something."

"Funny. What do you want?"

The question seems to throw him off balance much more than my counterattack. He shifts from one foot to another, his white Capoeira pants rustling and pulling across his thighs. Despite the cold, he's wearing only the light pants and a long-sleeved t-shirt, printed with something in Portuguese. He's barefoot, as usual, despite the cold.

Without tensing a single muscle or giving me any warning, Barata does a quick backflip, landing soundlessly on the concrete floor in a low crouch. Show-off. But the movement seems to loosen his tongue a bit.

"Hey Cherry, when was the last time you got out of this building? You're starting to look like some kind of underground mole creature. You need some sun and fresh air. Why don't we go for a walk and I can tell you about my new friend and how he's going to help us fight the Goddess of Destruction down the hall."

Underground mole creature? I know I'm pale and my hair hasn't been washed in a few days but that's pretty low. Then the last half of his sentence registers: 'Goddess of Destruction.'

"The goddess of what?"

"Just come with me."

Barata pulls a pair of floppy climbing shoes out of his pocket – he must have borrowed them from Brah downstairs. He grabs a foot and hoists it practically to his shoulders to slip on the shoes – flexibility I can only dream of. He gestures toward the window.

"Can't be any colder out there than in here, right?"

"I don't really want to go outside in this weather, actually. I get plenty of fresh air right here in the building, thanks to our drafty windows in the Aikido dojo. And we haven't pulled the shades down in weeks – no one to peek in and we count on the sun to warm up the space a bit on clear days. I don't need more sun and I'm not sure I want to test if it's warmer out there or not, frankly. I'm from California!"

"I don't care – you're coming with me, junior samurai. At least we can climb Mount Fuji together."

"Mount what? Nothing out there but parking lot."

"You've been in here too long, woman! Come out and explore with me."

"Is there something like a mountain out there? I've actually been trying to think of a way to summon this powerful bird-demon called a Tengu from Japanese mythology to help us out. He visited me on the fourth-floor earlier but I'm not sure how to get him back. In Japan they leave offerings for him on mountains."

"Not quite a mountain out there, slo-mo. But there's a pile big enough to leave something that won't get stolen right away. No one can see it from the street."

"OK, I guess I can try. At least it will be some exercise. I can substitute mountain-climbing for my stair-climbing."

"Sounds like plan!"

We head back to the dojo for me to suit up and find an

offering for the Tengu.

Barata is right: I haven't been outside in a while. There's a definite layer of dust on my "outside-outside shoes," the sturdy synthetic boots that I've been using. They feel a bit tight as I activate the straps on the boots – Sensei says your shoe size increases if you spend hours practicing in bare feet. Seems like I've gained at least a half-size. My coat has gotten more use in recent days as the temperature has plunged, but I still fumble a bit with the fasteners – I usually wear it like a cape inside over my winter kimono.

Now for a gift for the Tengu. I decided to break the rules on footwear in the dojo and shuffle over the storage cabinet in my boots for a quick peek at the top shelf. There they are, the many bottles of alcohol that students have given Sensei over the years on special occasions. Most of the bottles of sake have been opened and are half-empty as the rice wine is popular on dojo social nights. The half-dozen whiskey bottles are nearly empty. Wait – the last time I checked the shelf they were full: Has the Swordmaster been in here?

Near the back I see one unopened bottle: shochu, or sweet-potato liquor from the south of Japan. Sensei showed it to me one day and said it tasted like poison to her but was very popular in the village where she studied sword. She warned me never to hold an open container of shochu near a candle flame. This bottle was a gift from a visiting teacher and features a drawing of Saigo Takamori, "the Last Samurai," who fought against the modernization of Japan. Perfect. I tuck the dusty bottle of shochu into the big pockets of my coat. I'm not sure the Tengu will appreciate it but it will have to do for an offering as nothing else in the dojo right now would likely interest a crow goblin.

Barata is waiting by the shoe rack and gives me a playful kick to the head as we stand at the door and chat, bracing ourselves for the temperatures outside. He stops his foot at my temple, just in time for me to aim a fake punch at his groin. We both laugh a bit nervously and he spins away into a low cartwheel.

"Look at you – I see some sparkle in your eyes! You need to get out more often. How many times do I have to ask you to come play Capoeira with me? How many times before you say yes? I've played with your Sensei before and it was big fun, until she threw me on my butt. I'm not used to having both of my feet swept but I'll be ready next time."

"I promise I'll come over as soon as Sensei gets back. I just feel like I need to stick to Aikido training nonstop for now. It's kind of a test for myself. I'm seeing if I can live the Aikido life as a full-time mission. Do you know what I mean?"

"I guess, but you're a little young to be thinking about a life mission. University, career, family – that's all ahead before you think about a mission. You have years before you have to test yourself like this."

Can Barata handle my truth? He's looking much more interesting than usual in the light of the dojo, in some hallway-ambushing, head-kicking kind of way. I decide to try him out.

"No college, no career… absolutely no family. I want to do Aikido as a job and I want to start now. A year with Sensei, then five years or so studying Aikido and sword in Japan, then my own dojo. I tell my dad and stepmom this is just a gap year, but there is no way I'm going to spend any more time in a school."

"How will you survive doing Aikido? My Capoeira teacher is one of the best in North America but she can only feed herself, nothing more. I don't even feed myself with my art in these war-like days and I'm really good at Capoeira. Lucky for me I don't pay rent other than my practice space and like eating rice and beans every day. Better rice and beans than being mummified behind a computer in some other job, I guess."

Barata smiles then sweeps my leg with a lightning-fast kick. Luckily, Sensei loves to practice leg sweeps, and my fall is automatic and painless. My puffy jacket helps cushion my bad elbow as it slaps against the concrete. I dust myself off as I get up and aim a slow-mo kick at his shin. I'm not going to go down without a fight, even if we are just playing.

"Nice, heard of this great thing called a mat? You could have fractured my elbow. Anyway, I'm not afraid of the future. I'll get better at Aikido and I don't need much to survive, like you."

"OK. Let's just get through our epic climb first and see how you do at survival."

The chill deepens as we make our way down the stairs, past the levels of the building that seem to exhale their emptiness. From the first-floor lobby we can see outside through the glass door: pale sun reflects off the drifts on each side of the front walkway. A warm spell sometime in the past few days seems to have glazed them with ice and today's wind has pushed the new snow away. Barata pushes open the door to usher in a blast of frigid air along with a raw scent of something wet and moldy, laced with the tang of burning plastic. It's only a bit colder outside than inside, but the wind cuts through to the bone.

"Hey Barata, a you sure you want to do this? I'm not sure I have enough layers on and I can barely move. You're going to freeze without a jacket."

"Come on, Cherry. You'll warm up as soon as we start climbing. You need this. You're starting to look a little see-through. See my nice tan?"

"I am half-white, you realize."

"Hey, I'm half-white too, if you want to get technical about it, and I'm not *that* pale, girly. You're still alive, as far as I know."

"OK, OK. Here I go, into the wilderness."

My feet feel unsteady inside the boots – I'm not used to having something so thick between me and the ground. Socks and slippers at most for the last week. The sounds are also jarring – crunching from the ice and snow at my feet and the suddenly amplified sounds of traffic and wind and human activity. Cloudy as it is, the light scrapes at the inside of my skull with its intensity as it reflects off the whiteness. I slap on sunglasses, pull tight my hood and push myself forward, across the parking lot.

We edge around mounds of snow and between the dozen or so cars in the side lot and head for the back, where university dump trucks unload their hauls of snow and ice after storms. As we turn the corner at the end of the building I can't help but look back and up at the fifth floor: This is as far from the dojo as I've been in days.

Around another corner, past the long-shuttered loading docks, stands our destination – a mammoth pile of slush and ice frosted with several inches of recent snow. The warmth of earlier in the week has eroded the sides of the mound, exposing crusts of brown and yellow glittering with ice. A plow blade has packed a single facet into one side, smooth and multicolored and almost plasticky to the touch. The whole thing has to be 50 feet high. The building blocks most of the wind but some airborne trash and leaves swirl sluggishly at the base of the mountain.

Barata turns and waves me forward, guiding me onto the slopes. My boot punches through frozen crust on the first step, sinking into something slushy and bottomless.

"No fear, my samurai princess. See, the path is still nice and firm back here."

Barata heads to the other side of the snow pile, muttering about a trail he blazed last week. I abandon the sun-facing side and head to the back to join him. There's a brownish path packed into the sides of the mound back here. He hops up the first few steps and then turns, his hand extended. As much as I don't want to look wimpy, I decide to take it. His hand is big and wiry-strong, surprisingly warm even through my gloves. I climb with him up the trail, proud I can keep my footing despite the icy and lumpy pieces of trash packed into the surface.

Nearly at the top, we find a shelf carved by a melt just to the side of our path. Sheltered by the side of the building and out of the wind, it's almost warm up here. With a grand sweep of my arm, I pull out the bottle of shochu and shove it into the crusted snow, the glass clouding over immediately as the cold hits it. I tried a sip of shochu last year at a dojo party back home – it tasted like a blend of gasoline and muscle rub. Perfect to go down a crow goblin's throat: I hope the Tengu appreciates the offering.

A few steps higher up, the rough platform Barata stomped out on the top of the snowpile still holds. He spreads out a plastic bag he fished out of the slush on the way up and we sit down, settling ourselves like snow leopards surveying our domain. At least forty feet up, our perch allows views unobstructed by razor wire. Not much to see: Factory, worn-out neighborhood, university building to the far left. That one is windowless and brand-new, and Sensei says there's a rumor it's some kind of animal testing lab. No sounds from any of the buildings today, just the creak of tree branches, coughing of car engines and the distant roar of plow trucks.

"You can see it perfectly from here," Barata says, gesturing back toward our building. He points to the fifth floor, a set of windows at the back and all the way down the hall from the dojo. He pulls out an energy bar and offers me half, along with a swig from his water bottle. We settle in and watch in silence. After a bit, the background noise seems to intensify and build into something high-pitched and close by. Almost a screaming sound, and it seems to be coming from the side of our building. Barata and I stand up at the same moment to get a closer look at the windows. Our necks crane up and up – the sound is definitely coming from the fifth floor.

The roar deepens into a drawn-out moan and a quick movement from a window draws our eyes. It's got to be the big open studio next to Dar's lab. I exchange glances with Barata and we look back. Nothing seems to be moving now but there's a strange cast to the darkness up there. We watch for a few minutes in silence and dread seems to paralyze us both. I don't want to seem wimpy, but I feel like we'd be safer inside with the others.

"Should we go back inside? I may not be safe out here. Could be something demonic. We could bang on Brah's door and go up the stairs by the rock gym. Whatever is up there can see us clearly out here, Barata. Let's take those stairs."

"Not sure we should go in right now – look!" Barata gestures up.

High up in the window, an intense light has appeared, pulsing with glare that seems almost liquid. It could be a laser or some kind of high-powered energy beam. The concrete between the windows seem to fade and waver as the light grows stronger and spreads across the entire side of the building, creating a glowing bar of brilliant yellow.

The light is so strong my eyes start to water even with the sunglasses and I look away, only to see the pulsing beam reflected across Barata's cheekbones.

"What the hell is that?"

Barata's eyes don't leave the glow on the fifth floor. He lowers himself to a crouch then scuttles down the frozen face of the snow pile in a few seconds. He reaches a hand toward me as I make my way down, much more slowly.

"What are you waiting, for sister? We've got to go up there and fight."

* * *

"One question to everyone – have you seen any new demons today outside the building or in the hallways?"

All of us living here are sitting in Shai's office again, trying to figure out the plan. We chose his first-floor lair for its space heaters – a kind of graveyard chill has settled into the concrete walls of the building with the cloudy weather today and we spend the first ten minutes of our meeting complaining about the cold. Outside the sky is dead-gray and a rising, bitter wind seems to be forcing itself through all of the cracks and crevices in the concrete.

"Now that you mention it, I did see something strange outside my window, on the junkyard side of the building."

"Talk, Emma. What did you see?"

Barata is the one who has taken charge of our gathering this time, breaking through the complaining to get us focused on our mission.

Emma shifts in her chair and tells her story in her usual crisp, slightly bored tone of voice. Mere demons don't scare her.

"Well, I saw a woman in white with some kind of dust cloud around her. She had something on that looked like your Aikido costume, Cherry. That cultural appropriation of the kimono that you all do."

"It's not a costume, they're called Aikido gis. And they're based on kimonos, like in old Japan. But our uniform is not really a kimono, so you can't say it's direct cultural appropriation, so I'd appreciate it if you quit the snarky comments, Emma. Anyway, did the woman's robe hang long like a kimono or was it like a gi?"

"Definitely a kimono, now that you mention it. But don't you wear a skirt like that in Aikido?"

"It's not a skirt, Emma! My uniforms are no less silly than yours. Who ever heard of doing a martial art in red silk pajamas? What, are you modeling for a Victoria's Secret site? Lounge wear?"

"Sisters, enough!" Barata barks. "We need to figure this thing out so we can make it stop. Trust me, both of your outfits look silly to me. All I need for Capoeira is some lose pants and a t-shirt. Or no shirt at all, if you're the body-positive type."

Barata smirks a bit. He's so intensely annoying sometimes.

"So Emma, was it a kimono?"

"Yes, long and flowing behind the creature. She also seemed to have some kind of long black drape on her head. And lots of dust around her."

Of course, now that she's gotten past insulting me, I realize that Emma is describing Yuki-Onna, the snow witch.

"Actually, that was snow, not dust. That was a Japanese snow demon. You saw her walking on the ground? Last time I saw her she was outside my window on the fifth floor."

"She was kind of trotting along, I guess. Near the row of junked cars."

Barata takes charge again.

"OK, we've established that the creatures are getting outside the walls of the building during the daytime. Do they have physical form as well? Anything left behind in your space?"

Emma's calm shatters in an instant and her voice rises to a shrill pitch.

"My entire space is filled with towers made from clam spit! They don't go anywhere when the monster disappears now. I have to knock the spit castles down one by one and sweep them into the toilet before I do my workout every morning. I'm running out of space."

Shai can't help himself now.

"Into the toilet? You're putting demon spit in to the plumbing? What do you think this is – the city hazardous waste dump! Are you trying to trash my building?"

Barata sits up straighter and his voice positively booms in the tiny office. "Shai, calm down. I'm sure the crystals dissolve once they leave the vicinity of this energy field, whatever it is. But has anyone actually touched these demons? Are they solid like flesh and blood?"

My turn to lose my cool.

"You've seen my bruises, right? I've felt the frog demon's clammy hands on my butt, they are solid for sure. And the demon samurai has hit me so hard with a meditation stick that he gave me this."

The group mutters as I pull aside my coat to reveal the bright-red welt next to my neck. The bruise on my hand from the Tengu's beak has faded a bit, but I pull off a glove to show that off, too. We all sit back a bit and think about a future with demons attacking at any moment, causing real injuries and pain. Barata gets up, pours water from his bottle over a napkin, and hands it to me, gesturing to the welt. My eyes tear up a little at his kindness.

Now Barata is back to business. "So they can move, and they can hit and they can make things. Do you think they can be talked into doing something about the situation as a group? Are they happy here or do they want to go back to where they came from?"

Barata seems to be the only one now ready to push us forward, but he's looking to me for answers.

"Don't look at me: I have no clue. I haven't had time to ask a lot of questions when dodging the Swordmaster's attacks. But he seemed to understand that I needed help when he showed up earlier. I'm not sure I got through to him about actually doing something."

"Papa Legba seemed to understand too. He was reading things out of my mind if that makes sense. He knows that he doesn't belong in a biotech lab in a snowy wasteland." Jean-Baptiste seems to vibrate with outrage.

Everyone nods together now – even Brah, who has been braiding something out of parachute cord the entire meeting.

"Freddie Kruger's ready, sisters and bros! He sharpened his claws and everything!" he volunteers, slipping his new bracelet over his wrist to join about a dozen others.

Jean-Baptiste springs up from his chair.

"OK, let's do this!"

"Do what?" Emma can't help herself.

Jean-Baptiste sits down again, and we all look at each other. Barata breaks the silence with that bossy voice of his again. "We have to do something, Emma. I think we've all agreed that there is safety in numbers. So go back to your space, summon your demons and let's all meet on the fifth floor outside Cherry's unit at midnight tonight. That seems to be when all the demons are strongest."

We stay in our chairs for a minute or two, thinking about the showdown to come. Emma doesn't argue with the plan, as crazy as it sounds. No one seems to have a better idea. But no one seems eager to leave the warmth and company of Shai's office, either.

Shai looks around the circle of anxious faces then reaches below his desk for something.

"Cookies, anyone? And I can make green tea for you ninja types."

We settle back into our chairs and pass the cookies. The big confrontation is coming, but it's not here yet.

CHAPTER EIGHT

Thursday Night/Friday

White everywhere, white streaming across the windows as the building shudders and groans. This is a snowstorm for the ages, starting minutes after the last Aikido students left tonight. It began with the rattle of hail that seemed to rush the students out more quickly than usual.

Finishing up the last cleaning of the day, I see the hail become a spatter of sleet then soften into puffy flakes. My dinner rice warms up to the flakes splitting into pellets of ice, tiny grains that chatter against the glass as they gather force. Now I'm huddled in my bed as rivers of snow surge across the sky, the wind shrieking with rage. It might be a good time to visit Jean-Baptiste or Barata in their spaces, but I can't seem to leave my cocoon. The show outside and the intensity of the storm keep building, lit by a ghoulish pink glow from stoplights on distant streets. Not a good night to take on demons – or is it?

Now the chattering, howling and banging is at a volume where I can't even imagine a conversation with anyone. Snow scatters and amplifies what light there is outside so the outlines of the dojo space are etched in ghostly gray.

The constant movement and sound lulls me into an uneasy doze that seems to last only minutes when something touching my face jolts me awake. The clock at the bed says

11:59 pm: Hour of the Dog or Hour of the Pig, I can't remember which. A patter like the footsteps of a million of tiny creatures fills the dojo with sound – must be ice on the windows.

As the patter subsides, my ears pick up a rustling much nearer by… not quite on the bed next to me but on the other side, by the window. I ease myself over and push down the sleeping bag. Inches away, above me by the window, something is shifting and rustling, then stretching itself to a huge height above me, blotting out all light and sound as a scream builds in my throat.

Blackness paints itself across my eyeballs and all is darkness. Harsh screams erupt into the silence and I can't tell if it's me or the night visitor. I wriggle back away from the terror and a void opens up underneath me and pain lashes across my back – I've fallen off the edge of the bed.

The sleeping bag and futon slide after me and I'm smothering in bedding and panicking to the point I seem to lose consciousness for a few seconds. My eyes open and I shake loose from the blankets to see the dojo walls glowing with pinkish haze from the storm outside. The black shadow has shifted to the open concrete between my bed and the shoe rack.

My gloved hands swipe at my face as I struggle to stand up. Something's clinging to my hairline and it's not my hair. I pull at the irritant and work it free from my scarf and hoodie.

It's almost as long as my forearm, nearly pulsing with dark iridescence.

Another Tengu feather, this time delivered from much closer range. I turn to toward a rustling sound near the shoe rack – then really wish I hadn't.

At the door, the huge shape extends to the ceiling and seems to fill the entire dojo with darkness and an oily sheen. The beaked face emerges from the dimness and the Tengu's eyes catch mine – once again I'm overcome by some kind of ancient rage and grief channeled through pools of roiling black.

Minutes seem to pass with the Tengu standing and staring, then the images in my mind start to come together with flashes of Kappa, the Swordmaster and Yuki-Onna. Even as the visions dart through my mind, the demons themselves emerge from the shadows at the corners of the dojo, along with the long-neck demon and few creatures I don't remember meeting, like a one-eyed gargoyle that seems to be all head, and a scuttling spider-beast with a hairy body hanging on jointed legs and clacking fangs.

Hissing and clicking fills the air but all of the demons seemed focused on the Tengu as he turns. The rooms spins with feathers and snow and flashing beaks and talons. Before a split-second seems to pass, we're all together in the hallway. I'm out of my sleeping bag and standing in the hall with no memory of opening the door. I'm only in my first five layers or so of sleep-wear, standing on my feet in socks with no slippers, but I don't feel cold. My back where it's leaning against something soft is actually warm: I turn to see something hairy with two sets of yellow tentacles where its eyes should be – another yokai that looks like it could be useful in a fight. I turn back to Tengu at the head of the crowd.

Soft slurping comes from the left as the Clam Monster shuffles into place by the Tengu, Emma behind them with her fingers pinching her nose. More rustling and the dirt-caked Golem and a dreadlocked old man with a solemn expression and sparks flying from his eyes take their places nearby – that must be Papa Legba. I hear the voices of Shai and Jean-Baptiste whispering to each other from down the hall by the elevator. The entire situation should be weird, but somehow I'm filled with a calm, powerful energy.

More minutes seem to pass as the Tengu and the other demons glide down the hallway into the darkness toward Dar's unit. Everyone quiets down and the silence expands into a void like a vacuum, drawing in all energy and thought until even the pounding of my own heartbeat in my ears fades away into nothing. Minutes, hours seem to pass in the eerie silence.

Out of nowhere, something explodes into the space, stunning us all with a kind of mental scream.

The hallway fills with light, a reddish, pulsing glare that makes my eyes water. All the cracks in the wall and floors come into sharp focus, along with scraps of trash and tangles of cobweb along the space around the door frames. The demons are back in front of us, pierced with beams of light but holding their shapes, for the moment.

The hellish fire fills every corner of the passage then a shadow grows from the direction of Dar's unit. From a smudge of darkness, it steadily expands to form a shifting, dead-black hole surrounded by flames.

My eyes can't quite fix on it – I turn to see Brah squinting at my left. I pivot back to glimpse a huge lion-headed figure, but as I focus on it turns into a mass of squirming snakes, then a flaming goat-head, then a jagged black maw. The shape that stays the longest is a familiar tattooed figure, blue eyes gleaming from beneath a hood. My mother's killer – exploding into fire – is staring right at me, and I swear that I can see him smirk and give me the finger.

The light gets even brighter: One by one, the demons in the hallway seem to flare up to giant size, then snuff out. The Clam Monster explodes into a splash of sludge. Kappa's blown up with a moist popping sound. Freddy Kruger's claws clink against the wall as he's thrown back by some tremendous force. The Golem slumps into a mini-landslide of brown powder. Papa Legba holds on the longest, but then his shape contorts and collapses as his cane clatters to the floor.

A cloud of black feathers is blown back from the darkness onto the concrete floor – then each shimmering oblong blinks out into nothingness.

❋ ❋ ❋

I don't feel anything physical, just a ringing in my skull like I've just been thrown on my head in Aikido class. Darkness floods back into the hallway, and I'm standing there in shock as the roar fades away. Even with my eyes closed, spangles of light dance across my vision. All is dead silent. Then soft rustles and whispers start to escape from the humans in the hallway and my ears and eyes start working a bit again.

Barely visible as a silhouette next to me, Brah shakes his head and walks over to where Freddie Kruger's claw-marks stripe the paint on the wall.

From behind me, I hear Jean-Baptiste's voice, sharp with fear.

"What the hell was that?"

Emma's voice is pitched far above her usual annoyed tone. "Please, Cherry, tell me that's not one of your Japanese monsters. They're supposed to be on our side, right? Did that thing kill our demons?"

Shai and Barata crowd into the dojo doorway with the others as we huddle in confusion. They all seem to want answers from me. I push the door open and we stream inside, my desk lamp spotlighting tired-looking and wild-eyed faces. The dojo clock blinks helplessly – the explosion must have interrupted the power. Even so, it's a bit lighter inside and out, an orangish glow backlighting rivers of snow at the windows. It must be close to sunrise. The entire night passed in what seemed like seconds.

"That thing – whatever it was – wasn't Japanese, I'm pretty sure. Some kind of super demon. I don't recognize it from any of my reading. Did you all see... someone you know?"

"Yes, there was something from my past in there, along with goat-heads and snakes and everything. It's reading us and finding dark stuff from our past, somehow." Emma's shaking voice tells of something horrible in the visions, maybe even worse than the gangbanger that I saw. Shai puts his arm around her, and they pull close together.

"So because the power source is down the hall there, a monster demon shows up. Stronger than the others because it's closer to the source." Barata seems to be figuring things out faster than everyone else. His dark eyes are gleaming and he looks almost grown-up in this hazy light.

"That would be my guess. Closer to the power, the bigger and scarier it gets. We need to find out what that demon is. The storm knocked out my land line and Internet access last night so you'll have to look through that stack of books, Cherry," Jean-Baptiste says.

"How the hell do we fight that thing? It looks like all the other demons together don't have enough power," Shai says. "My Golem fell apart! I can consult my electrical plans downstairs to see if there's a way to upgrade the power for the rest of us but I'm afraid that goat demon is unstoppable."

"Everyone just come in here and sit down. We need time to figure this out."

For some reason, everyone is listening to me now and I usher the group into the dojo lounge, pushing the reluctant into taking off their shoes. In a kind of daze, I start making tea, pouring water from a plastic jug into the electric pot. As I go through the motions, my mind starts clicking away on what just happened.

"We don't know that that thing is unstoppable, we don't know anything. Anyway, our demons didn't exactly work together...they just sort of stood there and stared, right? We need to get them on the same team, doing something to take that thing down."

"Team Demon! Demon force 2025!" Barata can help himself: He cartwheels as punctuation and knocks over an empty teacup. He scrambles to pick up the shards and looks sheepish.

"Right, Barata, that's the idea. Now try not to trash my dojo."

Emma speaks up. "But they don't speak the same language, and I know that my demon thinks your Japanese ghosts are ignorant savages." She pulls her coat tight around her and smirks a little. Doesn't she realize how serious this is?

"I'm actually pretty offended that this device is reinforcing cultural stereotypes. I'm all for exploring my own culture, but that Golem is from a period of Jewish history I'm not interested in exploring. I'm sure you are all sick of dealing with the ignorant superstitions of your ancestors," Shai seems energized by his cultural criticism, and Emma looks on with approval. I have an answer ready.

"Come on, we can't let that stuff get in the way. That thing down the hall is going to kill us all if we don't work together. And I don't think it's really interested about how we feel about exploring the embarrassing parts of our cultures. Who knows, the way Dar was talking about unlimited energy and all, that thing could kill the whole city. The Swordmaster is the only demon tough enough to get everyone together. I don't know why he didn't show up tonight but I'm pretty sure he can make it work."

"What do you mean? Just because he's a Japanese warrior doesn't mean he's stronger than my Clam Monster." Emma's pride is wounded and her energy is back.

"My demon may have only one leg, but that Brazilian leg kicks ass," Barata says.

"Papa Legba is actually a kind of god, so I'd nominate him as the leader," Jean-Baptiste counters.

"My Golem saved all the Jews of Prague, so he's the obvious choice!" Shai shouts. "He's the only one with any experience in this kind of 'saving the world' thing."

"Enough, everyone calm down. If you think about it, my Japanese demons are the strongest because they're closest to the power source. And I've got more demons than anyone else, so if they get together they're even more powerful. We need to go back to our spaces and get everyone to agree to show up here again and take that beast down. Get your demons to overcome their nationalistic stuff and work together."

Muttering and grumbling follow my announcement, but everyone seems to agree at the end. When the tea is all drunk and the chill starts settling back into the dojo, shoes go back on and the crowd filters out.

Jean-Baptiste lingers after everyone else leaves. With the sun fully up and the dojo flooded with snow-bright light, I boil up another pot of water and we settle onto the futon. Neither one of says anything; we're both still a bit dazed after the morning's events. He sips at the tea as I flip through my library books.

"Wait! JB, look at this. Right here in the 'Religions of the Ancient Middle East' chapter."

"That's what we saw out there, kind of. Some kind of snake demon?"

"Much worse. It says it's Angra Mainyu, the god of darkness and destruction in the old Persian religion. It's where we get our whole idea in the West of the battle of good and evil, from these Persian stories. Dar's family is from around there, I think. Angra Mainyu is all the evil in the world in one package. 'Destruction, rage, all-consuming lust…' Wow, I don't think our quirky little demons can take this guy on."

"Well, what choice do we have?"

"This spirit is so evil they used to write his name upside-down in the books to disrespect him. They even blame him for giving women periods back in the beginning of time. Dar must have known about Angra Mainyu from childhood and his device brought it to life through his neuron machine.

"Look at this part: 'To aid him in attacking the god of light, Angra Mainyu created a horde of demons embodying envy, lust and all the other evils of the world.'"

"So you think that everything we've been seeing comes back to this guy?"

"Could be. This is really scaring me. I can't imagine Dar wanted to summon up the ultimate evil spirit from his culture. He's not in control of all this, I know it. He just wanted to create a new source of energy."

Even as the words leave my mouth, I know they're not quite true. Dar is just as angry as I am at the world, if not more. "Those bastards at the university" are as real to him as mother's murderer is to me. I recognize the look of rage in his eyes – I see it in my own eyes most of the time I look in the mirror.

Come to think of it, I could have summoned Angra Mainyu myself.

* * *

Shivering uncontrollably as the temperature drops, Jean-Baptiste finally flees the dojo, leaving me with the dregs of a pot of green tea and time to catch my breath. The bitter, lukewarm brew both snaps my situation into focus and at the same time triggers a wave of exhaustion. Fighting to stay awake, I pull a chair up to the windows.

With the sun up and the dojo practically blasted with light, the whole situation seems less urgent somehow. Outside, the view is transformed as the wind dies down. The storm has left enough new snow to airbrush out the busted factories and broken-down apartment buildings. The city has been transformed into a clean and peaceful place. No grinding of plows yet, only the murmur of the slowing wind across dunes, drifts and mountains of snow.

The dojo logbook lies on the window ledge and I flip through the pages, counting back to the day that Sensei left for Japan. Today is Friday, four days until Sensei is due to come back. It's only been six days since we drove her to the airport, but I feel like it's been a lifetime. Today's date rings a bell, bringing me back to California's parched moonscape and the day the police came to tell us about my mother's murder.

Six years ago, today.

My dad answered the door, then shooed me into the bedroom while he talked to the cops. His face had collapsed into a ruin by the time he came back and told me the news. Drawing on all my Aikido training and reading about calming the mind, I never let myself cry. Not at the funeral, not at the trial, not in the years since with anyone around. My face became a mask that day, hiding a volcano of fear and grief and rage.

I've reenacted the robbery scene in my head a thousand times. Instead of sitting there like a victim, I would have grabbed the gun, flipped the guy into a wall. Grabbed the gun and turned it back on the robber, pulling the trigger to send a bullet into his belly. Deflected the gun and smashed the heel of my hand into his chin, snapping the gangbanger's neck like a dry twig. All of my scenarios end in death – the gangbanger's death. Each victory fills me with a dark joy.

But only last year my dad finally told me that my mother *had* fought back, had tried to take the guy's gun. The robber didn't mean to kill her but the gun went off. He knows this because the gangster sent him a letter from jail. Likely story. My mom was fast and strong and would have been able to fight off that skinny loser. That's what I tell myself. But she could also have scared the guy into shooting when she should have just given him the $34 she had in her wallet. The money – and her purse – were found locked in a desk drawer.

My Aikido teacher in California said that was the ultimate lesson of martial arts: Knowing when to just run away or give the thug the money. All the techniques in the world are of no use against accidents and the forces of chaos.

A burning sensation in my skull startles me awake: I've nodded off and my forehead has fallen against the frigid window glass. I better keep moving or the exhaustion of the week's events is going to overtake me and this day will go to waste. First I check on my food stocks: Lots of ramen noodles and instant soups to get me through the next few days. Then some more cleaning as the day's harsh light uncovers pockets of dust and grime everywhere in the dojo space.

I'm halfway through a thorough wipe-down of all surfaces when there's a sharp knock at the door. It's Barata and Emma, who look as tired as I do. They file into the dojo and after a bit of small talk, I get a great idea. "Let's fight!"

* * *

About an hour has passed, and Barata is shifting from

foot to foot, humming a tune as his arms flash in front of his face, back and forth, back and forth. The *ginga* step in Capoeira doesn't look dangerous, but Barata's flowing movement and power are easy to see. He's also humming a tune that manages to sound both threatening and danceable at the same time.

To my right on the mat, Emma is shifting back and forth herself in the flowing circles of Tai Chi. Her arms are rising then falling as she exhales with a whoosh each time. I can almost see the energy gathering around her in electric circles as she swings her arms wide. Her feet are placed delicately in one movement, come down violently with a nasty stomping action in the next. The dojo floor seems to quiver with each step of her slipper-clad feet.

As for me, I'm standing on one foot, arms outstretched, as if I'm about to swan-dive into the mat. I balance there for a few seconds then let gravity take over to smash my entire 140 pounds into the thinly padded concrete. Only somewhere in midair, I round my arms and spine, and that curvature of spacetime that is gravity pulls me into a perfect Aikido forward roll. The fall is spending its force as angular momentum then bringing me back into a standing position with none of my own energy used. That's the explanation I give new students, and I'm sticking with it.

The other two take a look at my rolling practice but don't seem impressed.

The three of us are limbering up in anticipation for a free-style – a "super showdown" as Barata calls it. We've been testing each other's techniques and openings with kicks and strikes for a while. That's when Emma got the brilliant idea that perhaps the energy from our practice could summon the demons. So we decided to fight each other for real.

Watching Barata's feet lash out in deadly warm-up kicks and Emma's ultra-realistic eye-poking motions, I'm having my doubts about this plan. I've tested my Aikido against other Aikido people and untrained family friends, but never gone one-on-one with other martial artists. They do this all the time on

TV, but Aikido's meant for self-improvement, not ass-kicking, or so I've been told. In Aikido we don't aim to hurt people, so the energy never quite matches up with the more aggressive arts. But I'm feeling ready to let some of that peacefulness go to show these two what I've got.

We're all warmed up now. Barata starts the action by cartwheeling over to Emma, then aiming a spinning kick at her belly. Emma barely reacts, just turns and opens her arms to her sides, hooking Barata's ankle and flipping him over.

"White crane spreads its wings!" She smirks a bit. Barata quickly regains his stance and does a lightning-fast back walk-over, aiming another kick at Emma's legs.

Emma sweeps her arms across her body at knee level, but Barata's too fast and her leg gets kicked out from under her.

Rather than fall, she shifts her weight and hops back on one leg, squeaking out "Rooster stands on one leg!"

No clear winner, I'd say. Now I'm ready to enter the fight. I stretch myself up as tall as I can – then abruptly drop to my knees. Barata stands in a half-crouch a few feet away, shuffling his feet back and forth again in the *ginga* movement. Barata's not still for long, but I see an opening in his rhythm and lunge forward on my knees to aim a strike at the back of his left leg at the moment it's angled back in the *ginga*. All that knee-walking practice in Aikido, said to come from our roots as an ancient samurai art, pays off. Both Barata and Emma look surprised at my knee attack and that's enough to give me a momentary advantage.

Like I figured, my hand-blade hits Barata at just the right place and time to collapse his leg to the ground and I pivot fast to sweep his other knee and roll him onto his belly. But before I can submit him, Emma's behind me and hooking my neck with a backward sweep of her arm.

"Single Whip and Jade Maiden!" She crows. Nice to know the name of the form that's kicking my ass.

Emma's forearm is right against my neck and bright spots are starting to pop in my vision. All my training in choke defenses seems to fly out of my head as her grip tightens. By instinct, I start shifting my weight back in preparation for a sudden drop to loosen her hold. It will work. It's got to work.

But before my body starts responding to by brain's sluggish command, something slices across my view, faster than humanly possible. Faster than any human can move.

Of course, it's not human at all.

"What the hell!"

Emma lets out a shriek and drops me abruptly onto my back – only my years of falling practice save me from getting the wind knocked out of me. She's clutching at her shoulder and letting loose with a volley of curse words. Barata is also on his back for some reason, thrashing around and flailing his arms at something I can't quite make out.

"*BAKA!*"

That booming voice, that insulting word in Japanese – *baka* means "moron" – snap the situation into focus. The demon Swordmaster has turned up to rescue me. I'm a bit insulted on one hand, relieved on the other. A few more seconds and I would have broken free from Emma's grip, demon or not. But that's why we did the showdown in the first place, to summon some demons. I guess I should be honored that mine showed up first.

※ ※ ※

"Dar, hey are you there?"

I knock hard, my knuckles stinging from slamming them on the metal door, over and over. Funny, I never noticed that this unit has a solid metal door, unlike the rest on this floor. Iron-gray paint and big straps of steel wrap the surface – it looks like something that could be on a submarine. More like the blast partition near the elevator than an office door. Hmmm.

No sound emerges from the unit, but a band of light appears on the floor beneath the massive slab.

The demon Swordmaster didn't stay long back in the

dojo, but I think the three of us were able to communicate something about the growing trouble in the building before he faded out. Emma and Barata went back to their spaces to practice and see if their demons would show up as well. Lucky me – we all agreed that I should make another attempt to talk to Dar about the situation before things got out of hand. It seemed so logical a few minutes ago, but now I'm shivering with a combo of fear, embarrassment and guilt as I pound on his metal door.

"Dar? Hello? It's Cherry from down the hall. The woman in the dojo with the green tea…I need to talk to you."

The light beneath the door flickers, then a sudden flash of intense orange flashes from the crack and brightens the whole hallway. Was that an explosion of some kind? What kind of explosion makes no noise at all?

"Dar? Are you OK in there? Do I need to call 9-1-1? Is something burning in there?"

The massive slab of metal quivers slightly then cracks inward a tiny bit. Dar's brown eyes, a sweat-soaked slice of his face and a grayish expanse of lab coat are all that are visible.

"Everything OK in there? I saw a strange light coming under the door just now. Thought I'd check in."

"What are you doing here on a snow day?"

His voice is strained, with fright and annoyance mixing in the upper registers.

"What are you doing here yourself? I just wanted to make sure the place wasn't burning down. You can see that we don't exactly have high-tech fire suppression in here. We'd all be baked alive!"

I gesture down the hall to the "emergency alcoves" where the folded wool blankets, brittle with age, site behind glass in case of emergency. State-of-the-art safety measures, circa 1960 or so.

Dar turns to look behind him and seems to relax. The door shifts open another inch or so. All I can see is a jumble of desktops and widescreen monitors, a rank of chest-high cubicle dividers spanning the space and scrawls of what looks like graffiti along back wall.

"I'm fine. Everything is fine. See, no smoke at all! Smell anything? Just working hard and … playing with some lasers."

"Right."

We stare each other down for a few seconds. Not a trace of the humor he showed the other day. He seems guarded and just on the edge of unfriendly. This has to change.

"I'm sorry. I just get paranoid about the subject of fires. When Sensei lived in Japan, her apartment building burned down, with all her things. Her building had an electrical short and she lost everything. She always chews me out for leaving candles burning and stuff. After we meditate. We use candles when we meditate. To symbolize the briefness of life or something."

My voice trails off after what has to be the most stupid, rambling sentence ever in the history of the world.

Dar cracks a bit of a smile.

"I see." He seems a bit friendlier and I go for the opening.

"I'm sure everything is perfectly safe in here. I did want to talk to you about something to do with the building. Some of us have had some… disturbances in our spaces lately. Have you noticed anything weird?"

"What do you mean, weird? Why are you asking me about it?" His eyes have that suspicious gleam again.

"I'm not accusing you of anything, sorry. It's not about you at all. We've just been noticing some weird stuff. Those of us who live… spend a lot of time in the building. Nothing about you specifically. Just a general concern with some kind of not really normal activity around here. Paranormal activity, you might say."

Why am I babbling? Dar's face has shut down and he starts pulling the door closed.

"All is fine here. Normal, normal, normal. I have to get back to work."

"So you haven't seen anything strange? Strange people in your space?"

"Like intruders? Leprechauns? No one at all, except some nosy neighbors."

He's smiling again, but there's no humor in his eyes. I try one last time to negotiate with him.

"OK, fine. Sorry again. Listen, stop by tomorrow and I can explain a bit about what's been happening. I might be crazy, but there also might be something going on in here. Won't take too much time and I'll bring some Japanese cookies."

Dar nods curtly, glances behind him again, and turns away.

The metal door swings shut with an angry clang.

That was awkward.

As I walk back to my space, I pause in front of the fire blanket alcove. In the flicker of the lone hall light, I strain to read the old-timey warnings printed on the glass even as my eyes turn back toward Dar's unit. Nothing but darkness beneath the door now.

As my eyes turn back to the alcove, something bright and terrible jumps into my view. Reflected in the dusty glass of the fire cabinet is a pulsing starburst in orange and red, with snake-like arms and a fierce, fiery glare. My heart jumps in my chest as I turn to face what I'm certain is a form of death, a painful and scorching destruction of my entire being.

But when I turn, there is nothing in front of Dar's space but a lingering orange glow in the air and a steaming puddle of something on the floor. All I want to do is get back to the safety of the dojo. As I sprint away from his space, I'm sure of one thing – Dar is a liar.

Looks like he's got the worst demon problem of them all.

❊ ❊ ❊

First comes "woman" – a bent knee, a rounded belly then a slash across for arms. Next two lines that look like a table, one leg tapering into an elegant "harai" stroke. Last is "power," a thick line bending at the elbow like a flexed muscle, another slash across like a sword.

"More pressure, Cherry-Chan! Your strokes are weak and too skinny!"

Maruhito Sensei slaps her tiny hand on the table. She's about a hundred years old and shriveled up like a prune, but she scares the hell out of me. I quickly grab another sheet of rice paper, fold it in fourths, and dip my brush in ink for another try.

Only me and one other student have shown up for calligraphy class this afternoon – with the city buried in the aftermath of the blizzard, I'm not surprised. Maruhito Sensei doesn't let mere weather stop her from cracking the whip on her least-favorite student. With some Japanese blood, I'm expected to know each stroke and movement innately somehow. She hired a truck to plow her driveway so she could get to the dojo tonight and I better not slack off.

"Here, it's the stroke called *hane*. Put more pressure and then lift up the brush, like this." From the end of a downstroke, an exquisite little hook materializes to the left on her paper. My version looks more like a drop of drool. Actually, on closer inspection, it looks a lot like drool. That's not ink – a glob of what looks like congealed green tea has distorted my character. Before Maruhito Sensei can see the weird mark, I pull another sheet of paper from my stack of rejects. This one has a smear of something brown and sticky distorting the "woman" part of the character. A waft of something foul drifts up from the paper.

Damn him!

The bottom of the stack yields a clean if ungraceful attempt, which I swiftly submit to Maruhito Sensei.

"Make sure to use pressure on the brush." She grabs my paper, frowns, and then picks up a clean sheet to demonstrate. Her hand whips across the paper and perfectly formed, perfectly elegant lines appear on the snowy expanse. I don't see pressure, just complete control of arm, hand and fingers.

But even as Maruhito Sensei's characters seem to emerge perfectly from her brush, a glob of goo from above lands on her "woman" with an audible splat. We both look up at the same time. She's complained of failing eyesight in class – can she possibly see the dangling green thing hanging just at the edge of the light fixture overhead?

Kappa has been hanging around all day, and now he's dangling by one arm, letting the drool slide off his face onto the calligraphy class below. He's probably punishing me for earlier today, when I tried to teach him how to do an Aikido roll again. Everything was going great: I had him leaning over with his arms in a circle, ready to launch himself across the mat. Then I pushed his froggy head forward and a single drop of water splashed out of the dent on his head. He leapt up crying "*DAME!*" "Bad, bad, Cherry-San! Trying to trick Kappa to take away his power!"

True, I did want to see if the folktales were true, if Kappa would disappear if I got him to lose all his water. But the drop he spilled didn't seem to have much effect except to put him in a sulky mood and send him to the ceiling. Now this: Calligraphy with green slime for ink.

Maruhito Sensei's eyes narrow as she squints toward the ceiling, then her features seem to open up with wonder. Her head drops after a few seconds, and she thrusts her brush in my face.

"Cherry-San! Please rinse these in the bathroom – hold the brush end down. Don't you be messing up my brushes. Getting late, I need to go home. My eyes are getting strange with this weather."

For a few seconds, our eyes meet and she seems to be weighing another question. Before she can speak, I grab her brush and my own and jump to my feet.

"Quan! Come with me now to rinse brushes!"

Quan puts down his brush, his mouth twisted in regret. He excels at calligraphy, along with everything else, and Maruhito Sensei made a special stop to pick him up for class. An hour of practice isn't enough for him, although it feels like a century to me. He stands up and we head toward the hallway to clean brushes.

As the door closes behind me, I could swear I hear Maruhito Sensei's voice, pitched low but unmistakable.

"*Hisashiburi,*" she says.

It's been a long time.

There's no one human in the dojo for her to talk to, but it seems as if she's met an old friend.

❋ ❋ ❋

"Hey, it's me. Anyone home?"

I twist myself around to see Dar standing by the shoe rack, looking sheepish. He's opened the door to see me sitting on a meditation cushion, trying to empty my mind as another crazy night of demon-fighting gets closer. As the afternoon fades, darkness has gathered outside the windows as if massing for battle.

Dar slips off his shoes and strides over the mat, folding his legs into lotus posture and seating himself right in front of me. His eyes close, long lashes resting against his cheeks. We sit there for a few minutes, Dar's face slack, my eyes fixed on his features. Finally, the lashes flutter open and he catches me staring at him.

"OK, so what do you want to know? My work is about power sources and the collective unconscious, and yes, that might be causing some… side effects in the building."

I pull my cushion closer to him and try to ignore the aching in my knees. I decide to hear him out first before demanding that he shut down his operation. That way, if he refuses to stop, I'll know more about what we're up against.

"Power sources? That sounds pretty major. Why this building instead of at the university? Woudn't it be safer over there?"

"They're a bunch of sheep over there, not willing to take the risks to get the big rewards. They got rid of me but I left with something very valuable – my ideas and a tiny vial of this stuff that I helped create. It was my idea originally, so it's nothing like stealing. If I had stolen something the university would have sent its storm troopers over, right? As it is they're just pretending I never existed. They cut off my health care and everything."

"Wow, sorry about that. You look pretty healthy, though."

"Thanks." He pushes a lock of hair out of his eyes and twists his face into a big grin. It's like a light has gone on the room. As I watch, the smile slowly collapses and the light dims. Something like intense irritation recasts his features.

"It's just so frustrating that they can see what I'm on the edge of creating – those mediocrities at the university. My idea has so much potential for the entire world. They talk and talk over there about improving the planet but they're just scared of anything or anyone that is too disruptive."

We've both eased into slouches. I scoot back to lean against the wall and take some pressure off my aching knees. Dar follows and inches a bit closer to me. I'm feeling bold.

"So how were you going to disrupt things? What exactly are you doing over there?"

"OK, I'll try to simplify things for you. My idea was to use this compound of metals found in the human brain – actually the brains of people known to be mystical or crazy – to generate power. Elements combined in the precise proportions found in these brains create this synergistic field that acts something like a self-perpetuating power source. It's an incredible energy source that seems to pull power from the collective human consciousness of the entire ten billion members of our species. Infinite, inexhaustible, able to be shaped precisely to our needs… doesn't that sound like something worth funding?"

Sounds like something he should be telling a doctor in a mental hospital, actually.

"Um, yes. I guess. Sounds incredible. I mean, have you really made it work?"

"At least once." Dar starts absently rubbing at his arm and I glimpse what looks like a band of scar tissue just above his wrist. "Once at full power, and a bunch of times at lower power. That's what I'm working with now, scaling things up gradually.

"The problem is that we need a certain kind of trigger to set off the reaction. At the university we tapped into the magnetic generator, but that had some...side effects we didn't anticipate. The team split up and the administrators started getting involved in my work in an unacceptable way. But that tower up on the roof of this building – do you know what it is?"

"Not really. I just know that we aren't supposed to go up there and it does something that cuts off all wireless access to the internet. It also gives off these subsonic emissions that aren't great for you, I heard. People aren't supposed to be spending more hours than the work day in here, which is kind of a joke. Sensei says it's just the landlord's story to keep people from living in here full-time."

"Hmm, I hope people aren't working too late around here on a regular basis. That's a piezoelectric booster upstairs – it takes power from the vibration of every piece of glass and ceramic in the entire city and focuses into a concentrated beam. That beam then goes downtown to power the drones and everything. The university sold it to the city a few years ago when the technology was new. They've made the technology millions of times more efficient since then but haven't exactly made a big fuss about it. I've made a few fixes to that tower and now I have more than enough juice to get my device going at full speed."

"So what is your device, actually?"

"It's like a gate, using the mind as a gate into other realms of reality. Energy from the brain, from the collective mind of the species."

Right. Sounds completely insane. I trying to think of an intelligent question that won't set off Dar's alarm bells.

"Sounds kind of like *ki* – that's our idea in Aikido that you can channel universal energy that's more than the sum of your physical strength. Does that make sense? I always thought it was a silly superstition until one day I made guy fall down using it. He was pinching my shoulder really hard and I raised my arm and turned my hip and he flew through he air and almost crashed into the wall. It wasn't me at all, it was something else that was channeled through me. I though it was rage at the time but Sensei said it was ki. That probably sounds weird, not related at all, or is it?"

"Interesting. The concept of ki sounds like a religious or cultural interpretation of the same power source, which I have finally identified scientifically. Fascinating when culture and science come together like that."

"So what's the downside to this power source? Why is the university so scared of it?"

"I wouldn't call it a downside, really. More like a…complication that could turn out to be a real selling point. You see the metals we take from brains provide the energy, but it doesn't come in a pure form. It's not like plugging into an outlet or a charging dock. It's more like capturing lightning. There's lots of other stuff that comes with the energy."

"Other stuff like what?"

"Seems there's a gate out there somewhere that leads into this vast pool of human culture, if that makes any sense."

"Not really."

Dar pushes his hair aside then stretches his lanky frame across the vinyl. His eyes meet mine then range across the room to the smudged sky outside.

"It's really kind of complicated and I probably should explain the whole thing later, when we've got the process perfected. Let's just say that it turns out that people's brains are lot more than the sum of their parts. There's a gate in there to everything you, your parents, and your parents' parents have experienced. Like, exactly what ethnicity are you? I know your name is Japanese but you don't look completely Asian to me."

Great, the 'Where are you from' question. As in: 'What weird mix of races are you?' I try not to make a face as I prepare my answer when Dar interrupts.

"I don't mean 'where are you from' – I get that too and ob-viously we are both born and raised American. But my parents are from South Asia and there's some cultural imprint in there. But they are also a member of a centuries-old religion that is different from the major faiths, so there's more cultural data in there. It's imprinted in the collective consciousness."

"Imprinted in where? Your brain? Well my dad is Mexican and my mom is Japanese-American. Her ancestors came from Japan like three generations back. But she hates rice and doesn't speak a word of the language. I mean she *was* Japanese-Ameri-can. Hated rice. All that should in in the past tense. She's dead, actually."

A few beats of awkward silence. Dar looks at me, and I can see him weighing the "what happened" question. Those emo-tions don't need to come out right now, so I try to the steer the conversation back to the point.

"So how does Japanese culture stay in the brain of some-one who's never even set foot in the place?"

"Doesn't matter, there's some kind of residue in there, in the very nanoparticles of your being. So when we tap into the energy of the human brain, there's some weird cultural stuff that comes out."

"Like nachos or rice and miso soup? Sounds messy."

"I wish. More like Shinto gods for people with Japanese blood. Tree spirits and such."

"What do you know about Shinto gods? It's not that sim-ple and we don't exactly worship trees and rocks."

"There you go – you do have some cultural awareness, Miss Fourth Generation. We all pick it up a little at home, but what I'm saying is that 'Japaneseness' is actually present in some way in the energy fields your brain produces. If I tap into your neural circuitry, some of that might come out."

"That sounds really offensive, actually. Like my brain has memories of a geisha or a samurai? I'm mostly American, why wouldn't a football player or a cowgirl come out? I hate to say it, but you are talking some stereotypical garbage right now."

"Hey, calm down. Turns out that American culture is pretty superficial, energetically. The fields seem to grow stronger over the generations, so by far the most powerful source would be your ancestral DNA. Thousands of years of samural trump a century or so of cowboys. It's like cultural DNA."

"But what about my dad's side? He's mostly Mexican, but there's some Irish, Hungarian, all kinds of stuff. He speaks a little Spanish but his Mexican ancestors came here a hundred years ago."

"Seems like the biggest proportion wins. Fights off the other influences, so to speak. The most aggressive culture is the one that makes itself known. But if I used the technology on you, you might want to watch out for Quetzalcoatl. He's nothing to mess around with – ask the university!"

"Quetzal who? Isn't that the guy from *Dune*?"

"No, it's one of the gods from Aztec culture. Theoretically some of your dad's Mexican heritage could come out in the shape of a featured serpent god. Don't ask me how I know, really."

Hmm, when I think of it, the bird-man that I've been seeing doesn't look so much like the tengu pictured in my books, and has some serpent qualities.

"Is it possible the brain can mix the cultures up, like blend Mexican and Japanese into some kind of Asian fusion?"

"Could happen, potentially. I'd have to work the algorithms."

This whole conversation is making me confused and a bit dizzy, so I sprawl out on the mat myself.

"So I'm still not getting how this 'cultural energy' comes out. Is it like Kabuki dancing or … sorry, I can't really think of a South Asian cultural dance right now."

"Actually, every country in the region and every state within those countries has its own dance. Not sure what my parents' hometown does, but I'm sure it's very cool."

Dar leaps up from the futon and capers around a bit, waving his arms and wiggling his hips.

"Like it? I'm feeling the Bollywood cultural energy!"

Of course I jump up then and start my own version of Ka-buki dance, waving around invisible fans and taking tiny stut-ter-steps. We circle around each other a bit until the cultural en-ergy wanes and I sag back down to the mat. Dar stays standing, his eyes fixed on the door. I should be asking him to shut his de-vice down, but I feel like I missed the opening, somehow.

"Sorry, it's all hard to explain and I'm feeling pretty ex-hausted right now. Probably said too much already. Do you think I'm crazy? Don't answer that! Thanks for the chance to stretch out."

"Crazy people are welcome here, the crazier the better. Stop by later and I'll make you some of my world-famous rice-cooker ramen noodles. My cultural DNA makes me awesome at boiling water and opening flavor packets."

"Great, I can't wait. I has been nice talking to you by the way. It helps me clarify my thoughts to explain things to a lay-person."

"Happy to help, and get some rest. I have a bunch more things to ask you, will you be around later?"

"Of course, I'll expect you."

Dar smiles and closes the door carefully behind him this time. I stretch out again on the mat, feeling the cold settling into my bones the longer I keep still. My conversation with Dar has helped clarify what's going on in the building, but he doesn't sound worried about the side effects at all, more like he's proud of making it rain demons.

Whose side is he on? Will he help us fight the demons or fight to keep them alive? My brain is muddled with a thousand thoughts and conflicting impulses. I force myself to sit back on the meditation cushion.

In the year before I moved out here I started doing at least twenty minutes a day of Zazen, the meditation method prac-ticed by great Japanese swordsmen from centuries past. These guys sat for hours every day on the cushion and said that Zazen was vital training for a swordsman in preparing to face death. I downloaded everything I could about Zazen to my phone in the months before I left home and forced myself to practice every day.

Now I'm looking for meditation to calm the confusion I'm feeling about what I should do next. Not quite the same as facing death by sword, but some kind of pain and death seem likely from the demon battle ahead. I plop down then edge my butt forward on the round cushion so my knees touch the mat. I lean a little forward so my sitting weight is supported in a triangular fashion at three points –– knee, knee and butt. Then a big bow forward to straighten out my spine, then I rock back with my hands in mudra, right cupped under left, palms to the ceiling.

A smudge of something brownish on the wall is right at eye level and I try to focus on it without staring and tiring out my eyes, closing my lids half-way. A swarm of intrusive thoughts immediately flood into mind: What would Dar think of this session of meditation? Will meditation wake up the demons? Can meditation make the demons go away? How exactly does this brain matter work as an energy source?

The "monkey mind" chatter intensifies as my body settles into the meditation posture and my breathing slows.

Time for a step back – a trick I use to zoom my awareness out above the chatter and watch as my thoughts bounce back and forth. Now it's time to count breaths, slowly centering my focus on each inhale and exhale.

Ichi, exhale. *Ni*, exhale. *San*, exhale. *Shi*, exhale.

OK, the monkey mind is refusing to settle down. Time for the big guns: counting in an older system of Japanese numbering that requires me to actually concentrate. Lucky for me, the Japanese can count in a bunch of ways.

Hi, exhale. *Fu*, exhale. *Mi*, exhale.

Exhale. Exhale. Exhale.

CHAPTER NINE

Friday Night/Saturday

A blow to the head, brutal and ice-cold. My eyes snap open and I fall back in shock, not exactly ready to face an attacker. Nothing in front of me, nothing above. Just my legs, aching knees and a black cushion flung across the mat.

Waves of shock and cold rattle through my sluggish brain as I put things together – I fell asleep during meditation and my head hit the wall. Nice. I was supposed to be emptying my mind to communicate better with demons. Instead I'm half-collapsed on the mat, probably with a big red mark on my forehead, after falling asleep in lotus posture. What if the mark turns into a bruise, yellow and purple with red dots? And I can't blame it on a demon? Barata will probably say something snarky.

Funny that I'm thinking of Barata's reaction before I think of Dar's reaction. Dar is definitely more mysterious and mature, but Barata isn't as annoying as I first thought. As my mind wanders, my fingers find the spot on my forehead that hit the concrete. Some swelling has already started. I'm trying to remember where I put my pocket mirror so I can check the damage when my eyes catch movement at the wall, right above where my head smashed forward.

It's that brown smudge I was focusing on before I fell

asleep.

It's moving.

Not exactly moving, more like swelling – ballooning into something malignant and pulsing and monstrous right before my eyes. Cracks in the concrete twist into giant snakes, wriggling and hissing. The brown spot becomes a mouth with bone-white fangs, bared and then snapping shut. Light blasts through the dojo space and the sound of millions of angry wasps erupts from the wall, pushing me away across the mat as I scramble backward like a crab.

Bigger and bigger, the monster grows to cover the entire wall and starts spreading up the ceiling as fear pushes me to the limit. I'm going to pass out, I think, as my scrambling takes me to the far wall even as twisting shapes and hungry mouths grow to trap me.

Then the hissing and buzzing is broken by a mighty shout – "MEN!"

The voice is coming from the corner of the dojo near the kamiza, where another shadowy shape has risen up.

"MEN!"

It's the kiai shout used kendo, or Japanese fencing, a yell that's supposed to shock or distract the enemy when you attack the head, or so Sensei explained to us.

As the shout and its meaning take shape in my mind, something spinning flies out of the corner of the dojo and into the center of the swirling mass on the wall, striking it right at the spot my head hit earlier. My eyes take in the sight of the suburito, the heavy wooden sword used for building your wrists, cartwheeling as it rockets across the room.

My eyes also take in a familiar figure: The demon Swordmaster – outlined in brilliant blue light – has hurled the wooden sword right at the monster on the wall. Now my mind takes in the horror of that monstrosity and calls it by its name.

Angra Mainyu.

The spirit of destruction has moved down the hall, right into my dojo.

208

The suburito hits the wall, and a wave of energy seems to ripple across the cinderblock. Snaky shapes that were reaching out to grab me seem to pull back. The huge fanged mouth snaps shut and fades into a grayish swirl. A few seconds later, all of the shapes and colors fade. Then a cloud of mist spits out of the wall, floating upward and clinging to the dojo ceiling for a few seconds more. All that's left in the end is a sword-shaped shadow, etched in charcoal black, tagged across the cinderblock.

And, of course, the Swordmaster, turning back to me with a look of pure rage on his face.

All in white, from head to toe, the Swordmaster stands in the center of the dojo, looking much taller than I remember from his earlier visits. His shoulders seem impossibly wide, draped in a kimono top that seems to glitter as he turns. At the waist he wears white hakama pants, etched with pleats and shimmering like a mound of newly fallen snow. In Aikido, only the highest-level masters wear all white, the color of both purity and death in Japanese culture. His face is twisting and his eyes burn with an ancient rage.

Without thinking about it, I arrange myself into the formal *seiza* kneeling posture to face him, ready to make my case.

When he showed up late at night to make me practice earlier in the week, the Swordmaster barely spoke, just barking quick commands in Japanese. Now half-awake and still stunned by what I've just witnessed, the only Japanese word I can remember is *"gomen nasai"* – "excuse me." Not much help in trying to tell him that we need his power to fighter the big demon up the hall.

Without seeming to take a step, the Swordmaster is suddenly right in front of me, the overwhelming whiteness of his robes filling my field of vision even as his eyes seem to burn black and red. His beard and hair are now completely colorless, but his eyebrows lie stark and sooty against his sallow skin. What looks like sweat gives his face another kind of shimmer.

"Excuse me..."

The words are barely out when my mind is assaulted with images from the past few days, shards of Kappa and Papa Legba and Angra Mainyu reflected back in the Swordmaster's coal-black eyes. He's inside my head, seeing what's been going on, and he understands. He's ready to join with the Tengu and the rest of us to fight.

Exhaustion and relief flood through my body, and I can't help but slump a bit in my kneeling position. Before I can self-correct, the blow lands with a thump on my shoulder. The sub-urito wooden sword is back in the Demon Swordmaster's hand and he won't tolerate bad posture. The thwack hits with just a sting this time, barely a slap, more energizing than painful.

"Namakemono!"

The Swordmaster is calling me "lazybones," but I recognize that it's not an insult as much as a call to action.

We've got to get ready for a fight.

✳ ✳ ✳

I'm still rubbing at my shoulder where the Swordmaster hit me when Shai pushes his way into the dojo, his hair wild and clothes all rumpled.

"Karate girl, we need to do something, now! These… creatures seem to be getting stronger. Mine are staying all night bothering me now, can't you tell?"

"It's Aikido, not Karate." I can't help myself, even in a state of shock after the evening's events.

Shai's eyes are bloodshot and big bags have opened up under his eyes.

"Judo, Jujitsu, Hapkido, whatever! I need help here, lady!"

"Did you say creatures, like with an 's'? Do you have more than one now?"

"Yes, at least two or three! The Golem spent last night fighting with some kind of thing with many heads that smelled like a stable."

"What are you talking about? That sounds like something new. That's all we need, more demons in this building. What was it?"

"I'm not really sure, I couldn't get a good look at it. But something about it reminded me of a story my grandmother used to tell about a monster in Hungary, a kind of dragon man."

"Oh, interesting. Do you have anything of your grandmother's in the space?"

Shai shucks off his shoes and sprints toward the couch, where he collapses. He grabs at the cup of cold tea I left earlier and gulps it down.

"Actually, I have my grandmother's *mezuzah* on my office door. She brought it from the old country. Do these things get in through objects?"

"Mezu-what?"

"It's a thing we put on the door with a verse from the Torah in it...Never mind. It's a religious thing we do Didn't you see the one on the first floor? By the door frame with some Hebrew letters on it?"

"Right. Well, if you have something with those old memories in it, that may be causing the dragon demon to appear."

"So do these demons get in through physical things like the *mezuzah*?"

"That's what we're trying to figure out. But it seems everyone who is infested has something with some kind of ... stuff from their culture, either in their heads or in something physical. Something old and from the old country like your mezuzah. Most of them are coming from our minds but they could be sneaking in through other portals. It's all very confusing and makes no sense at all. We might all be going nuts because of the asbestos in the walls or some fumes from the old boiler or something. Especially the guy down the hall who started this whole thing."

"Fumes? I run a clean facility here, lady. This place was inspected and cleaned out years ago when we bought the building. Yes, there's some asbestos here and there, but no magical vapors that make people see golems and dragons!"

"Okay, okay. I wasn't accusing you of anything. But it is weird that these creatures all turned up at the same time and that they seem to be hanging around more since the storm closed off the building."

"Why do you think these things are staying longer now? I can't get anything done and this has to stop."

"I'm not really sure, but from what I can figure out, a door keeps being opened. Or maybe it's being left open. The door opens, and these demons come in."

"A door from where to where? Is it a real door, like that?" Shai gestures toward the dojo entrance.

"No, I'm thinking it's at the cellular level. Or the neural pathway level or some physics stuff I don't really understand."

"We don't need to understand it, Taekwondo Girl. We need to stop it. Any progress with that crazy sword guy who hits you with a stick? Was that him I saw running down the hall just now?"

"Actually, the Swordmaster is on our team, I think. He's ready to help us get together and take the building back. We're ready to take the next step."

Now if we could only figure out what the next step is supposed to be.

❊ ❊ ❊

"So tell me again what happened when that bird thing tried to bite you, Cherry."

"It wasn't really a bird – more like a bird-demon."

Everyone's gathered in the Aikido dojo this time, one disheveled figure after another following Shai up the stairs to my space as weak morning light floods the building. We're spread out around the lounge, talking at the same time. My head hurts from the racket and I'm ready to explode. Last night was one demon visit after another until the sun came up.

Shai won't wait his turn.

"Whatever! Now these things are starting to get a bit rough with all of us, right? Emma got her arm slashed by the Clam Monster."

Emma looks tired but her voice is as loud as ever.

"It was an accident! He didn't mean it and he was very sorry afterward. I blame myself, really. I was the one reading the Chinese classics to expand my cultural horizons and brought him to life here. He's not happy at all in this cold weather, by the way. He's a tropical monster."

"Right, whatever," Shai waves his arms in dismay. "And the one-legged guy's been acting up in the hallways, punching people out!"

Barata shrugs and rolls his eyes, one of them all bloodshot in a greenish socket.

"I snuck up on him, so it isn't totally his fault."

"He kicked you right in the face!"

"I should have done *esquiva* – moved my head out of the way. It's really my fault for being so slow and sluggish. His name is Saci, by the way. I called my mom back home and she told me my grandma used to tell me stories about him. He's kind of a prankster in Brazil but he's only been a little annoying so far."

"Enablers, all of you!"

A new voice from the doorway, unexpectedly booming. Jean-Baptiste's so angry he shakes off his puffy coat. I've never seen him without it and he looks like a newborn chick, gangly and scrawny even covered in layers of thermal underwear. Nothing baby-like about his frustration right now, however.

"I won't hear any more excuses for these monsters! Just because they're from your own culture doesn't mean they should be cutting us up and smacking us. That samurai demon beats you up for real, right Cherry? I've seen the bruises."

"Well, he's not strictly a samurai. Samurai were like the palace guard for Japanese noblemen. This guy's more like strict sensei, or teacher. In the samurai tradition, of course."

"Enough! For a small guy, Jean-Baptiste can generate an

impressive shout. He slams his fist on the table then sits back for a few seconds as we all recover from the shock.

Brah is the first to stir, opening his eyes as he wakes from what looks like a relaxing nap.

"My brother, you've got to relax. You're releasing all kinds of toxins into your system right now. I'm worried about you."

Something about Brah's gentle tone and crumpled face seems to drain the tension out of the room. Jean-Baptiste reaches for his coat and burrows back in.

Barata starts talking as Shai collapses into a sprawl on a chair.

"OK, no more judgments. Let's just get back to the story of how Cherry survived that killer bird-man and then the snake-beast. The big bird was about to bite your head off, right? Then he disappeared. What exactly happened to scare him away?"

"I don't really remember. It was just really sudden. Happened with a cracking noise…wait – it was the power! The storm was really going nuts outside and the wind was screaming – the power went out and the bird-man was gone. I was this close to a serious injury but the power went out."

Jean-Baptiste shifts forward, pulling the attention of everyone in the room.

"Power! We've all seen the creatures appear and disappear, almost like someone's flicking a switch. Makes sense that they need Dar's machine on to appear and take physical form. If we can somehow shut the power off, maybe we can stop this madness."

Barata snorts. "That guy's some kind of genius hacker dude. I'm sure he's got backup generators and stuff. He'll just figure out how to get the power on again and let our creatures run wild until they kill us or we leave him alone. We should never have bought that story about 'alternative energy' in the first place. What do you think, JB?"

Jean-Baptiste pops up his jacket hood and seems to retreat into himself. We all sit back and wait. If I'm the brawn of the operation and Brah's the heart, JB is definitely the brains.

"We just need the power off long enough to get our guys into position to go after Dar's demons later tonight. Should be a fair fight and then we can shut off his tech for good. I'm ready to see the last of Papa Legba."

Shai perks right up. "I know where the main breaker box is – let's go at midnight. We're ready to try this again."

❋ ❋ ❋

Our breath trails us in wispy white puffs in the frigid stairwell as Jean-Baptiste and I climb our way down to his space. He's agreed to meditate with me for a bit in preparation for our big night but insisted that we do it in his heated office. I'm the one who's supposed to be in shape, but Jean-Baptiste is the one who can talk and stair-climb at the same time.

"I've been thinking about all of this. These monsters are all forms of the same thing, some kind of darkness and fear in us. We each shape that darkness in a different way and it's linked somehow to our past and our consciousness and our individual cultures."

Pulling the icy air into my lungs, I squeeze out a reply.

"How can a clam monster and a golem be the same thing?"

"Think about it – what scares you the most? Like in the real world. Climate change? Volcanoes? Disappointing your parents? Vampires?"

"Nothing from mythology, really. My mom was killed by a gangbanger six years ago and I haven't really been scared of anything since. Angry, yes. Scared, no."

We pause on the third-floor landing, then both edge around the corner to peer at the wasteland of broken furniture beyond. Jean-Baptiste turns and looks me directly in the eye.

"You're not afraid of anything. Wow, that scares me more than any demon I've seen this week. Run away from your fear and it turns into a soul-destroying rage. Does that sound familiar? Your sensei told me that a few years ago."

All of a sudden tears are pooling in my eyes and I take a few steps away from JB into the dusty chaos beyond the lobby. This is the floor where the city police practice urban assault tactics using paintball guns, and all the doors are off. Around me are tipped-over file cabinets, broken chairs, office dividers ripped into shreds. Paint smears streak the walls with neon red and orange like the blood of some dying technicolor beast.

Everywhere I look I see the destruction inside of me caused by my anger and pain. And fear. Yes, fear.

"Ok, I get it. Just stop talking, OK?"

Both silent, we watch scraps of paper on the floor shudder in an icy draft. My tears puddle below my eyes, then fall in streams across my cheeks. I stand there until the tears stop and then head back for the stairs again. Jean-Baptiste puts his hand on my shoulder for a few seconds, and we walk together toward the warmth.

* * *

Down I go, my face pushed into the cold vinyl. Then, as I struggle to get up, an arm goes straight into my face to lift my chin and I'm thrown backward with incredible force, my hand slapping the mat with a stinging thwack. The fall is so hard this time that the wind gets knocked out of me a bit and my head is microns from hitting the ground. Microns from concussion, brain damage, death.

Up again, to get smashed forward, then back again. And again. And one more time.

This class is taking forever, and Ellie Sempai is showing me no mercy. Only she and Quan showed up for the afternoon free practice, a time for dojo members to get ready for tests and try out new moves. Morning classes were canceled due to the storm but these two dug themselve out to get to the dojo. Lucky me.

As uchideshi, I have to practice in every class, and I can

really use the test preparation. Quan is looking ahead to black belt next year. Ellie may go for her third-degree back belt. I'm not even a second kyu in Aikido yet, two ranks before black belt. Probably two years before Sensei lets me test. But I'm certainly good enough to take the falls for other people's tests, and Ellie Sempai is letting loose today.

Now it's Quan's turn. My hand comes down with all the force I can muster in a shomen attack, meant to have the same angle and power as an overhead sword cut. A week with the demon Swordmaster has sharpened my shomen to something fast and mighty. Quan quickly side-steps, then times his downward counter-strike so that the power of my attack sends me into an abrupt sprawl, face-first, to the mat. My forearm stretches out to slap just in time, sending pins and needles up my arm with the shock. Ugh. Remind me not to attack harder than I want to fall down. The secret of Aikido is that you use an opponent's force against them, so don't hit harder than you want to hit the ground.

Back up again, I strike at Quan again... another trip to the floor. I can't seem to dial back my intensity to strike at a normal speed, but my body isn't ready for the crushing falls that result. Bit by bit, I realize that the crushing falls are where the energy can come from. Ten more minutes of hard Aikido practice, followed by final stretches and bows. Afterward, we gather at the edge of the mat where I've assembled the cleaning tools. Saturday afternoon is the designated intensive clean-up time. Brooms, rags, mops, buckets and dusters sit in a heap, outnumbering us by a lot.

Too much cleaning, not enough people. It's going to be a long session of *samu*, or mindful work. I should have lined the mops and stuff up more mindfully, but I was too tired to care. The dirty cups and plates from the earlier session with tea and snacks are also piled in a heap on the table in the lounge, ready for washing when I've got a few minutes.

Ellie Sempai glances at the messy pile of cleaning tools and glances back at me with disapproval. No need to say anything. She reaches for a broom – and the broom rolls away across the floor. I snap awake a bit. Ellie was reaching over from the mat for the broom, and the handle was still inches from her fingers when it moved.

It moved. It moved itself.

Tired or not, I know I saw the broom roll itself away. A sudden gust of wind? Kappa? Another demon? I sniff the air and all I get are the building's usual burnt gunpowder and moldy furniture smells. No swamp, no low tide, no dead fish behind the fridge. No minty Swordmaster fumes. No demons in here, at least. Who else would play such a silly prank?

Ellie mutters a bit, bows as she steps off the mat, leans over and reaches for the broom again.

This time, the broom rolls a few inches – then lifts itself off the floor, angles back and swings itself forward to whack Ellie on the side of the head.

The hollow thud echoes off the dojo walls, and Quan and I both gasp. He's been watching too, it seems, and he gives me a wondering look. I shrug and he grimaces a bit. Ellie staggers back, taking a few steps to the wall. Her face is blank but her eyes are focused, a look I recognize from when Sensei turns on the pressure in class. It wasn't that hard a hit, but she's trying to figure out what's going on.

Before Ellie can move, Quan springs from a crouch at the edge of the mat and grabs a rag hanging off a bucket, only to have the rag pull itself out of his hand, fling itself at his head and then crawl across his face like a clinging octopus. Seconds later, the bucket heaves itself off the floor, flies into the air and slams itself down on Quan's cloth-covered head.

Now there's movement all over the dojo and I can't take it all in. Teacups are clattering across the table. The clock on the wall is spinning. Shapes and colors whirl across the glass of the mirror used in sword practice. New-student forms snake their way out of the file cabinet and swirl together in a rustling tornado of paper. The brooms and mops are the most aggressive, bobbing in the air just out of reach and swinging forward to thwack me and Ellie every few seconds on our heads and shoulders. I shrink back to the other end of the mat, but the cleaning tools follow me.

Thunk.

Ellie gets it in the head again from a broom.

Plink!

That's my elbow, being rapped by a mop handle. Didn't sound like much, but I drop to the mat and howl in pain. Right on the funny bone.

Quan is still struggling with the bucket on his head as rags pelt his arms and a second bucket rams him behind the knee, trying to take him down.

I scramble for the edge of the mat on my hands and knees only to see something sharp and threatening zoom across the floor to slash at my fingers. The metal dustpan is probably the only thing out here that could do some real damage, and that slicing motion doesn't look friendly.

I fake to the right and the dustpan streaks across the floor to scrape at my knuckles. Fake the left, and it spanks me briskly across the forearm. That really stings! Quan is still thrashing nearby and Ellie is in a defensive crouch against the wall, parrying blows from brooms and a particularly nasty sponge mop. She's grabbed a wooden sword from the weapons rack and is holding her own.

"*YAMEH!*"

All of the cleaning tools and tea things seem to freeze in mid-air, shivering in the breeze that rockets through the dojo with the open door.

"*YAME!*"

The demon Swordmaster shouts again, and his voice seems to cut the strings holding the objects aloft. With a crashing, clattering thump, everything drops to the ground – brooms, teacups, mops, rags and bucket.

The Swordmaster strides into the center of the dojo, bows to the kamiza and stands there for a few seconds. I turn my head and notice that both Quan and Ellie are transfixed, staring at the middle of the room.

I can't help myself.

"Do you see him? He's right there! The Swordmaster!"

Ellie and Quan both nod slightly, then slump to the ground at the same time, as if the strings holding them standing upright have been cut. They are sprawled in a heap, eyes closed.

The Swordmaster turns to me.

"*YAMEH!*"

Images flood my head of the other demons, the other tenants gathered in the dojo. He's yelling "stop!" – is he asking me to stop our plan to fight the monster down the hall?

More images this time, of just the demons, moving together in a silent horde toward the end of the building.

We humans need to stop. We need to stay out of it. Our energy is fueling the monster.

The Swordmaster is so sure, so angry. But I can help but ask him a question, projecting the words toward him in mind.

But isn't our energy also fueling you demons who are going to fight the monster?

His face, already clouded, glows with rage at my disrespect. The brooms and buckets on the floor start to clatter and shimmy, woken up again by the Swordmaster's anger.

With a swirl of kimono and an explosion of sparks, the Swordmaster sweeps from the room.

The brooms and mops give a final death rattle then lie still.

Quan and Ellie open their eyes and sit up, both turning to me in confusion.

He's gone, but the Swordmaster's answer still rings in my head.

Aren't we humans important in this final fight?

Maybe.

✳ ✳ ✳

"The sky has never been this dark during the day the entire time I've been in this town...which is like a hundred years."

Ellie snorts a bit. She and Quan haven't asked too many questions, just helped me gather up the cleaning stuff. We went through the motions of a total dojo scrubbing, but as soon as possible took a break for some tea. From the back of the cabinet I dug out a bag of rolled butter cookies in tiny packets, and now we're all munching and sipping green tea as snowflakes start spurting from an ashy black sky.

Not even the end of the day yet, and I feel like it's been weeks since I woke up after hitting my head on the wall in meditation.

"You guys better get home, this look like the big one."

Ellie, for once, doesn't argue, just sips her tea with a scrunched-up forehead. No stories about Japan, no words of wisdom.

"You need our help."

Quan's voice is strong and loud, and both Ellie and I jump a little. That's about as much as I've heard Quan say in the last three months that hasn't been an answer to a direct question. He's not asking a question now, just stating the facts.

We all take a few minutes to think, and the flakes outside start streaming past in blurry stripes as the wind picks up.

"Thanks, Quan, I do need help. But all of the people who live in the building now are getting together. We've been here all week and we know what needs to be done. I'm not alone."

Ellie shifts forward and gestures at the door.

"Sensei would want you to be safe, Cherry. You can come home with me right now. You'll be on your own here once this next storm gets going."

"As I said, I'm not alone. We've got it figured out and we're going to do something to solve this problem. All of us. JB and Emma and Barata and Brah and Shai. Those are the other people staying in the building right now and we're all working together."

Ellie and Quan give me questioning looks and Ellie stands

up, pointing to the roiling rivers of snow now streaming against the windows.

"Are you absolutely sure? I need to get Quan home right now."

As if on cue, the sky seems to get darker and the dojo seems to shiver with an unhealthy, shifting grayness. Squealing and roaring and squeaking fill the room as the snow squall batters the glass of the windows. The lamp on the shoe rack sputters and flickers out. Ellie walks over and flips the light switch for the whole dojo – nothing. The power has gone out.

No power, no real plan, a building full of crazy people, nasty demons and a great evil. And a Swordmaster-general who wants his human soldiers to sit out the battle.

Am I really ready for this?

A sharp cracking sound at the door makes us all jump.

"Cherry! I need you!"

Dar steps into the dojo, his parka open and his face gleaming with sweat. He takes in the group then settles himself a bit.

"Oh. Sorry about scaring you. I just need a quick chat with Cherry."

Ellie glares at Dar for what seems like an hour and shifts an exasperated gaze toward me.

"I'm going to regret this, Cherry, but you are an adult and Sensei told me that you were ready for this…experience. I can't force you to leave and I've got to get out of here. Good luck. I really can't waste time with the snow falling this fast."

Her face shifts into a resigned mask. Quan shakes his head, looking all of a sudden more like my dad than a high-school kid. Quan and Ellie change out of their gis, gather their bags and hustle out to the parking lot, trying to get home in a brief break in the storm before the roads get worse.

Dar, his frantic energy seemingly spent, collapses onto the couch and grabs the last cookie. We finish the rest of the tea as the sound of Ellie's car briefly flares above the wind, then fades into the general clatter. That was probably the last car in the lot.

We're all alone here.
Now what?

* * *

"I want to be honest with you: I'm afraid I've unleashed Angra Mainyu – it's kind of the spirit of destruction from my ancestral culture. We don't think of it as the devil or something real, it's more like a force of evil that coexists with all that's good in the world. There's also something that for some reason it's taken the form of one of your Japanese demons – what is that bird thing? Anyway, it's kind of a big deal."

I can't help but snort at what Dar's telling me, although he does look pretty scared. Is he trying to tell me he's unleashed the forces of evil in our building? Like, I already know. Shouldn't he have known that his device was going to cause some kind of trouble? And he's decided to do this the week that Sensei's away and there's a big storm and I have to deal with this by myself? Or by myself with just the help of all these crazies in the building?

Dar sees the frustration on my face and fills the silence with some noisy tea-slurping. I decide to answer his question before chewing him out about his reckless tinkering.

"Bird thing – do you mean the bird-slash-homicidal maniac that was in my space a few nights ago? It's Japanese and it's called a Karasu Tengu and it's supposed to signal that war is coming. That Tengu is part of the plan... our plan. All of us living in the building know about your recklessness and your monster and we've got a plan to put it back where it belongs."

Dar jumps up, sending a flurry of cookie wrappers to the floor. His face is twisted with rage.

"What are you talking about? What are you guys planning? How many people are living here, actually?"

"There are about five... six of us and we've all been noticing bizarre stuff in the last week or so. We know there's something serious happening in your space. We saw the burning from the parking lot yesterday. Whatever 'collective unconscious' insanity you've got going on in there has got to stop." Dar is looming over me, but I'm calm and centered for a change. Thank you, Demon Swordmaster.

"Stop? Wait a minute…now? You don't know what you're talking about. You'll ruin everything. And we're talking about Angra Mainyu, the god of destruction. A bunch of losers who live in a busted-up factory aren't going to stop it."

Dar face is shiny with sweat, etching the strong lines of his features. His eyes are practically black with anger. Did he just call me a loser? I push back the anger that is rising in me and find myself reaching for Dar's hand as he sits and edges toward me on the couch. He doesn't seem to notice as his voice rises. But his hand stays in mine.

"You can't do this now, not yet! I can control Angra Mainyu, really I can. We're working it out day by day but it's getting more… cooperative. I've got it under control! I was just getting a bit frustrated with the whole situation."

My anger floods back and I can't help but twist Dar's hand a little in the beginnings of an Aikido joint lock.

"Under control? All the demons in the building are talking about the end of the world. We humans feel the bad energy growing every day. We can't sleep anymore, we can't work – we can't even close our eyes without demons popping out of the walls and physically attacking us. We also don't have anywhere else to go – we're losers, right? How can you say this is under control?"

Dar twists his hand out of my grip, jumps up and heads toward the window. "Did you say 'demons'? Like ghosts? Are you all going insane? Wow, I can't believe this is happening again."

Again?

I get up and stand next to him at the window. A few miles off, the towers of the university stamp their gray outlines on the skyline, blurred by at the edges the blowing snow.

Dar points to the towers, his voice low and angry.

224

"They were all such mediocrities over there, those fools who stopped my research. They didn't mind their business and they didn't trust the technology. You all in this building were supposed to be different. You're all breaking the law – none of you have real jobs or careers. Why can't you just stay in your rooms and stay out of my research? It really has nothing to do with you."

He's in my face now, his skin nearly glowing with rage and his features distorted. Seeing him like this, knowing that he thinks of me and my friends as disposable losers, I feel my respect for him shift to scorn. He stands in front of me now as an arrogant, self-absorbed nut job. In desperation I shove the backs of my hands toward him, the parts that are striped with bruises and hash-marked with bandaged cuts from the Swordmaster's painful "lessons."

"You expect us to live like this until your research pans out? Have you seen my hands? They bleed all over everything, and they hurt like hell. This is your research in action, and it hurts. The woman down the hall has a big gash from her demon. Another guy has a black eye, and it's getting more intense every day. It's got to stop, and if you're not going stop it, we will."

Dar moves closer to me, staring into my eyes. A smell of burnt meat and singed plastic wafts up from his body, tensed to the breaking point. He stares at me for what seems like an hour and reaches out. For a second there I think it might be the beginning of a hug. Instead, he shoves sharply at my shoulder and brushes past me. He stomps into his shoes and slams his way out the open door and into the hall. I walk to the door and watch him stalk down the hallway into the darkness. Looking after him for longer than I should, I see a hellish light flare from his end of the building. Then an electric crackling echoes through the darkness in several short bursts – it almost could be a laugh of some kind.

I feel like I should cry, or at least do some meditation to sit with my pain. Instead, I rub at my shoulder when Dar shoved me.

Time to forget the talking and get ready for battle.

✳ ✳ ✳

"Stop counting out loud! I can hear you!"

"Hai, Sensei!"

I know the Japanese response will annoy Emma, and sure enough, she swings a hand-blade at me from across the room at slow-mo Tai Chi speed. I stick out my tongue at her, and she stomps the mat.

"Quiet!"

Barata swings his leg out from his handstand, spins in place and collapses to the mat in a heap. He lies there groaning.

"What is going on around here?"

We're all wasting time in the dojo as the afternoon fades away and dies, with no demons and no action in sight.

Outside, the snowstorms seems to have taken a break for a coughing fit, with brief flurries and wind gusts chattering out of a poisonous green-black sky. There's just enough ambient light to practice in the Aikido dojo, but the three of us look like reanimated corpses in the sickly glow. Hours have passed since our meeting, but it seems like weeks. We're all ready for a big battle, but neither side has shown up yet, it seems.

I'm still a bit warm from my last climb up the stairs a half-hour or so ago. One the second floor, Jean-Baptiste was entering all our demons and their attributes into a spreadsheet. On the ground floor, Shai was searching through volumes of some kind of religious reference book to find a way to power up the Golem on demand. The book has been digitized but Shai insists that he's more efficient looking it up by hand.

Brah is down in the basement hunting for "psychic energy conduits" or something like that. We all listened to him talk about horror movie plots for a while, then just started nodding and urged him to get started. The trip he and Shai took to the basement earlier was a bust: Dar's energy source is the rooftop transmitter, not the main breaker, they concluded.

Barata, Emma and I couldn't think of anything to do to get ready, as our demons are missing in action. There's nothing but a puddle of spit on Emma's floor where the Clam Monster used to be. Saci, Barata's one-legged Brazilian demon, seems to be staying just out of sight around corners and in doorways. Here in the dojo, I can smell Kappa, but he's staying under the futon for now and won't respond when I call out for him.

In frustration, we all decided to hang out in the dojo and practice our martial arts for a while. I'm doing cuts with the wooden sword, hoping the Swordmaster is watching somehow and approving. Sure enough, when I let my cut wobble a bit just now I felt a light slap across my shoulder. He's here, somewhere, disapproving of my form. He just won't show up in full and get us going.

Barata springs up from his sprawl across the mat and lets out a yelp.

"The roof! We should go up there now before the storm gets bad again. Maybe the clouds block Dar's power transmission somehow and this is our chance to get in there. All of the demons seem to go into hiding during the worst of storms, don't they? If we go up there, maybe we can pull out the plug or something without that big nasty beast taking us down. The roof is where we need to be, not fooling around in here."

Emma and I freeze in mid-kata and look toward the windows. The shaky little flurries have turned into a gale again out there, with a steady white torrent rolling across the glass and blackness beyond. Whatever sun there was is gone, whatever break in the storm we saw earlier has ended. It's a nightmare out there. And Barata wants us to go out on the roof?

"Too late, buddy."

Emma shivers and hugs herself, turning away from the window.

"I've got a better idea: We could just stay in here and wait for something to happen. The demons might even be fighting right now and we don't know it. It's not about us humans, children. Remember what the Swordmaster told Cherry?"

Barata shakes his head. He grabs a coat from a shelf then walks over the shoe rack and slips on a big pair of dojo sandals. Putting on shoes means he must be thinking of something drastic.

"It's not that bad yet. We have to do something. Cherry's not even sure the Swordmaster understands her completely. We need to do what we can to stop this thing."

His voice hasn't even trailed off before he is at the door, fumbling with the zipper of Sensei's spare winter coat. I'm next, pulling another puffy jacket from a cabinet below Sensei's desk.

"Whatever, I can't let you two uncoordinated clowns fall off the roof without a witness." Emma's coat is already on and she's rifling through the shoes on the rack, looking for something sturdier than her Tai Chi slippers. Thankfully, Sensei brought all her old boots to the dojo last week so I could find a pair that fit in case of deep snow.

Emma leads us out into the hallway, fitfully lit from the lobby and so cold it makes my face hurt. It takes us all a minute to get used to moving quietly in the boots, but we've all been trained in stealth in our arts, so before long we're passing Dar's door like a posse of ghosts. No shuffling, no talking, nothing but a few meaningful glances between us as our eyes adjust to the dimness.

We're past Dar's lab now, tiptoeing through the huge space beyond that was once a photographer's studio. At the end of that room, a door on the right takes us to the far stairwell and the hatch to the roof. As we get closer, Emma starts coughing and gagging. She turns to me and hisses.

"What is that smell? Did you one of you eat a bunch of rotten eggs?"

Barata jumps and wipes at his neck. He doesn't bother whispering.

"Something just leaked on me! It was warm!"

Well, it looks like not all of the demons are resting up for the big battle. Scuttling out of the shadows, Kappa launches himself right at Emma's leg.

"Get off me, you little …. What the hell is wrong with that thing?"

"Kappa likes legs, likes climbing up people's legs… We don't have time to go into the whole thing right now, do we? He's been helping me out so I don't think he'll cause any trouble."

As if he's been listening and understands the English, Kappa starts pawing at Emma's exposed ankle, as if to crawl up her pant leg.

"What the hell is it doing?"

Emma launches a well-aimed kick. As her foot hits, Kappa curls himself up into a armadillo-like ball and rolls over toward me. I dribble him a bit like a soccer ball with my feet, which he doesn't seem to mind, then I pass him to Barata, who launches him airborne with a flip of his sandaled foot. Kappa lands with splat, then uncurls and totters onto his legs with a smirk at Emma.

"Fun time! Can I play with you?"

"Behave yourself!" I hiss in Japanese. Kappa responses with a wet-sounding fart. Great, we're trying to sneak around to fight the bad guys and the noisiest and least dangerous demon of them all decides to tag along.

* * *

"News alert, the door's stuck."

Emma has taken the lead as we edge into the top landing of the stairwell, probably to get as far away as possible from Kappa and his smells. She's settled into a deep Tai Chi stance, knees bent, and is pushing at the door to the roof. Barata steps up to join her. There's not enough room for all three of us, so I stand back with Kappa and offer words of advice.

"Use your center. Engage your lower body, that's where the biggest muscles are. Don't think about your arms. In Aikido we always try to engage the center to generate power."

Barata and Emma give me withering looks. Right, all martial arts use those principles, I guess.

With both of them pushing with what I have to admit is perfect form, the rusting door squeals and stutters forward a few inches, then a few more. It's finally enough for us all of to squeeze through, one at a time. Kappa trails behind, rubbing against the wall and hocking globs of spit at our backs.

A few steps up a staircase in near darkness and we come to another door that opens with only a slight shove, releasing a mini-avalanche of snow but little wind. We've lucked into another break in the storm. At last we are on the roof, five and half stories above the city. Around us street lights flicker on as the last pinkish light of day throbs at the horizon like a low-grade fever. Snow is falling gently in tattered shreds at the border where the light shades into darkness. The wind has calmed for the moment and the city shimmers gently around us.

Flakes barely cover the whitish gravel and stretches of roofing tar up here, with the heat of building likely melting what doesn't blow away in the wind. Across the roof, tarps are nailed down in patches, perhaps to cover holes. The power transmitter towers above us at the right, its energy field almost palpable in the freezing air. Beyond the tower I glimpse a flash of white, so intense and electric that it makes the fresh snow look dark gray.

"Over there! Kappa, get your paws off me and look over there."

Sticky hands detach from my pant leg and Kappa's beak swings to the right.

"I see it. Not pretty. That lady is always trying to freeze you up."

"Go over there and see if you can talk to her."

Barata and Emma are behind me now, sensing that what's waiting for us up here isn't quite natural. I'm the demon expert now, I guess.

The three of us squeeze together and try to keep ourselves

out of sight against the stairwell wall. Another flash of white, this time at the edge of the roof on the other side of the tower. Kappa drops to the ground and takes his turtle form to crawl forward, then scuttles back toward us.

"Dangerous! I'm scared!" he hisses, then evaporates in a cloud of green mist. Gone, completely gone, even his stink whipped away by the wind. So much for our loyal demon soldier.

Barata turns toward me, then to Emma.

"I'll go check it out."

Again, like we're some kind of twins, Emma and I talk at the same time.

"No, I'll go." We stare each other down for a bit as Barata shrugs and settles into a squat against the wall. No macho hero, this guy. He's going to let me and Emma fight it out.

Before we can figure out who is the toughest Asian-American up on the roof, a cloud of white froth seems to pour out of sky onto a spot right in front of us, taking a familiar form.

"That's her!" Emma says, stepping back into a defensive stance.

The creature's kimono sparkles like fresh snow, setting off inky hair in impossibly long cascades. Her eyes burn black, if that's possible in the real world. Lips are a red blossom, cheekbones etched with a razor.

Yuki-Onna, the demon snow woman, has decided to drop in on our little party.

Emma flashes me a look – she's seen this demon but only from afar. For some reason, the snow woman seems to piss her off, and Emma's face twists up into rage. For me, each swirl of the crystalline-white kimono fills me with terror; the demon's rosy lips are hiding huge fangs, I'm sure of it. But it is Barata who has the strongest reaction to our visitor.

"Wow!" He stumbles forward from a crouch, skidding a bit on the icy gravel.

"She's so beautiful!"

He's still quite close to us, so Emma and I get a full view

of Barata's face, open and wondering and completely in thrall to the snow-witch.

I'm so terrified right now that I can't even turn my head. Gusts of icy breath that smells of death billow across the rooftop from the demon's fanged mouth. I try to make myself smaller, even as a tiny, hidden part of my brain tries to shake the terror loose. I've seen this creature before, and she's no danger to me. Somehow, this time she has infected me with fear and frozen me into inaction. Emma, I suspect, is paralyzed as well – by anger instead of fear. This demon is tapping into our thoughts and amplifying our emotions, rendering us helpless. But why? And what's going on with Barata?

Even as I ask the question, I see the answer. Barata, his face wreathed with a dopey smile, is now stumbling across the gravel toward the swirling evil in white. It's only twenty feet or so before the roof ends, and the demon is drifting back toward the edge slowly and deliberately. Barata is making progress, walking more assuredly now on the hem of the white kimono, inch by inch, stepping toward his doom. The demon's leering smile is for Emma and me, I'm sure of it. She's gloating about her power over Barata as she lures him ever closer to the edge. Her smile must be visible only to us, because it splits open her ashy skull to reveal a nest of hissing snakes and worms behind her lips.

Barata doesn't seem to notice the ghastly sight and takes a few more steps – he can't be more than a foot or two from a hundred-foot fall to a certain death on the pavement below.

My voice won't come out of my fear-locked throat, and I can't seem to move. Emma is equally helpless, hunched over and pounding the roof with her fists. Barata takes another step with his arms outstretched, reaching for the silvery vision just out of reach. He's still in a trance but his feet seem to be hesitating – we can save him if we act soon. Another two steps and he'll be dead.

The voice of the Swordmaster booms in my head.

"*Yame!*" Stop!

It's as if someone speeds up the video – Emma and I both leap up, sprinting forward and reaching out to grab at Barata's coat,

Yuki-Onna thrashes and howls above. A claw rakes across my face before I can react and Emma claps a hand to her wrist as blood splashes all over the back of one of her gloves. But we both get a grip on the coat and manage to yank Barata away from the edge just in time – he sprawls back on to the roof even as his foot steps out into empty air. The demon's kimono is a maelstrom of snow and wind above us now and we're pelted by a barrage of hail that pricks our skin like needles.

Barata's face looks like it's been in the freezer too long – ice crystals spangle his eyelashes and the straggly beard he's been sporting the last few days and his skin is bluish under his usual brown complexion. His feet are still dangling off the building as I pat at his cheeks and blow warm breath into his open mouth.

"Wake up, Barata! You need to snap out of this right now!"

Emma leans over to help, bellowing at the top of her lungs.

"Barata, time to wake up! Rise and shine, we have to get out of here!"

I stand up and we each take one of Barata's arms to drag him to the roof hatch. The storm seems to have shaken itself awake during our struggle with Yuki-Onna and flakes begin to blow into my eyes and mouth. A moaning like a dying animal starts to rise around us as wind rockets across the roof and past the building. Emma and I stagger a bit as the wind hits us.

"We need to get inside, right now."

Emma yanks hard on Barata's arm just as he starts to stir, muttering as his eyes open and his legs start to thrash.

"*Itai...itai!*" His voice is strong and his accent in Japanese is surprisingly good. Emma swats away his kicking legs and reaches again for his upper arms, all business.

"That's not English...What is he saying?"

"Sounds like 'It hurts' in Japanese. Maybe the snow demon

scratched him – see any blood?

"Wow, Cherry, look at this! That bitch."

Barata's glove has slipped off and his fingers underneath are stiff and dead-white, like a doll hand. The snow demon gave him frostbite, and from what I know about that from mountain-climbing videos, it looks pretty bad. He won't have much of a career in martial arts with no fingers.

"Now! We need to get him back inside now!"

CHAPTER TEN

Sunday and beyond

"**S**he may be a demon, but that lady is hot."

Emma and I have been taking turns rubbing Barata's arms and hands to warm him up, and I'm glad it's my turn. A pinch can only help, right?

"Ouch! What are you doing?" Barata's face is back to its normal caramel color and he pushes himself up to seated position on the landing. Emma and I are still puffing a bit from dragging his body across the roof, through the door and into the stairwell. Plumes of snow are pushing through the crack we left in the door to the outside, and the roar of the storm echoes through the space. Now that I'm sure Barata will live, I stand up and pull the door shut.

Emma's had enough.

"You're lucky to be alive, fool. That hottie tried to get you to step off the roof – like falling five stories where you die when you hit the concrete down below. I can't believe how shallow you men are!"

Emma's the only one who can talk right now: I'm fighting back tears of relief that Barata is alive. I busy myself rubbing his frozen hands and brushing the flakes off his jacket. Then I start rubbing my own hands and brushing the snow off my own jacket when I realize that's a weird thing to do to someone you hardly know. At least Barata's hands now have some color in them again.

Emma picks up one hand and gives it a gentle slap. "Great, you're alive and it looks like your hands just got chilled a little. But I regret to inform you that your romance with the snow demon ruined our plan to shut down the tower, loverboy."

"How is that my fault? She's a demon! I couldn't help it!"

Emma snorts, and Barata himself doesn't look totally convinced. Emma and exchange looks, then grab Barata's arms and haul him to his feet. The trip back down the stairs and through the hallway is silent except for the shuffling of our boots and an occasional sneeze from Emma. No sound or light from Dar's space, only the faintest glow from the streetlights leaking from in the windows in the photo studio.

Moaning and creaking come from all sides as the building shudders in the storm. We make it past the dojo to the lobby, where a smell something like wet dog and ancient freezer puffs up from the stairwell with each gust. Barata shuffles over to the window and presses his face against the glass, peering up into the darkness.

"So maybe the storm is damping down the demon energy, even for that snow babe. Makes sense that she digs blizzards – that wind makes her hair look all swirly and stuff. But you guys were able to fight her on your own, so she's not at full power."

Now Barata is just baiting us, but he's got a point. The excitement of the roof battle seems to ebb away as the realization sinks in: No point in any big showdown right now. Our demons will be underpowered even as Dar's is underpowered. Emma and I exchange glances: She looks as drained as I feel.

"We're all tired and it looks like none of the other demons are around, so it makes sense to rest for a bit. No way I'm going back to that roof until the storm is over. I'm heading back to my space for a nap."

In the lobby light I see that Barata's face has collapsed into exhaustion. That demon encounter must have taken a lot of out him. I reach for his hand without thinking and hold it between my own, trying to warm it up some more. His face opens and his other arm encloses me. We stand there together for a long minute or two before Emma snorts and starts striding down the hall.

"Right, you guys rest, but don't take too long. I'll chill for about a half-hour then do some training. We can't be wasting time here, people."

She can't stop being competitive for a minute. Barata seems to rouse himself and follows her down the left hallway, muttering a muted good-bye. I watch them as they pass into the darkness, listening for the doors of their spaces opening and closing. Two slams follow. Nothing looms out of the dark, no sounds of struggle or surprise. I brace myself for something nasty when I open the dojo door, but nothing greets me but the screech of wind from outside and the occasional sound of a piece of falling ceiling plaster on the mat as the building sways. My eyes close almost as soon as I stretch out on the futon, before I can wriggle out of my outside clothes. I burrow into the sleeping bag and blankets and wait for the next battle.

❊ ❊ ❊

The rustle of a gi top. The snap of a sports bra from very close range.

The sounds are familiar and yet deeply strange.

My eyes ease open as I realize why those sounds are so close – they're coming from me. I'm standing half-dressed at the edge of the mat in the dojo, and I have no idea how I got there. It's like I'm watching myself from a distance going through my routine: Gi top on, gi pants cinched, my white belt looped behind me then tied into a flat knot at the front. Now my hakama – shaken open so the baggy pant-legs gape wide, then I step into it and start lacing up the straps. As I'm doing these familiar actions, I also feel like I'm watching myself from a distance.

Who is this Aikido robot who looks just like me? Is this

me or myself in some kind of dream? Slowly, I wake to the reality that I'm here, but something outside of me is controlling my every movement.

Completely dressed and ready for Aikido practice, I take in the scene.

The dojo interior is lit by a cool blue light as if it's underwater. My breath sends up puffs of vapor, but I can't feel the cold even though my forearms are bare below my gi sleeves and I'm not wearing socks, a hat or a scarf. My body feels warmed up and ready for practice, although I have no memory of stretching. A strong smell of burned plastic and fireworks fills my nose, along with the dead, stale stink like the back of a freezer so familiar from the building stairwells.

Outside, just visible below the highest window frame, a huge moon hangs over the city, the source of the blue light. No snow flurries, no lingering storm winds, no movement at all for miles, just the glow of the moon and some glints of reflection off fresh snow. The moonlight is so bright the city lies pale and helpless before it. Silence, total and eerie, both inside and out.

My attention snaps back to ... me... as I find myself on the edge of the mat, bowing in. First a bow to the kamiza and the picture of the founder of Aikido, then a bow the center of the mat, where my training partners would be. No one is there now, of course. I'm not quite in complete control, but my consciousness seems to have settled back into my body as I go through the familiar motions of breathing and stretching before Aikido class.

Under my hands, the mat surface feels smooth and a bit warm, which makes no sense at all since it's been like a slab of ice every day this week. And that's during the day, after I've run the heater for a bit. But my hands and bare feet find the surface comfortable. It even feels like I'm drawing strength from the floor beneath, sending energy through my legs and arms and out of the top of my head. I feel like I'm super-powered and ready for anything right now. Still no sound in the space but the slight swish of my cotton hakama against the vinyl. Now I find myself knee-walking forward to stop at dead-center, in front of the kamiza, as if class is about to begin.

As I start my bow, the mat erupts with movement on each side of me. There are at least half a dozen disturbances in the air along the center of the mat – almost as if there are lots of people bowing in to join the class. Or lots of enemies around me.

What kind of class is this, and who... what are these things practicing with me? Panic floods my brain for a brief instant. I feel the urge to jump up, sprint off the mat and get the hell out of here.

Then all my fear intensifies in an instant with a phrase that echoes in my brain, even if I don't quite hear it with my ears – "Time for randori!"

Randori, the multiple attack in Aikido, the ultimate test of your technique. Can you handle a group of attackers swarming you and attempting to take you down? Can you stay upright and keep the opponent off balance? I know how to do randori. I did this practice earlier in the week in Thierry's class. I've got this.

But who – or what – will be attacking me?

I stand and move to the absolute center of the mat. Around me are swirls and pulses of energy, but nothing or no one that I can see in any detail. Just blue light and movement. Terror, panic, fear – anxiety of all kinds rises up and chills me to the bone, even though the air against my face feels charged with an otherworldly warmth.

"Keep your center. Fear is not an option."

The voice in my head starts out sounding like Thierry, then Sensei, then my mom. With each word, a little of the panic subsides. Finally I'm ready to face the attackers. I still myself and let the energy flow up from the ground through my feet and into my body.

Ready to rumble.

At my left, a blurred outline rears up to twice my height, then takes shape into something familiar: white kimono, black hair, wormy twisting lips – and fangs.

It's Yuki-Onna again, and she's really angry this time. Her mouth gapes open and the worms and snakes writhe into full view. Her kimono whirls and unfolds to fill the entire dojo space with a raw, chilling mist. As the whitish spray hits me, I find my energy ebbing away; my legs don't obey me when I try to step back.

The fear surges back, but Sensei's words echo loud enough to push it away.

Keep your center.

Yuki-Onna hisses when she sees that I can move again. She draws her kimono tight to her body and her hair streams back like an oil spill on water. Her rage gathers into itself into a swirling, impossible attack on the diagonal – her outstretched claws are aimed right at the side of my head in a classic Aikido yokomen attack. Yokomen is meant to whack at the temples with a hand-blade moving at maximum speed. If a yokomen strike hits your head at the right spot, it can kill you. And that's if your attacker is human and doesn't have actual claws.

Yuki-Onna's yokomen is like a spiked throwing star, her blood-red talons outstretched as her arm swings at me like a whip. If she makes contact, she'll cut my head in half like a ripe watermelon hit by a katana.

I react before I can take in the outlandishness of the whole scenario: I'm being attacked by a demon using Aikido techniques in my own dojo. My Aikido instincts kick in and I whirl inward, toward the attack, a seemingly suicidal move. But instead of slashing me to ribbons, Yuki-Onna's claws whiz past my head as I move to the safe space inside of her strike. Then I swing my own arms around to hammer at her skull with my left elbow. She collapses inward, claws scrabbling at my head.

A sickening crunch, a spray of what feels like slush, and the white kimono floats to the mat, empty. My sleeves look wet, but the fabric of my gi still glows blue-white in the moonlight, not black with blood.

Only after I sink to my knees in shock do I realize that a stray talon has raked my forehead just above my eye. A red mist falls over my vision as the blood blends with sweat to flow into my eye socket. No time to take care of it now... another blurred spot near the back of the mat has taken form – a form that still horrifies me, even though the only emotion coming from the creature is regret. I wipe the blood off with my gi sleeve, roll myself up to standing and turn to face the horror.

Up, up, up toward the ceiling the shape rises, taking on its full, snakelike, hissing form. This is Rokurokubi, the long-necked demon who likes to scold people for not being religious enough. There's the familiar female-like head on the end of the 20-foot neck, but the sound coming from its mouth is more like a mash-up of a scream and a fire alarm this time. Topped by rag-like swaths of hair, the head whips around on the end of the neck and rockets toward me, the screaming reaching an unbearable pitch.

No time to think again, just move.

I find myself sprinting toward the beast this time at full speed, my bare feet skating across the mat's surface like it's made of glass. Before I can even blink, I'm a few yards from the demon's feet – or where its feet would be if it *had* feet. Like most Japanese ghosts I've read about, the long-neck demon seems to float a bit off the ground, nothing foot- or ankle-like below the kimono hem. Never mind, I've committed to this technique, so feet or no feet, I'm going in.

The creature's head on its snaky neck flies toward me as the torso rockets ahead at a slightly slower pace. Before I can decide if it's a really stupid move or not, I find myself diving at where the monster's knees would be, in a kind of sutemi waza, or sacrifice throw. The creature's head on its snaky neck flies above me – I'm hurling my own body at the demon's "legs," in the hopes I can take it down.

The screaming gets abruptly louder, and I clap my hands to my ears from my crouched-low position on the mat. Something like a bag of squirming eels or maggots passes over my shoulders and neck, making enough contact to make me feel like puking. I force myself to open my eyes and watch as the long-necked demon is launched into the air and catapults through the dojo window with an explosive screech. Broken glass and twisted metal shower onto the mat surface. A blast of air that stinks like rotting roadkill rolls over me, nearly bowling me over.

My eyes squeeze shut to block the flying shards, which rake across my face, shredding it.

Seconds later, I open my eyes to find the windows and wall back to normal, no cuts on my face. Whatever happened just now, it didn't really affect the real world of brick and mortar. But the shock and the sensation of that wormy, squirmy nightmare against my back lingers, and I fight to keep from screaming. My ears are also ringing from the demon's final screech. I stagger as I stand up, half-deaf and sick to my stomach, all of that calm power I felt earlier draining away. I can sense the cold now, too, and my face and arms ache like they've been dipped in liquid nitrogen. Yuki-Onna's dying embrace has chilled me to the core. All I want to do is crawl into my futon and hide.

It's got to be over, right? This randori was only two attackers, but I'm ready for it to be done.

No such luck.

A shimmer in the back corner of the mat catches my eye, then another in the front corner – wait, there are more swirls in the air to the left and right of the kamiza. Basically the entire mat area at about waist-level is going out of focus as globs the size of Kappa take shape all around me. Say what? All of those blobs aren't the size of Kappa, they *are* kappas. Not the goofy, farting little frog-beast I know, but some kind of snarling, snaggle-toothed version of Kappa with an evil glint in its eyes. Eyes as in dozens of eyes, as in a dozen or more of the nasty little beasts all shuffling toward me at surprising speed.

Don't lose your center.

My Aikido training kicks in again. With so many attackers at once, I can't afford to stay in the middle of the mat, surrounded by enemies. These little demons are fast and look like they'd love to chomp on my ankles, so a sprint won't do it. Without turning my head, I fling myself backward into a reverse roll, flipping my upper body around and diving into the mat into an elongated somersault. By sheer luck, my arms as I land hit a patch of mat free from a gibbering green frog-demon, but my feet slam into the face of one as I pike over into the fall.

Once again, the demons must have taken physical form because my feet landing in bad-kappa face feels just like stepping barefoot into a pile of dog poop: slimy, goopy and weirdly gelatinous. A stink not unlike a pile of poop forces its way into my nose and once again my ramen noodle dinner from last night starts the return trip up my gullet. But the space where my feet hit the demon's face is empty – nothing but a cloud of stink and a quickly scattering green vapor.

One down.

I take a second to quiet my stomach and survey the dojo. These things can be beaten, just like the rest of my attackers tonight. I take a position with my back to the wall and plot my strategy to take them all down. The bad-kappa horde emits a raucous chorus of croaks, burps and farts and slithers toward me, each beast licking its lips. The stink and the wormy motions again tickle my gag reflex and I turn away for a second, just as a slimy kappa hand pulls at my ankle. Down I go into a pile of gooey grossness – looks like disgust is my enemy when dealing with this challenge. I kick free and stand up again, facing down a belching pack of ten or so arranging themselves around me.

Best plan is not to wait for them to start moving again – I charge toward the nearest kappa as his face twists up in a horrific snarl. He lurches toward me, grabbing at my hakama pants at waist level. Fighting my disgust at touching his slimy hide, I wrap my arms around him, step back and pivot. The wriggling demon goes flying, hitting the front wall of the dojo with a sickening splat.

Another one down, nine to go. I use the same move over and over: Let the kappa-beast grab my waist, hug it to my body, step back, pivot, drop my center and chuck it across the room.

One by one, they splatter out of existence, thrown against the walls, windows and once, to my horror, against the kamiza. But each blubbery bag of nastiness leaves no trace of its doom, only a stink and some green mist. The kamiza isn't even dusty when I check it later, although the reek of swamp still lingers.

The last kappa-beast seems to be a bit smarter than the rest, hanging back when I stand still and scampering away when I approach. That's when randori practice breaks down, when the attackers stop attacking. This is when a teacher would clap to end things if we were in class, but there's no one here but the hunter and the hunted, and I'm not sure which is which as the kappa-beast bares a set of pointy-looking fangs and stretches its talons toward my side of the mat. Is he going to try to tire me out? Sneak up on me? Wait until I give him an opening?

Look over here, slobbering little monster. Check this out.

My front foot starts to turn as slowly, inch by inch, I start pivoting toward the window, pretending there's something outside attracting my attention. Actually, there is something outside, huge and impossibly fast, that just blacked out part of the moon as it rocketed past the windows. So I'm not exactly pretending as I turn away from the kappa-beast, presenting him with my back and what any kappa demon prizes the most – access to my intestines. Each inch that I turn away, the shuffling and farting and gobbling sounds get closer. With each degree that I turn, I also shift my weight to my back foot and bend my knee, winding up my hip and storing power in my torso in preparation for a quick defensive move.

The kappa-beast slows his approach as a blot spreads across the moon again – something huge and airborne is hovering just feet away from the dojo window. Gibbering and whimpering explodes from behind me, but before long, shuffling steps start up again. I shift forward as if to start escaping and sure enough, the beast grabs at my waist from behind.

My stored energy explodes into windmill pivot, elbows flying and hips turning sharply to send the glob of green stench splattering against the windows, high up this time.

Even as the green mist poufs up from the final kappa's impact, the dark shape beyond the glass gets larger. The kappa-dust disperses with a flap of massive wings as Tengu emerges through the wall, pushing itself through glass, metal and asbestos like a swimmer breaking through the surface of a pool.

It stands before me now, as tall as the top window twenty feet up, its wings outstretched and resting against each corner of the mat. Power and malice pour off its snakelike form like an acidic downpour. I had been revved up from my kappa-beast victory, but I feel my power and energy fading away as the chief demon envelops me in his ancient hatred. There's no Aikido technique, no technique of any kind or no weapon that I know of in this world that will work against this monster.

Again I seem to lose conscious control of my movements: I drop to my knees into the *seiza* seated posture and gather myself to bow with my head down, the traditional samurai signal that I've surrendered and am ready to get my head chopped off. Even as I find myself giving up, I can't pull my eyes away from the majestic, horrible spectacle in front of me.

Tengu's form and wings seem to block all the light from the waning moon, but each of the demon's two-foot-long feathers glows from within with a kind of oily sheen. As its presence extends itself outward, I feel darkness blooming in every corner of the dojo, inking out the mat and the kamiza and leaving me stranded on the edge of what feels like a hundred-foot drop. From the chasm all around me something dead and corrupt seems to exhale, buffeting me with a rotten wind.

Swaying in my seated position, I ready for the suicide signal and place my hands on the mat, only to catch the glint of something metallic only a few inches from my left hand. Not an iridescent Tengu feather but a little bit longer and with a familiar scrolling detail on the outside surface: Sensei's live blade, an antique sword at least four centuries old. Does the Tengu want me to commit suicide with this, cutting my stomach open in hara-kiri? Can't be: A samurai would use a knife or short sword for this job, and the Tengu would know that. What does the demon want, to kill me with my teacher's weapon?

Before I can prepare myself for a quick death, I'm jerked onto my feet by a powerful yank on my gi collar, as if I'm a kitten being yanked upright by its mother. My hand drifts to my belt area and I feel the sword already there, in position for battle. Standing on unsteady legs in pitch blackness, I'm swept with the feeling of standing on a cliff or narrow ledge – there is void around me and below me, I know it. One wrong step and I'm splattering on the pavement five stories down, or onto some rocks in hell. My right hand grips the *tsuka*, or hilt, of the sword and my left holds fast to the scabbard.

All at once, four glowing shapes pop out of the void, arrayed around me in a familiar pattern. Samurai demons this time, grunting and clanking in their armor and lit with a pale red glow in the black emptiness. Four opponents, coming from four directions, all with their swords sheathed and at the ready.

Where have I seen this scenario before? Just last week, but that time I was visualizing the samurai as I practiced sword forms. Now those imaginary attackers are here in the flesh, and they stink of stale sweat and violence. Their faces are twisted and beast-like, looking more like the bad kappas than any samurai I've ever seen in a book.

No time to think – the guy at my right is closest, and reaching for his own blade. I step forward, trusting that the abyss I sense around me is a few steps beyond. My left hand curls up with the scabbard turned flat and I stomp down as I smash the sword's heavy handle on the guy's wrist. He staggers back against the windows, giving me a moment to respond to the other three.

Sensing another enemy sneaking up on me from behind, I pull out my blade and stab backward blindly, shifting my weight to my left foot as I hear the satisfying squish of metal passing through demon guts. That samurai slides back off my blade and into the void, his frustrated scream dwindling into nothing as he falls. My eyes and body pivot back to the first guy as he lunges forward, just in time to meet my blade as it slices down in a full-power shomen strike, cutting him neatly in half. Neatly, that is, except for a spray of brains and hot blood. No scream this time, just oddly timed thwacks as the two halves of his body topple down into the abyss.

Now from the right rear of the mat, a woman this time, in a silvery kimono with a sword that seems to be giving off sparks. Or perhaps those are the sparks of our swords clashing together as I meet her overhead shomen strike with mine, turning her blade to the side and cleaving the softer metal of her hand-guard to chop at her wrists. Another moaning that fades with her plunge into the depths.

Last is a giant warrior looming from my left, nearly the size of the watching Tengu and exploding into movement and a mighty *kiai* shout as he charges at me. My sword is at my side, blade down, in the *waki-gamae* position, meant to hide the length of my weapon from the attacker. Not much use against an enemy with a sword that looks like a telephone pole, but the stance gives me a moment to gather myself and focus everything I have at the charging demon.

My mind is calm. My stance is strong and my step is determined. As I step forward, my sword comes down in another shomen with everything I've got, my fear and anger and frustration united into a single strike.

The giant doesn't even last long enough to fall down the abyss, just winks out with a hiss and a sun-bright burst of light. Now it's my turn to stagger back, blinded and off-balance, hoping I can recover before falling into the pit. Staggering in shock, my bare foot steps into empty air and I tumble downward, into blackness.

Upside-down, downside-up, spinning and twisting and clenching my eyes shut to recover from the light blast. The fall seems to take hours, long enough for my eyes to recover a bit and allow me to force open my lids a crack. With the first dim images that hit my eyes I feel myself yanked out of free-fall and planted back on the mat, this time in seated meditation posture, legs crossed and hands clasped in front of me. Eyes forced open a bit more and I'm nearly blinded by a tsunami of light, coming from the palest, hugest moon I've ever seen.

I'm seated, the entire surface of the mat glowing bone-white as if I'm sitting on a blanket made of moonlight. The abyss around me is gone. The Tengu is gone. The bodies of the samurai that I just defeated are gone, if they were ever there. No brains, no blood, no piles of slashed kimono.

Still stinging, my eyes want to close, so I let my lids fall halfway, as if I'm settling into to a meditation session. My view now is just a thin strip of mat and the concrete floor, burnished platinum by the orb outside.

My body is seated still, but another... version of me rises to standing position nearby, fully visible in my mind's eye. The other Cherry holds a wooden sword and stands in *migi hamni* stance, right foot forward, readying for more opponents. My eyes close briefly and reopen to my shadow-twin's view, zoomed back to the center of the mat and taking in the whole room with ten-direction eyes. My enemies this time are the barest outlines, ripples in the blinding light all around me.

I start my form. Slide forward to cut shomen to the top of a shadow's head. As I cut through, it's gone. No resistance, no contact. Then I pivot behind me to block an overhead blow in the nick of time – again my enemy is cut down with no blood, no impact, just a fading away. Now to my left as I turn my sword to parry any incoming blow. A third enemy is cut into nothingness. Then another pivot behind, a fourth victory in my four-direction cutting form.

No time to pause as another form rises from my right – I turn and cut. Four directions, four cuts. Again and again, over and over, the attackers come faster. I fight to hold my form and my stance as the attackers speed up. Each cut must be strong and centered, each step must be grounded, or one of these shadows is going to get through. I don't know exactly why, but I'm totally sure that's a bad thing.

Cut, cut, cut, cut. Turn. Cut, cut, cut, cut. Turn. Ichi, ni, san, shi. The Japanese numbers start booming in my head as the attackers come faster and faster. ICHI, NI, SAN, SHI. I'm at my limit now, cutting and turning so fast that my form is unraveling. The cuts are coming in on a diagonal. I'm tripping a bit as I step. The shadowy forms are moving closer each time and one brushes against my wrist, chilling my soul to the bone even as it burns like acid. More stumbles, a near-miss as I swing the bokken like a baseball bat.

Keep your center.

Even as I continue to thrash at the shadows, something shifts. My turns get smoother again, as if I'm on wheels. My cuts straighten out and add some power, cleaving the shadows without hesitation. Speeding up steadily, I cut down shadow after shadow, my mind completely quiet and focused. Any tiredness and muscle strain fades away as my body starts calibrating itself to perfect form at top speed.

One more turn to the right and... nothing. No shadow, no samurai, no enemy. To the left, still nothing. Front, back, left, right. Nothing, nothing, nothing, nothing. No enemy. No shadow. No form. Nothingness.

I drop the tip of my bokken to the mat, exhaustion overtaking me. Outside the moon has faded to a pale shadow, and the mat and dojo walls are barely visible in the tapped-out glow that's left. I consider collapsing to the mat to rest, but something swims its way out of the gloom right in front of me, a few steps away.

One more opponent.

No shadow this time – a solid figure coalesces out of the gloom, tattooed and pudgy-faced and shrouded in a hoodie and baggy sweats. My stomach drops, where do I know him from? Is this a demon or something much more strange... I lift the tip of my bokken and take a defensive stance.

"Yo, bitch, give me the money."

He's holding something dark and glinting, swinging it toward me.

"Fucking Chinese bitch, hand it over!"

Now I recognize him, the soft features, the baby face, the

tattoos across his neck. My mother's killer. I've never seen him before, but this is really him, not just what I imagined from his mug shot. My mother's voice rings out in the silence.

"I'm not Chinese, I'm Japanese. Japanese-American! And I don't have anything. Look around, don't you see this place? I don't have anything worth stealing!"

The thief is still looking in my direction, and I meet his jittery gaze. My voice rises in a scream of rage before I can consciously process that a scream would be exactly the wrong thing. His eyes break and scatter to the door, to the window. He's no criminal mastermind, just scared, and holding a weapon he's only fired out in the desert at empty cans. Something bucks in his hand and his entire body convulses. I feel nothing but a ripping through time and space as a spasm of shock ricochets across his face.

He's shot me.

My sword drops to the mat. I collapse to my knees, a white-hot pain searing itself into my gut. Through the pain, my mind reels from what I've just seen.

My mother's killer didn't mean it, it was a mistake. It's not her fault; it's not really his fault. He was just a stupid kid and things got out of hand. Hating him was just a waste of time.

"Sorry lady, really! Are you OK? He rushes toward me, and whatever energy that created him rushes forward then pulls back into a glowing nimbus. The killer is gone, along with the pain in my gut. Also gone is most of my hate and anger, replaced by a grief so oceanic I'm afraid I might drown.

All I can think to do is fold my legs under me, take the meditation posture, and close my eyes.

✳ ✳ ✳

I wake with a start – it should be light out by now but the dojo is still dim and gray. I'm sitting cross-legged on the mat, cold and stiff. The moon hangs low in the sky in the window in front of me, shrouded in a crystalline halo. It feels like this night has lasted for centuries. The sun should have come up long ago.

The aches from the randori and all my ordeals of the night punish me as I rock to one side then slowly, painfully push myself into a standing position. The sky is lead gray, except for a band of yellow to the east just above the horizon. I lean against the wall and watch as the world lightens a bit, not exactly a sunrise but more like a fever inflaming the air above the city.

First to arrive in the dojo is Jean-Baptiste, his jacket half off and his head bare. Clearly visibly is a huge red welt across his forehead and scalp. He pushes open the dojo door, takes one look and me and kicks his shoes off. He takes his hat off and points at his head.

"Lightning from Papa Legba." He collapses on the couch. I don't press for more details.

Next comes Brah, his hair caked with blood on the left side. His words come out in a pained trickle.

"Ear. Gone. Freddy was rough."

Emma is next, limping but smiling. I almost don't recognize her, she looks so happy. She shuffles over to the mat, sits down and stretches out her leg.

"Just a flesh wound, ha-ha. Actually, it was my mistake. The Clam Monster stepped on my foot. He didn't mean it. I should have been more aware. Either way, I think he's gone now. Back to my practice!"

Brah tosses her a packet of green-tea-flavored pretzels. Then he tosses me a bag. We all crunch in silence for a few minutes.

Now Shai comes knocking, his face caked with dirt.

"Hope I never see that stupid Golem again. He just didn't listen."

That makes as much sense as everything else, I guess. He grabs some pretzels and sits next to Emma. Kind of close to Emma, if you ask me.

But still no Barata, and I'm starting to get worried. A few minutes later the pretzels are starting to churn in my stomach and my concern for Barata is at red alert when a voice erupts from the couch area.

"OK, now we have to go confront Dar. The fights we all had tonight were some kind of test, but you all feel that it's not over, right? Freddie's gone but whatever was making him crazy is still around, for sure!"

Everyone turns in surprise to Brah, who looks like he's been brought back to life by the pretzels and tea. He's obviously been doing a lot more thinking than the rest of us after our nighttime adventures.

Another voice has our heads swiveling to the door.

"He's right, you know. We haven't beaten this thing. It's not over."

Thank god, it's Barata. He's barefoot and his arm is wrapped up in a kind of bandage, but he's alive.

"What do you mean it's not over? I kicked that monster's ass!" Emma shakes her fist and pulls her sleeve up to show off a bracelet of bruises.

"Of course it's not over. We've all been sitting here, and I'm the only one who's noticed… that?"

Shai gestures toward the far wall of the dojo, which most of us are facing away from. We turn together and I let out a gasp.

"What the hell? This is my dojo!"

A red glow has set the corner of the dojo on fire with almost blinding intensity, revealing a pulsing tunnel of light. An energy field seems to have cut through the building like an x-ray, with beams and ducts showing up as dark patches in the glare. Clearly, something major is going on in Dar's space, at least 100 feet and multiple walls away, and it's cutting right through the walls.

"OK, one more showdown." Jean-Baptiste sounds like he's ready for it all to end, like now. "I hate to say it, but I had a feeling Papa Legba was still around, somewhere. And we do need to unplug whatever it is that Dar is using to keep the consciousness gate open. That power company data that Shai gave me shows that our demon outbreaks coincide with heavy electrical usage from the fifth floor. I'm pretty sure that's not your rice cooker, Cherry."

"Do you have any leftover rice sitting around, by the way?" Brah's food stash must be running low again. I dig out some energy bars and we all take a few minutes to carbo-load. Then we gather our coats, our demons and our determination to face the final showdown.

* * *

Instead of meeting on a battlefield, we all stand together in the hallway, looking toward the fiery glow coming from Dar's space. No demons, just the ragged, beat-up lot of us humans.

Barata has grabbed Sensei's *wakazashi* short sword from the rack behind the kamiza, a razor-sharp live blade that dates from the last century that I've never dared to touch. I've got her katana in my belt, liberated from the safe at the bottom of the cabinet. Shai has a wooden staff and Emma has a nasty-looking Tai Chi stick with a handle on the side. She swings it at my head with vicious backhand that I'm sure could crack my skull, but I've decided to trust her, and sure enough, she stops just in time to save me a concussion.

Sound explodes around us – a droning blare somewhere between an emergency broadcast signal and a bagpipe.

No demons, no light from outside. We creep down the hallway toward the light, and somehow, I'm in the lead. As we get closer, the light seems to dim and the noise subsides to an angry hum from behind Dar's door.

Now I'm in front of the door, and it seems our big show-down has to start with a knock. I grab Shai's staff and pound the scarred metal with it. Before I complete my third bang, the door swings open.

"Hi, perfect timing!"

Dar's in shirtsleeves and his hair is wild. His eyes look

glassy and his smile is empty and cold. From behind him the horrible blare sounds again, pounding on my eardrums and causing my brave fellow soldiers to retreat down the hall a bit.

"What the hell is that?" I scream as soon as the sound fades a bit.

Dar frowns then replies with something between excitement and dread. "I think it's a conch horn, made from those big shells. They used it in India back in the day for battles. Must be from the Kali side."

"Side? You mean there's like a battle going on in there?"

I don't see anything in the crack in the door, but a kind of electricity is pouring into the hallway from the lab. Even as I feel my skin prickle, I feel my ankle grabbed by an astonishingly strong Kappa claw. Not just any kappa, my Kappa. He lets out a friendly fart and looks up at me with a beaky smile. Dar doesn't even seem to notice that a Japanese frog demon is stinking up the air outside his door. He starts babbling and the reflected red glow glints off his sweaty forehead.

"Armies shaped like eagles and fish, lining up for battle… it's all in the *Mahabarata*, the Hindu bible from India. I can't believe there's room in my lab for all this!"

"Wow! Sounds cool. Can I watch?" I'm hoping my phony enthusiasm will keep his door open. Now, I need to get in there and stop all this madness. Screeches and gurgles are building from the hallway, where the full squad of demons has appeared. Freddie Kruger pushes Saci the one-legged Brazilian demon aside as the Clam Monster slimes up the concrete. Papa Legba raps his cane against the Golem when he gets too close, unleashing a splash of dirt. Down by the dojo door, Yuki-Onna and Rokurokubi seeming to be having some kind of fistfight.

"Cherry, let's get this thing going! This bunch isn't going to keep from busting out for long." Barata stands at my side, his short-sword in hand.

Dar looks angry and dances from one foot to the other, nervous but seemingly reluctant to go back into his space. He doesn't seem to notice the growing horde down the hall, but keeps glancing behind him. I move closer, but he edges away and pulls the door so it's open just a crack.

I try to keep him talking. "So who is the main... god in there? You keep calling it 'her,' but all I see is a bunch of fire."

Dar glances behind him, his face glowing with a kind of crazy joy.

"I'm not completely sure what's there now – it keeps changing forms. Angra Mainyu was here a few days back. But I think that's Kali, the Hindu goddess of death and destruction. She came through the portal earlier today. They're all possible considering my ethnic background. But don't worry – I've got them under control. Isn't this amazing?"

Amazing, right. I try not to snort, since that's going to make my bruised ribs hurt. I also try not to think of the squirmy, slimy monstrosities everyone in the building battled all night long and the cranky demons waiting a few yards away.

"Goddess? Wow, that's a big upgrade from our demons and monsters over there."

"It's not that clear, actually. In Hinduism we have thousands of gods and some are like your demons and ghosts. Kali is actually the embodied anger of the main female goddess, as I recall. In the stories she's out there on the battlefield or in the cemetery raising hell."

"So is Kali dangerous to the rest of us?"

"I'm pretty sure in this form she is dangerous to some people. But I can definitely contain her at this point. She's getting stronger the longer I leave the portal open, though. I seem to remember that she ends up destroying the world. Don't worry, I won't let that happen!"

Dar's eyes are bloodshot nightmares and his face is dripping with sweat. I can't believe I ever thought he was interesting.

"Er, destroying the world? Don't you think it's time to shut this thing down?"

"Didn't I explain that it doesn't really matter what the legend actually is? Kali is in my head as the destroyer of the world, so that's what she becomes on this side of the gate. She's drawing power from somewhere other than my consciousness right now though, and it's really fascinating. We can't shut it down. We need to see how it ends."

"Sorry, Dar. I appreciate your scientific curiosity, but that's sounds kind of alarming. How much has Kali grown since she…emerged?"

"At first she was a little ball of light on the floor in the corner of my lab. Like the size of a lit match. Then she got a little bit bigger and grew some arms and I recognized her. The arms kept multiplying and then she was hurting my eyes. That's why I'm out here talking to you, to give myself a break! I'll wait a bit and check in with her later. My eyes need a rest."

Jean-Baptiste snorts audibly from down the hall and even Brah looks disgusted. My frustration breaks through, my voice drops a bit and I sound like my mom for a second.

"How about checking on her now? All of us stranded here would like to take a look. See, they're all down the hall there. We need to come in and see what you're up to in person. We're all affected by this! You owe us a look at the portal."

Dar's craziness has made him a bit less confident, and he looks down the hall on command at the gathered crowd and seems almost ready to let us in. Then, as if jerked on a chain, he shuffles back into the doorway, pushing the door open wider as he retreats.

"Well, let's just say I can't show you the portal itself right now. This is what happened when I got near it earlier."

Dar pulls up his sleeve as he pushes down his right glove. The skin of his hand and arm looks like it's been held over an open flame on a stove, puckered and scorched.

"I just pushed my arm toward and this is what happened. I tied a shirt over my head and still I'm seeing little flashes out of the corner of my eyes just from the light that leaked through! I'm going to have to wait to shut it off until things cool down."

"So you can't shut it off right now?"

Jean-Baptiste and the rest have crowded in around me in

front of Dar's door.

Emma's the first to take action, smacking Dar with her Tai Chi stick right in the kneecap. He grunts and falls the ground – it's painfully clear that he's never taken martial arts. Any of the rest of us could have taken the strike and stayed standing. I bet Barata could have leaped up to avoid it completely. My mind keeps spinning as the demons flow into the doorway to Dar's space, one by one, in what seems like fractions of a second. It's as if they've been sucked in by a vacuum. The door slams shut.

We humans stand in the hallway alone for a few seconds, then push forward. Emma gets there first, shoving the door open. The red glare inside blinds us all to everything but the glowing, pulsing forms of our demons, standing the edge of what looks like a giant vat of lava.

Kappa leads the parade of creatures toward the vat, growing larger and more present with every froggy shuffle-step. Dar clutches at my arm as I pass him at the threshold.

"Just a few more days and the portal will stay open permanently, Cherry! Just give me a few more days. The balance will be restored! All the evil in the world will yield to the one true power! No more of these stupid demons – only the one true power. It will rule over it all! You'll get justice for your mom!"

I close my eyes and see Sensei's sword at my waist, then slicing through the neck of the robber who shot my mother, in whatever broken-down hell he's hiding. Or the sword could just slice through the power cable I see along the floor and end it all. End the demons. Snuff out Kappa and the Swordmaster forever. Close the door on the Clam Monster and Papa Legba, all the cultural relics who have been tormenting us in the building.

"I need your help, Cherry! None of these mediocrities understand what I'm trying to do here."

Dar's voice cuts through the crowd of demons. The space seems infinite now, filled with shapes and writhing flames. The other humans seem paralyzed, frozen by the flames. The thought of revenge against my mom's killer fills me with pure rage and righteousness. The feeling reminds me of the dark joy I feel when twisting someone's wrist just a little bit too much, or making someone yelp for challenging my strength on the mat.

I know this feeling.

I draw my sword. Sensei's live blade feels infinitely powerful in my hands as I raise it above my head in jodan position, the cutting edge aimed at the top of Barata's skull. Dar's voice rises in an unearthly wail.

"Do it, Cherry! Get rid of these people so we can watch the end of the world!"

My sword falls as I pull my foot back in a tenkan turn, shifting the direction of the blade as I strike. Instead of cleaving Barata's skull, the blade slices through the power cable with a metallic clunk. I expect to be instantly killed by the electric shock, but my hands feel like they're pushed off the sword at the last possible second, even as smell like swampy farts hits my nose. The severed ends of the power cable coil and twist like living things.

Wailing sounds rise as one by one, the demons fade into nothingness. Only the flames behind Dar remain, pulsing and intensifying even as the cables twist and shimmy across the concrete.

A final intense burst of light and one end of the cable rises into the air, like a snake that's been charmed. It rises up and up, then lashes across the lab, hitting Dar with incredible force across his forehead. He staggers back to the corner of the room.

"Dar, no!"

He collapses like a broken doll, blood splashing onto the concrete. The remaining light seems to contract around him to snuff his life out. By the time I get across the room, he's starting to get cold.

* * *

It's been a week since the big showdown, but I still feel a little stunned. Right away the snowstorms seemed to ease and the building and dojo life returned to normal: Classes, cleaning, sleeping. Day by day it's been getting warmer and today melting snow is making a racket outside as it drips onto the window ledges from above. Every new sound startles me: I expect to see Kappa or the Swordmaster after every crackle and plop.

This morning huge black wings flashed past the far window and I could have sworn I glimpsed Tengu's terrifying, gaping beak. But then I saw another dark shape circling above the abandoned building next door. It had a bullet head and wings in the shape of a tapered "V" and I remembered Dar's last wish.

"If something happens to me, put me on the roof," he told me in a dream the night after the showdown. "Just leave me there and the vultures will take me. I have no human family, so leave me there for a few weeks and my friends will take me away."

I didn't know what he meant, but in our exhaustion after the battle, we couldn't decide what to do with Dar right away. As if in a trance, we all went back to our spaces and slept for hours. I have't seen most of the other tenants since.

The next day, JB and Barata showed up in the dojo and I told them about my dream. We talked about calling the police but that didn't seem to make sense, somehow. How would we explain everything that went down? When I explained what Dar told me in the dream, JB and Barata agreed to honor his request. We put him in a sleeping bag, slid him down the hall and then dragged him up to the roof. There we hoisted him on top of the shed beside the transmission tower. A few shoves and the sleeping bag skidded across the stillfrozen crust of snow and out of sight.

With the voices of demons and the screams of Kali still ringing in our ears, it seemed like the right thing to do. If anyone showed up looking for Dar and found him up there, we reasoned it would look like he picked a bad night to camp out on the roof and froze to death. We then went down to Dar's workspace and started dismantling his equipment, piece by piece. Barata had the best approach in the end, taking a section of pipe from the junk pile in an empty unit and smashing the hard drives and monitors into scrap. Jean-Baptiste then dug the chips out of everything and Barata reduced them to silicon slag in a bonfire. As the chips were burning, they sent up some shadows that looked awfully familiar. We had thought the demons had disappeared completely as soon as the power was cut, but I guess there was some lingering energy in the building.

The muttering, slithering, moaning crowd gathered as all of Dar's work was turned to rubble. Kappa chortled a bit with each blow as Yuki-Onna sulked and the Clam Monster blubbered. Papa Legba was the first to completely flicker out, to Jean-Baptiste's relief. He managed to issue a booming command in Creole before his cane clattered to the floor for the last time. Jean-Baptiste nodded seriously and barked out a "oui" in response.

"What did he say?"

"He told me to work hard and get my company going, basically."

Kappa was the last to go, sitting on my shoulder and yanking at my hair until the last chip melted. His sloshy weight was on my shoulder one minute, nothing but a slimy spot on my coat the next. My eyes teared up a bit in the minutes after he blinked out as a rush of loneliness filled me. Yes, he was an annoying demon from old Japan who wanted nothing more than to pull my intestines out of my butthole. But he was also kind of my friend.

* * *

Later, alone in the dojo and watching the snowmelt stream down the window near my futon, I thought about Dar's body on the roof. It was already getting warmer – was he going to rot up there and fall apart? Are the vultures going to carry him off piece by piece?

I'm not sure why Dar wanted that, but one of my books

on world religions says vultures play a role in what's called a "sky burial" in mountainous parts of Asia. It makes sense to let nature take its course in areas where it's too cold and rocky to bury someone underground, I guess. In most of the world the giant birds have been made extinct by chemicals, but here they flourish on road kill. With the warmer weather, the vultures will follow noses senses to Dar. They won't take long.

No one came looking for Dar in the days to follow, as he predicted. The building was still mostly empty, so Barata and I took turns at night carting his broken equipment to the basement and emptying out his space. Once his Internet access was restored, Jean-Baptiste hacked into Dar's online accounts started erasing things. He found old posts from concerned professors and angry colleagues, but nothing personal for months. Nothing from friends or family for far longer. Dar's last year was one of complete separation – from family, colleagues and society.

An enforcement team from the university – outfitted in body armor – did turn up at the building a few days later. By then there was nothing in Dar's space but dust and burn marks on the ceiling. The team scraped the walls for samples, took our statements and left.

Sure enough, by the end of the week the vultures started coming, in twos and threes. The massive birds are silent as they soar in across the sky, but on quiet afternoons I hear them scrabbling and squawking above. I know Dar would be pleased that they're keeping him company.

❋ ❋ ❋

The snow is coming in big fat globs today, a sign that winter is coming to an end, Barata says. It's been two weeks now and we've finally decided to go up on the roof to see if any signs of Dar's body remain. Some guy working on the tower this spring might find it and ask some awkward questions. Thierry just smiled and let us leave the dojo together – he's just happy we're all alive and hasn't asked too many questions about what's been going on.

I'm nervous about going up to the roof but Barata's oversized presence – he's wrapped himself in a giant puffy coat – steadies me on the climb up the stairs. Something about him has changed in the past week or so. He's wearing shoes, making more sense and I'm finding myself really looking forward to his visits. He's even agreed to teach the Aikido students a few Capoeira techniques. We talked about having dinner at his space next week and he's promised to cook up authentic Brazilian cassava mash in his toaster oven. I tried to sound enthusiastic.

We push through the hatch at the top of the stairs and hunker down as we climb up on the roof – ice glazes every surface up here now with all the melting and refreezing. Barata edges ahead and shimmies himself along the side of the transmitter then extends a hand. I don't hesitate; I grab on and let him lead me across the slick tarpaper.

Soon we're at the edge of the shed where we left Dar's body; Barata launches himself into a twisting leap and pulls himself up the roof. I grab his wrists and he hoists me up there with him. We look out at the snowy cityscape for a while, then turn toward where Dar's body should be. All that's left are some singed scraps of fabric and a few shards of what could be bone, could be ice.

Barata and I crawl over, pushed and shoved by a raw wind, and take a closer look. The snowflakes, lumpy and clotted, drift onto the singed spot and disappear. No zap, no sizzle, they just seem to blink out of existence where Dar's body once lay. The weirdness of it all and the bitter chill set off a violent bout of shivers as I crouch there.

Behind me, I hear a velcro ripping noise and before I know it, Barata has pulled me into the warm circle of his arms, wrapping me in his jacket. My shivering stops, and we stay up there a while, watching the flakes sputter into nothingness.

* * *

"*Tadaima.*"

"*Okaeri nasai.* Welcome back, Sensei."

I try to sound enthusiastic, but I'm petrified. Despite hours of cleaning and a full week of stair-climbing and sword cuts, I can't shake the word "*namakemono*" – lazy bum – out of my head. Some energy from the Swordmaster lingers in this space, I'm sure of it. Sensei walks into the dojo and it's like he's back in the dojo again.

Sensei's return from Japan was delayed several weeks by storms in Japan and her eyes are hollow with exhaustion, but her movements are quick as she stalks around the dojo. The Clam Monster slime in the corner is gone, as are Papa Legba's cane marks and the mark from Swordmaster's *suburito*. Freddy's claw marks were painted over just a few days ago. Kappa's fishy stink has been replaced by the citrus scent of cleanser.

Sensei turns toward me, her inspection complete. Before I can say anything, she grabs my left hand and brings it up to her face. Her fingers, strong as talons, push across the top of my palm.

"Nice, there's a good callous here on your hand. You've been doing your thousand cuts a day with the suburito and using the correct grip. Left hand is the power hand."

My luck – if she grabbed the right hand she'd see the burn left by Kali. If it was a bit warmer in here and I weren't mummified in sweaters and leggings, she'd likely see the lingering bruises left by Golem's grip on my forearm and the kappa bite marks healing near my ankle.

"The only thing is, this place is not as clean as I'd hoped, with all your days off due to the storms. See this?"

She holds out a finger smeared with grime.

"This was on top of the door frame outside. Remember what I said about making sure the *genkan* area was spotless? The door frame is part of the entryway to this dojo, the boundary between inside and outside, civilization and savagery, life and death. Do I have to repeat that it should be cleaned at least twice a day?"

"Right, sorry about that."

Why is it so hard to look sorry for something you're really not sorry about?

Gee, Sensei, sorry about that cataclysmic demon battle that nearly took the whole building down and ended the world. Guess that Kali's wrath left some ashes on the doorframe, in addition to the huge scorch marks in the hallway that we had to paint over. We saved the world, but I missed a spot. My bad!

Saying nothing is my best option.

"Don't be casual, Cherry. I expect you to be training every second that you're here in the dojo, understand? Training means noticing every inch of this sacred space and make sure it's spotless. I've only got nine more months to turn you into some kind of martial artist, and I'm still not convinced you've got what it takes to become an Aikido teacher. As my old teacher said: 'Clean most where people look the least.'"

Her words are harsh, but there's warmth in her eyes and she's almost smiling.

"Anyway, look what I brought you. Pickled plums from my sword teacher and this incredible little thing I found in an antique shop."

Sensei's not much for wrapping things, so she hands me a bag covered in characters and gestures toward it.

I reach in and pull out a tiny lump of clay, green and glossy. There is the plate on its head, a froggy grin, beak and grabby arms.

"It's called a kappa; you might have read about it for your presentation. It's this funny creature from Japanese folklore that has the most amazing superpower. It wants to pull your intestines out of your butt!"

"Right, I think I've read something about that."

As I examine the little figure, the smell of a fresh fart drifts across the dojo.

Sensei gives me a look.

"We're going out for lunch today," she announces. "You've probably had enough ramen noodles."

* * *

First her fist comes at my head. I lift my hands to block, step back and drop my weight into her elbow to take her to the mat. Then her fist comes at my stomach. I pivot off my front foot, grab her hand, step back again and then bend her wrist, forcing her to flip or watch her bones break.

Last, Sensei comes at me with a flurry of punches and kicks. I deflect, block, pivot and then step back in to bowl her over in an explosive forward throw. Sensei's rested now and in peak condition, but I've spent the last few weeks dealing with demons.

She gives me a funny look – kind of admiring, kind of suspicious.

"So you've been training hard while I've been away, I see."

"You could say that. Not too many people in class but there's been a lot of... after-hours training."

"Anything to do with cartwheel boy from down the hall? What's his name?"

"Er, Ramon, actually. But his Capoeira name is Barata. That means 'cockroach' in Brazilian Portuguese. I'm actually learning some Portuguese, too. And some Capoeira moves. Tai Chi, too, from Emma down the hall. Cross-training."

I figure if I talk enough, Sensei won't notice that I'm blushing.

She takes another look at me, and she's smiling now.

"Emma is teaching you? Well, ask her and Barata if they want to come try an Aikido class. All of us martial artists can learn from each other. It's great that you're getting to know our neighbors, but you're going to be pretty busy in the next few months. I've been meaning to tell you some great news! My swordmaster in Japan said he might consider taking on one more foreign student before he retires. You need to get the basics of sword training, but you might be ready by spring for some uchideshi time in the mountains. What do you think?"

"You think I'm almost ready for Japan? Wow. My mom would be so proud."

Sensei gives me a concerned look this time. I'm sad, but something angry and twisted inside me about my mom's death seems to have faded away in the last few weeks. I'll always be grieving, but I'm also happy thinking about how proud my mom would be about the things I've accomplished so far. Me in Japan, studying sword with a great master.

"I'll do my best to train harder with the sword."

Sensei looks relieved, and then her face transforms in a split-second.

"*Namakemono!* That means lazy in Japanese. Take a bokken and let's see a thousand cuts. Now!"

After a thousand cuts or so, we finish our class and stop for a tea break. Sensei sips her hojicha as she talks.

"You are going to love Japan, Cherry. The Iaido dojo where I train is more than a hundred years old and it's full of *ki* energy. Some say there are ghosts there, believe it or not. That's just superstition, but the last practice before I left, I could have sworn I saw a samurai on the back mat at the end of a three-hour practice. He was standing there covered in blood – I even smelled him! Like metal and sweat."

"Wow, sounds... epic."

Ghost samurai, three-hour practices, grumpy Japanese swordmasters and a dojo in the mountains.

I can't wait.

The End

About the Author

A writer and journalist, Liese Klein is the author of the biography *The Life Giving Sword: Kazuo Chiba's Life in Aikido.* She teaches Aikido at New Haven Aikikai in New Haven, Conn.

26850414R00166

Made in the USA
San Bernardino, CA
22 February 2019